CANDLELIGHT REGENCY SPECIAL

CANDLELIGHT REGENCIES

LOVE'S
A
STAGE

Laura London

A CANDLELIGHT REGENCY SPECIAL

Published by
Dell Publishing Co., Inc.
1 Dag Hammarskjold Plaza
New York, New York 10017

Dedicated, with Love, to Lanny and Summer

Dell ® TM 681510, Dell Publishing Co., Inc.

ISBN: 0-440-15387-5

Printed in the United States of America
First printing—April 1980

Chapter One

Miss Frances Atherton, the parson's daughter, stepped from the hired hackney carriage onto the busy marketplace corner of Charles and Russell Streets. A whimsical spring breeze dandled the long ties of her old-fashioned straw bonnet as if to undo their neat arrangement, and molded her shapeless gray traveler's cape to her trim young figure, causing more than one head to turn in her direction. Bustling herds of shoppers, hawkers, and costermongers schooled around her as she gazed with innocent awe on the spires of St. Paul's Cathedral, gilded like a chapel shrine by the late afternoon sun. It was a stirring view for a young lady who had lived her nineteen summers in Beachy Hill, Sussex, a fishing village so small that when Mrs. Brantley's baby cried on the west side of town, cross old Mrs. Betterton on the east side would shut her window. Miss Atherton's previous definition of a crowd had been the parish packed into her father's church on Easter Sunday, but this single London corner contained more souls than her father had had a chance to save in the last decade.

The corner contained more vegetables, too, thought Frances, glancing about—not, of course, that her father had ever tried to save the soul of a vegetable. Frances felt a tiny smile tighten her lips at the idea of her Reverend Papa sermonizing earnestly from his pulpit to-

5

ward pews packed with hefty radishes. But if Miss Atherton had been spared the company of vegetables at Sunday service, she was certainly surrounded by them now. A dusty mountain of potatoes was heaped on the pavement with a hill of crisp turnips rising at its side. Maroon pickling cabbages fought piled onions and bundles of glossy leeks for space on busy market stalls. Down the street an herbalist's shop was getting a fresh coat of whitewash from a trio of rowdy youths, who paused to tease a group of apple-women sitting nearby on their porter's knots sharing a pipe.

The day had been a long and tiring one for Miss Atherton. She had come from Eastbourne on the public stagecoach in a grueling ride that had begun at four o'clock that morning. The other two passengers had been a baker's widow in black bombazine and a frail stay-maker's wife with her overweight bulldog. After three hours of battering over rutty spring roads, their stage had become mired in a lowland road near a swollen river bank. Pulling the bulky stage through the knee-high mud had been a hard enough task for the horses even with the coachmen leading them; the passengers had been forced to get out and walk. Frances had descended bravely into the muck, saying that she was sure she wouldn't mind a chance to stretch her legs. Her two lady companions had followed her with loud complaints, but the fat bulldog had steadfastly refused to leave the carriage. The coachman had angrily announced that he wouldn't have his horses drag the coach another step with that bulky brute inside, the staymaker's wife had begun to cry that it wasn't Doggie's fault that he didn't like to walk in the mud, and the widow in black bombazine began a shrill for the return of her ticket price. Frances, with an inward sigh and all the good-natured cheer that she could muster,

6

had offered to carry Doggie. She had marched the next three miles in wet sucking mud carrying a forty-pound bulldog, who alleviated his tedium by struggling and licking Frances vigorously on the side of her face.

No sooner had the bedraggled and weary travelers returned to the cramped interior of the stagecoach when the baker's widow insisted that there was too much draft and ordered the scuffed leather curtains pulled down to cover the windows. Frances had sat in increasingly stuffy discomfort while the staymaker's wife enumerated the outstanding qualities of her son, currently apprenticed to a snuff-box painter, and then went on to describe his advent into the world, which, it seemed, had been accomplished in miraculously short order. Not to be outdone, the baker's wife had offered the tale of her own confinement, some forty years past, which, she said smugly, had been remarkable for its length and difficulty. The staymaker's wife quickly countered with the claim that, of course, *everyone* knew that short confinements were more taxing and risky than long ones. The baker's widow did not take well to a suggestion that any confinement could have been more risky or taxing than her own, and from thence the two ladies began a prolonged and detailed exchange of obstetrical histories that caused Miss Atherton to lose what little appetite she had left for the roll and hard cheese she had brought for lunch, and might have (had she not been a young woman of common sense and character) caused her to enter a nunnery forthwith and eschew the company of men not likewise celibate.

Frances had found no emotion within herself stronger than that of relief when the stagecoach had finally pulled into the hopping courtyard of the London's Great George Coaching Inn. She had hired a hackney

7

carriage, seen to the transfer of her case, and within minutes here she was among the vegetables.

The picturesque hustle about her filled Frances with fresh energy. She smoothed a wisp of her soft brown hair under her bonnet and gave her crumpled skirts a brisk shake. A sparkle returned to her hazel eyes as she filled her lungs determinedly with the dense acrid air of the metropolis. Tilting her head back, she smiled politely at the hackney driver.

"This is my first trip to the capital," she said. "But I can see that it's a city of which England can be proud."

The hackney driver was a surly man in a green felt cap and a double-breasted cloth frock coat with a turned-up collar. He looked contemptuously at Frances and muttered a reply largely indistinguishable, but which sounded suspiciously like "Sure, girlie, and me old dad was a kidney pie." In more audible tones he said, "Fare."

Miss Atherton opened her purse, selected the coins, and handed them up to the driver. "Here you are, one shilling and sixpence. If you please, you may set my case here on the pavement."

The driver looked at the fare in his cracked palm as if someone had presented him with a cockroach corpse. The other hand he lifted to scratch his unshaven chin, and he looked down at Frances with an intimidating frown.

"Ain't enough," he growled.

"But it is," she answered, taken aback. "I counted it out most carefully, one and sixpence."

"One and six ain't enough," returned the driver, with the air of one talking to a dimwit.

"Most certainly it is," said Miss Atherton stoutly. " 'Tis the fare on which we agreed at the coaching inn not twenty minutes ago."

8

"One and six was enough *then*. If yer don't like it, yer can come and get yer own trunk," said the driver, smirking unpleasantly.

As Miss Atherton's case was strapped onto a baggage rack behind the hack driver and more than six feet off the ground, its retrieval would have called for her to clamber up the side of the coach on widely spaced footholds and kneel over the driver's lap. Miss Atherton stood back and reassessed the situation.

"Sir, you are not behaving well," she observed.

The hack driver cleared his throat with disgusting, and quite unnecessary, resonance and spat upon the pavement.

The three youths who had been whitewashing the herb shop saw the exchange and, sensing that better amusement was to be had near the coach, trotted over to gape at Frances and nudge each other suggestively.

Ignoring her chortling audience, Frances said firmly, "I shall have my trunk now, please."

The driver squashed his cap further down on his grizzled head and fixed Frances with a cold stare.

"Ye can come and get it," he said, with tight-mouthed satisfaction.

Nothing draws a crowd like a crowd, and before Miss Atherton had time to think of an adequate retort, the watching group had swelled to include a bevy of sooty chimney sweeps, a greengrocer in a blue apron bulging with carrots, and a red-faced woman with a gaudy gypsy scarf and a basket of crimson love apples on her head. A youth with a long, pointed nose and coarse ginger bowl-cut hair made a saucy comment that drew snickering approval from the gathering. The Golden Rule and chivalry aside, a young, unaccompanied female on the London streets was considered fair game.

A less resolute young lady might have let prudence

9

win over principle and paid the hack driver his demanded due, but Miss Atherton was made of sterner stuff. Turn and run? Not she, the girl who, at the tender age of eleven, had taken the village smithy to task for drinking away his good wife's market money at the county fair.

Frances shook her finger reprovingly at the hack driver. "I suppose because I am from out of town that you think I'm to be easily bamboozled," she said, adopting a tone one would use with a refractory child. "You're quite wrong! I won't allow you to take advantage of me."

To the crowd's heartily expressed enjoyment, several voices inquired if *they* might be allowed to take advantage of the young lady. A burly giant with curly black hair and enormous shoulders in a coster's corduroy was inspired by the uproar to drop his bundle of beets with their dirty dangling roots and step toward Frances with a foolish grin that stretched from one stumpy ear to the other.

"I'll help you get your case, missie," he proclaimed. "Let me put my hands on yer waist and I'll lifts ye right up to your case and in no time, too."

Miss Atherton barely had time to say "thank you, no," when the rough giant slipped his hammy hands under her cape, taking her in a bruising grip. With real alarm, she jerked away from him and took a step back, and the rough fellow came after her, arms outstretched as if to get a better hold on the situation. She stumbled, her heel striking an upturned flagstone, and fell backwards.

A pair of light, strong hands steadied her from behind, releasing her when it was plain that she had regained her footing.

She turned instinctively, looking backward over her shoulder, and found herself gazing into a young, vividly male face so attractive as to be almost startling. Miss Atherton was not one who allowed her knees to turn to pudding every time she met a handsome gentleman (which, it must be admitted, was not often), but however immune one might be to the Hollowness of mortal Beauty, Frances was aware of a rather intense, if brief, sensation somewhere in her middle that Modesty forbade her to name, even to herself. The gentleman was tall, fashionably dressed, and sensuously slender, with hair the color of melted gold touching his collar. His eyes had been painted by the same brush that decorates the first sweet greens of spring; they held an expression that was at once mocking and friendly. Frances was far too inexperienced to see the serenely calculating admiration in them. She didn't know that she was face to face with one of her country's foremost and most fascinating rakes. She might not know it, but the watching crowd did. They gave a cheerful shout of recognition, which further disoriented Frances, and she failed to understand its cause.

The black-haired knave who had been so willing to offer Frances unwanted assistance gave the blond stranger an affable salute, and gestured toward the driver of the hackney carriage, saying, "This son of a whip has been tryin' to take advantage of the dimber mort" (this with a lewd wink toward Frances), "so her says."

"Does she?" said the golden-haired stranger, his wonderful green eyes alive with interest. He gave Frances a smile that was famous throughout London for its irresistibly engaging tenderness. It quite completed the job on her. "What happened?"

The black-haired man seemed to consider himself the party who had been applied to for information. He hitched his hairy thumbs through his belt, looking as pleased as the schoolboy winner of a running contest.

" 'Er driver says 'e won't give up 'er case until she gives 'im 'is fare," the fellow chuckled proudly, "and I says I'm gonna 'elp 'er by liftin' 'er belly up to board."

Miss Atherton had not yet recovered from the shock that she, noted in her family from the cradle for her sensible attitudes, could react to a member of the opposite sex like a giddy miss. It did nothing to assist her composure to hear herself publicly proclaimed to possess so vulgar a member as a "belly." With an effort that can only be described as heroic, she gathered her not inconsiderable mental resources, blocked the blond stranger from her mind, ignored the crowd's gay jibes, delivered a quick, reproving frown to the black-haired lout, and stepped toward the hackney carriage.

"I shall summon a magistrate," she announced valiantly, not having the faintest notion where in this vast city one was to be found.

The hackney driver had been deriving a fair measure of sour enjoyment watching Miss Atherton's discomfiture, but at the mention of the law, his pleasure evaporated. "Oh, you will, will you?" he snarled. "Damned if I'll take sauce from a snooty little curtezan like yourself. If you don't pay your fare, see if I don't take it out in trade before you're much older."

The black-haired lout captured the spotlight. He made a rude gesture toward the hack driver shouting, "That ya couldn't, old Domine Do-little!" The crowd roared its approval. "This kitten needs to take her aqua vitae from a Johnny Ready like meself!" The fellow made a lunge for Frances, attempting to envelop her in his bearlike embrace.

Again Frances felt light, experienced hands encircle her waist as the golden-haired man laughingly plucked her from her attacker's path, setting her down behind him. Her rescuer held a restraining hand toward the black-haired giant.

"Oh, no, my friend," said the gentleman, giving the giant a dose of that curiously affectionate smile. "You may be ready for her, but I very much doubt that she's ready for you."

As if by magic, the lout stopped fast in his tracks, scratching awkwardly at the shaggy hair above his ear. He grinned shyly back at Miss Atherton's champion.

"I was jest funnin' loike. Didn't mean 'er any 'arm," said the lout in sheepish apology.

"No," said the man with the golden hair, subjecting Frances to a swift, intimate appraisal. "And I don't think you did her any, either, because she doesn't appear to have understood half of what you've been saying to her." He flipped a coin of generous denomination to the hack driver, and said good-naturedly, "The lady's case, please."

The size of the coin rendered the hack driver's lugubrious aspect into something approaching happiness.

"As ya say, guv." Twisting behind him, he unstrapped the heavy traveling case, handing it to the black-haired giant, who set it before Miss Atherton, saying, "There you are, missie, all's right now."

Miss Atherton, however, did not share his opinion. She nerved herself to look the blond man directly in the eye.

"That was wrong," she said severely. "Very wrong."

"Oh, I'm sorry; did you want Johnny Ready to hug you?"

She regarded him with a searing eye. The gentleman, it seemed, meant trouble. She hadn't liked the effect his more than pleasant aspect had on her heart rhythm; she hadn't liked the obligation that his unsolicited gallantry placed on her; she hadn't liked the casual manner in which he discussed the level of her understanding with her black-haired pest; and she hadn't liked the way he'd taken the situation with the hack driver into his own hands. "I am referring, sir, to the monies you have dispensed on my behalf and without consultation with me. I had already paid the driver the agreed-upon fare, and to concede to his extortionate demands encourages him to expect more than the justly agreed-upon rate."

"A well-done speech," smiled her rescuer, "considering that you couldn't possibly have rehearsed it. There is the merest hint of a staccato, though, which it probably wouldn't hurt to watch. Still, overall as an impromptu recitation, I would rate it decidedly above the average."

Only the strong conviction that she had already bandied too many words about on a street corner kept Miss Atherton from advising the blond gentleman to mind his own staccatos. She would give him no further opportunity to make game of her and turned her attention to the wayward hackney driver, who was gathering his reins preparing to depart.

"Sir," Frances addressed the driver, "you know you *ought* to return that coin to this gentleman." From the expression on the hack driver's face, not the most dyed-in-the-wool optimist could have held the hope that this was his intention. Miss Atherton decided not to pursue this almost certainly fruitless line of conversation, instead continuing: "You must let your conscience guide you. I hope that when you've thought more on the matter you will change your attitude and remit that money to charity."

"Ain't likely," said the driver with a raspy chuckle. He gave the blond gentleman a knowing grin, nodded, and drove away.

14

Frances shook her head in resignation, and being careful not to look in the direction of the golden-haired man, she bent to pick up her case, giving a firm refusal to the giant's offer to carry it for her. The giant shrugged, winked at the gentleman and, grabbing his bundle of beets, was off down the street. Seeing that the show was finally over, the gathered crowd melted into the bustle as easily as it had appeared.

Frances began to thread her way down Charles Street, perusing the numbers over each door for Number 59. It took both hands wrapped around the handle of her heavy dressing case to drag it beside her. The handle bit through her wool traveling gloves to sting her palms, and the case banged mercilessly against her knees. How in the world had the case become so heavy? She had originally intended to bring a few necessities in a small jute bag, but that was before the members of a large and dear family had each added their own article to her packing. Eight younger brothers and sisters had contributed such indispensable objects as a ponderous stone paperweight lovingly hand-painted with flowers, a large notebook of press-dried wild herbs, a driftwood carving of a fishing bark.

Mother had touchingly presented Frances with the old Bible Papa had used at Seminary (it was what Papa would wish, after all), and the jute bag had grown to a round valise. Frances was congratulating herself on being able to fit everything in when Grandma Atherton had arrived with a warming pan *and* a bed brick. Nothing could convince Grandma that her London daughter-in-law would be sure to keep a fire burning in Frances' bedchamber. The valise had been returned to the attic and the unwieldy dressing case chosen. When Frances' brother Joe had handed it to the stagecoach driver that morning he had said:

"God forbid you should have to carry this thing, Fran. It weighs like a cheese wheel."

Frances looked at the doorway above her. Number 62. She set down her bag on the pavement, clapping her palms to rekindle the circulation. Suddenly, she realized that she was not alone, and turned to look into the eyes of her blond rescuer. With some indignation, she said:

"You've been following me."

He smiled. "Actually, I've been walking beside you, but you've been so busy scowling at the doorways that I'm afraid you haven't noticed."

Miss Atherton fought the urge to deny that she'd been scowling.

"If you have been walking beside me, then please don't do so anymore. I don't walk with gentlemen to whom I haven't been introduced."

"I'm glad to hear that," he said, "because you strike one as being a little untutored."

"Untutored! What, pray, do you mean by that?"

"Do you realize that your eyes lighten almost to amber when you're angry? It's very unusual. Was your father by any chance a Moor?"

"Certainly not! I wish you will go away." Frances grabbed her case, hoping fervently that he would ask if he could carry it so that she would have the pleasure of refusing. Unfortunately, the gentleman was either too perceptive or too lazy to offer his assistance, and Frances was forced to endure him strolling beside her while she tugged at the heavy baggage.

"Do you know, Prudence . . ." he began.

"My name is not Prudence!"

"No? What is it?"

Not so easily tricked, Frances remained silent. He gave her a sidelong glance and smiled inwardly.

"As I'd begun to say, and believe me, I wouldn't mention the matter if it were not that you might encounter this problem again . . . You see, in London we have a quaint custom called the gratuity. Believe me, it's very pervasive."

Frances would have liked to discard this verbal tidbit, but the import of his words began to penetrate her tired mind. She set down her case, rubbing arms that felt as though they had been pulled from their sockets, and allowed herself the luxury of one more glance at her companion.

"Do you mean," she asked slowly, "that the hack driver was angry because I didn't give him a tip?"

"Something like that."

She got a new grip on her case and dragged it a few more feet. "Very well, you've told me, so you can go away. If you're waiting for me to admit I was in the wrong, you're wasting your time, because I won't. I hate admitting it when I'm wrong."

"An admirable quality."

"You know it's not," she said with a gulp of exertion. "Everyone knows that it's a terrible weakness, besides being a sin of pride."

She heard his soft laughter as he stepped in front of her, bringing her painful trek to a rest. He placed one caressing hand on her shoulder and, with the other hand, lifted the tip of her chin between the thumb and forefinger.

"I find your pride enchanting, Prudence, and I would never consider it a sin. Will you let me carry your case, or are you going to drop first?"

Frances had already more than noticed his attractiveness, and felt the tug of its magnetism. But nothing in her previous experience with men had prepared her for a swift transition from magnetism to this captivating

17

force. The shock of his touch on her face caused for her a suspension of rational thought, as though someone had thrown a bucket of icewater on her. His expression radiated a charm so supple that it flowed about her like a golden net. It was lethal, that combination of sympathy and humor, and it had led to the undoing of far more canny women than she. And Frances was exhausted and vulnerable. But years of being the practical eldest daughter of a vicar were not compatible with the frivolous heady emotion she was experiencing. Miss Atherton came to earth with a bang. What in the world had gotten into her? Grimly, she instructed the too-helpful gentleman to remove his hands. She readjusted her grip on the case and began to lug it forward, free again. He stepped out of the way.

"Don't you like my tactics, Prudence?" he asked conversationally. "I had a suspicion that it might not work."

Frances swallowed, a hard task considering the dryness of her throat. Rather abruptly, she said, "Why do you keep following me?"

"Two reasons," he said easily. "The first is that you don't look like a person who would arrive safely at her destination."

Miss Atherton was inclined to take umbrage. "I have arrived safely," she informed him, "at every destination in my life for which I have ever embarked."

"I know a very good drama teacher who could get rid of that staccato within two weeks."

Miss Atherton was not sorry to see that the tile above the next doorway bore Number 59.

"Here I am, arrived *safely* at my destination. Good evening!"

She prided herself on having just the right note of finality in the good evening, and without a backward glance she set her case against the brick balustrade leading to the door and ran up six marble steps. Frances gave the tarnished brass door knocker a lusty whack. Nothing. She tried again, feeling a miserable trepidation grip her heart. Homesickness, a fat bulldog, and a muddy walk had not been the only trials of her ride to London. Uppermost in her mind had been the ever present fear that her great-aunt might not be home, but instead on one of her jaunts to the continent. What would come of Frances' plans then?

The sound of a slow shuffle came from behind the door. There was a loud clank and the door opened a crack, letting a bar of light into the darkening street. A shiny, gray-fringed head poked quickly around the door, preceded by a squat hooked nose and a bristling mustache. A ratty pair of eyes darted back and forth.

"What is it? What do you want?" asked the mustache.

Frances stared back nonplussed. What could this man have to do with her great aunt? Could Aunt Sophie have possibly married in the three years since she had last corresponded with Miss Atherton's mother?

"I would like to see Miss Sophie Isles, if you please," she said.

"If you'd like to see her, why'd you come here?" he said unpleasantly, and blew his nose on a big white handkerchief.

"This is Number fifty-nine Charles Street, is it not? And the residence of Miss Isles?"

"H'mph." He twitched the hooked nose. "It's fifty-nine Charles Street all right, but there's no Isles woman here."

"But that can only mean she's moved! Perhaps you know . . . ?"

"Don't know and I don't want to know. Don't know who she is, where she is, and don't care to. And what's

19

more, don't like the way you inconsiderate young folk come pesterin' an old man with a bunch of foolish questions. In my day a decent woman would *know* who she was lookin' for and *know* where to find 'em." He snapped the door shut in her face.

Frances stared quietly at the unresponsive door knocker before turning to walk down the steps. She sat wearily on her case. The sun had vanished behind the block of townhouses rendering the severe Palladian façades of Charles Street colder and more austere than they had been in the kindly afternoon light. The pavement was still crowded, though less than it had been earlier, and faces carried the impatient preoccupation of those returning home from their labors. Across the street, a woman in a large crowned cap was pulling the chock pegs from under a cart piled high with baskets and covering her merchandise with a red wool blanket. A postman hurried by thrusting his brass bell through the leather straps of an empty canvas letter bag. One by one, a row of bright dots appeared, following the slow progress of the lamplighter.

The man with the golden hair was leaning against the balustrade, his elbows resting comfortably on the stone newel.

"Prudence," he said musingly, ". . . Sweetsteeple."

Frances roused from her self-counsel to say, "That is *not* my name!"

"Prudence Sweetsteeple," he continued, ignoring her indignant outburst, "leaves the remote hamlet where she was reared and travels to the Great and Terrible Capital only to find herself stranded friendless and hungry without so much as the price of a return ticket or a night's lodging."

"How," she said suspiciously, "do you know that?"

Age had softened the fabric of her cape, permitting

the top button to slip, at times, from its hole. It was loose now and he reached down, refastening it. "If you could afford a room, you would have rented one to shake off your dried mud before arriving at the home of a lady you don't know well enough to be sure of her address."

Frances smiled reluctantly. "Very clever. You must have been a source of continual amazement to your tutor."

The man leaned back against the newel post, crossing his finely muscled legs at the ankles. The searching hand of the soft evening breeze stroked through his hair. He smiled at Frances in his odd, affectionate way.

"I never had a tutor. My parents held that public school was superior for the development of character."

"Did they? How do you know I come from a remote village?"

"Your clothes are twenty years out of fashion."

Frances frowned at the serviceable gray cape that her own mother had worn at Frances' age. Then she looked at the stranger in his beautifully cut blue jacket, tight buckskins, and shiny Hessians. "It's wasteful to throw out perfectly good clothing simply because the style is no longer the current thing. I don't care a fig about being fashionable."

"Very proper," he said affably. "Frills and furbelows won't get you into heaven."

She stood, emphatically brushing at the mud on her cape. "Going to heaven is nothing to joke about," she said primly.

The gentleman did not appear in the least chastened. "And I knew you were hungry," he said, "because you're so cross. Let me take you somewhere and feed you."

Miss Atherton ignored the wheedling of her stomach.

21

"Absolutely not! I don't know you. Now, if you'll pardon me, I'll have to think of a plan."

"I believe you could." Smiling, he came to stand close to her. "But you won't have to, I know where Sophie Isles lives."

"You . . how could you know that?"

"She lives in an apartment above a young male relative of mine, on Long Acre, about ten blocks from here. How would you prefer to travel?" Green devils danced in his eyes. "Shall I call a hack for you?"

"For ten blocks? I should say not. Although I can see you are funning. If you would be so kind as to give me directions," she said formally, "I shall do very well on foot."

"You will, if Miss Sophie doesn't go to bed before two A.M. I'm afraid that's how long it will take you to drag your case there."

She looked at her boot tops and kicked at the caked mud on the hem of her cape, so that a tiny piece fell off and crumbled on the sidewalk. Pride had carried her case down Charles Street. She wondered if a miracle might give her the strength to carry it another ten blocks. Her arms and legs ached miserably. Mayhap the Lord had provided this stranger to carry her traveling case, although any virtuous young lady would have wished that the Lord had provided someone a little less spectacular.

"I'm not weak," she said. "It's just that this case is very heavy."

He reached for her bag and lifted it with irritating ease. "A Herculean weight," he agreed. "What's in here?" He started walking toward Russell Street, carrying the case, and she went beside him.

"Lots of things. But mostly, a brass bed warmer."

22

"I wouldn't have thought you would need that to keep you warm in bed."

"I didn't think so either, but then Grandma said she wouldn't sleep nights if she wasn't sure I had it with me."

"Grandma Sweetsteeple?"

This time she laughed, a musical rippling sound that caused a boy pushing a cart heaped with broccoli to stare after the girl who was lighting the evening with laughter. "No, Atherton. That's my name as well. What's yours?"

"David," he said easily. "So you were named after your grandmother. My felicitations. Atherton is an unusual name for a girl." He was pleased to hear her laugh again.

"How can you be so absurd? Atherton is my *surname*. And you were very bad to joke me by not saying immediately that you know where Miss Isles lives."

Privately, the man with the golden hair marveled at the relative ease with which he had won her trust. It spoke volumes for the depth of her naïveté that she so readily accepted his word that he was taking her to the residence of Miss Sophia Isles.

"I admit to being very bad." They were walking through a circle of lamplight that glimmered on his shiny hair. "I ought to warn you that your reluctance to tell me your first name leads me to believe that you are too embarrassed to tell me. What could it be . . . Bathsheba? Armilla?"

"It's nothing like that." They were separated briefly by a man carrying a giant stick of bread who shouldered his way hurriedly between them.

"Jarita?" he asked after they were reunited by the man's passing.

23

"That is not a name!"

"Ah, but it is. I can see you haven't studied Hindi."

A certain twinkle danced in Frances' eyes. She peeped sideways at her companion. "I confess I haven't. Does that sink me utterly beneath reproach?"

"Not for a moment. I'm the soul of tolerance. What have you studied? Painting? Do you know who Cooper was? That's right, the miniaturist that Mrs. Pepys sat for. That apartment house above the coffee-seller's was Cooper's home."

Long, long ago, the surrounding nineteen acres had been the garden of the Westminster Abbey monks. The Convent Garden, folks had called it; but since, it had known a transformation to the Duke of Bedford's garden, then into a fashionable piazza, and finally, to its current earthy and colorful incarnation. Somewhere in history's unthinking plunge, some unsung innovator with an eye for abbreviation had shortened the obsolete name and restyled the area Covent Garden.

The gentleman knew the area well. He entertained Frances with an enthralling walking tour of this historic place. Frances could almost see the beloved actress Nell Gwynn viewing a parade from her lodgings as the cavaliers of the Stuart Restoration saluted her from horseback. The gentleman beside her seemed to be one of the rare people who can bring history to life and turn a stroll through busy streets into an adventure. Frances began to forget her earlier caution. She had never met anyone like this man before—so charmingly animate, with such unselfconscious ease.

It was not Miss Atherton's habit to be easily impressed. However, by the time she had walked from the corner of Charles Street, down Russell, and over to James, she realized that he possessed a degree of erudition, wit, and education that placed him on a level of sophistication far above her own. She was not intimidated, she told herself, but as they turned the corner of Long Acre, she began to wonder why he should have taken the trouble to befriend and assist a nobody like herself, especially as she'd been less than polite to him earlier. He had said there were two reasons he had been following her on Charles Street, the first being that he was concerned about her safely reaching her destination. It was true, Frances thought, that she might have had a difficult time locating her great-aunt's new address without him.

"But what was the second?"

"I beg your pardon?" he said, sending his sweet smiling glance to her.

"The second reason you followed me."

He looked, if not precisely surprised, then a little curious; he studied her face as if to revise a prior impression. His eyes were bright and kind as he said:

"Miss Atherton, surely you must know."

The wind's mischievous fingers had loosened her bonnet strings. She retied them rapidly as she walked.

"Well, I don't. And as we've been walking along, it occurs to me to wonder why you would want to spend your time helping strangers around the streets, because I can see now, even if I did not at first, that you are quite a brilliant man."

It was his turn to be amused. "*Thank* you, Miss Atherton. You honor me too much. Do you know, though, that if you continue in that vein, I will find myself revising my previous estimate on the size of your hamlet downward. Hasn't anyone ever tried to seduce you?"

Seduce. She knew the word, of course, but it had previously played so minute a part in her vocabulary that she was forced to think a moment to recall its mean-

ing. She gasped when she remembered and said simply:
"No."

"That's quite an oversight on somebody's part." A crowded street corner was not the setting a man of his vast experience would have chosen to make a declaration of desire, nor was a bald statement of fact as likely to produce a successful result as were patience and attentive intimacy. To have ignored her direct appeal for an explanation, though, would have amounted to a deception alien to his nature.

A grin touched his lips as he noted they had arrived almost at the ornamental porch that marked the entrance to Miss Isles' apartments—at least, when she demanded the return of her case, she would have only a short space to carry it. "Miss Atherton," he said gently, "I would like to be more than friends with you."

Frances' young life had been devoted to Duty and Service. She was Assistant Mother to eight younger siblings, confidante and soul mate to her Papa and aide-de-camp to her unworldly, domestically inclined Mama. Excepting her brothers, the only young men Frances knew were the fishermen's sons from her village, any one of whom would have been too shy to woo the Parson's lovely, intelligent daughter. There had been no proposals, proper or improper, in Miss Atherton's life; and while she might daydream in modesty of the former, it had never crossed her mind that she might ever be in a position to receive the latter. So unexpected was the declaration that Miss Atherton was not completely sure of his intention until he said helpfully:

"Yes, Miss Atherton, I meant precisely what you think I meant."

To say that Frances was shocked would have been greatly to understate the case; in fact, she was astonished. She had never been encouraged to think of herself as pretty. As a result, she did not, and it came as a surprise to her that she could somehow have inspired those sentiments in any gentleman, particularly one who, it was quite obvious, could hardly have suffered from a lack of feminine companionship. Her incredulous surprise, however, was soon trampled by a flaming wrath.

"I suppose you think," she said dangerously, "that because I *allowed* you to talk to me on the street you can insult me!"

Capped in her shabby brown bonnet and cloaked in her puritanical morality, she had for him the quaint charm of a delightfully apt cliché. They had reached Miss Isles' building, so he set her case on the low porch before the door and took Miss Atherton's flushed cheeks leisurely between his palms, forcing her to look into his sparkling green eyes.

"Never, Prudence," he said, with what Frances regarded as an odious tranquility, "is it an insult to tell a woman that you find her so attractive that you would like to . . ."

Miss Atherton stopped his words by clapping her mittened hands over her ears in a gesture rendered unfortunately inefficient by the oversized contours of her bonnet. She removed her face from his hold with so forceful a back-step that if it were not for his steadying hands on her shoulders she would surely have fallen.

"It is always, *al-ways*," she said furiously, "an insult unless preceded by a marriage vow."

Releasing her shoulders, he walked to the heavy oak door and held it open for her. Miss Atherton marched past and found they had entered a narrow hall lined with marble wallpaper in yellows and browns. An interior door lay to the right of the entrance, and a wooden open-newel stair lit by a single lamp led to an upper landing. He lifted her case inside the threshold and shut the outer door behind them.

There was both rueful self-knowledge and compassion in his smile as he said, "That's one game I don't play, Prudence. I doubt if I'll ever be able to make that type of commitment to a woman. Honestly, sweetheart, there's very little chance I'd marry you."

Miss Atherton came to a full rolling boil. "Well, there is *NO* chance that I would marry you!" She stormed to the door like a tidal wave and pounded against it with her fist.

Diverted, he watched her for a moment, then said, "Miss Isles lives upstairs, Prudence."

Frances stopped her assault on the door and saw with painful embarrassment that it was opening. A tall man wearing a red silk dressing gown stepped into the hallway. The man was in his early twenties; and while his looks were not the show-stopping extreme of the man with the golden hair, they had caused flutters in the heart of many a young lady. His hair was brown and curled in the classical manner; his blue eyes were intense and alive. He studied Frances curiously before the blue eyes lit up in a smile.

"Come in!" he said enthusiastically, making an expansive gesture of welcome.

Miss Atherton suddenly remembered that this person was a "young relative" of her detested escort. She turned in one space, snatched her case, and began to bump it, one step at a time, to the second floor. The man looked puzzled and ventured:

"Did I say something wrong?" It dawned on him that there was a third party present. "David! Hello!" He indicated Miss Atherton, who was halfway on the climb to her aunt's door, the suitcase rhythmically hitting each step as she went. "A friend of yours?"

The noise of her suitcase obscured the words of Landry's reply.

"Oughtn't we to be carrying her case for her?"

"I wouldn't try if I were you," was Landry's amused rejoinder. "You're likely to get it back in your face."

Chapter Two

Miss Atherton was admitted to the apartments of her great-aunt Miss Sophia Isles by a hefty and rather deaf maid in a lacy bibless apron. After several loud repetitions Frances succeeded in making known her name and her wish to see Miss Isles and was shown promptly to a parlor hung in pastel-blue damask. It was a small room, rendered smaller by a large, hot fire in the carved marble hearth and by a hotchpotch of surplus furnishings. Silver cloth upholstered settees, piecrust tea tables, and tripod stands bearing porcelain fruit dishes littered the cramped space in such abundance that Frances was forced to thread her way gingerly to a seat. She had nearly a half hour to recover from the hateful conduct of the dissipated Mr. David before Great-Aunt Sophie appeared at the parlor door.

"The only thing worse than arriving during dinner," Aunt Sophie remarked as she entered, "is arriving while one is dressing for dinner. Which one of the Atherton brood are you?"

"The eldest girl, ma'am. Frances." Frances had beheld her great aunt on only one previous occasion, nine years earlier, but her memory of that time was vivid, and she could see that her aunt was little changed. Miss Atherton was too well reared to offend the dignity of a fellow being even in her thoughts by applying so demeaning an adjective as "fat," but she couldn't suppress a recollection of her graceless brother Jim saying Aunt Sophie was as big as a haystack and had more chins than a Greek chorus. The lady thus alluded to was clad this evening in a bright-jonquil dinner gown, and sailed across the furniture-packed room with the smooth, flowing motion of a flower-bedecked man-of-war entering a harbor filled with fishing boats. Contrary to every expectation of age and fashion, her hair was worn long and straight, and the flowing brown locks, white at the temples, were accented by the addition of a single daffodil tucked behind one ear.

Frances continued, " 'Tis very nice to see you again, and looking so well! I apologize for the inconvenience, but there wasn't time to let you know that I was coming. Last night I decided that this was the right thing to do, and early this morning I boarded the public stage!"

"What you want, then, Miss Frances, is tea. You're white as a mainsail." Sophia reached behind her and took in hand a speaking funnel and clearly enunciated the single word:

"TEA!"

The maid was entering the room carrying a painstakingly arranged dish of peaches. She looked at her mistress, puzzled.

"I thought I gave you the key," she said.

Aunt Sophia shook her head, pointed at Frances, and said with careful articulation, "She'll have some tea," and took a pantomime sip from a cup. The maid replied with a sapient look and hurried from the room. Aunt Sophia nodded with satisfaction.

"That's Henrietta," she confided, gesturing toward the disappearing maid. "She's a gem." The settee groaned as Sophia sat next to Frances. "Here you are with your dressing case. Run away from home?"

"It's nothing like that, Aunt. I've come to help Papa."

"Help him?" replied Sophia. "You mean someone's finally going to persuade him to take the university chancellorship that your uncle, Bishop Ambarrow, has been trying to convince him to accept these twenty-one years?"

"Papa would never willingly leave Beachy Hill! His work is there, among his people. Only . . . Aunt, can it be Uncle Ambarrow hasn't told you what's happened?"

"I never go next or nigh the Bishop unless I'm tricked into it. Haven't seen him in a year."

"Then you can't know," Frances said, her hazel eyes serious. "Papa is in the King's Prison at Bristol!"

"Your father, the saint? Short of boring someone to death with a sermon, I can't imagine what he could have done!"

"It was a plot, Aunt, a wicked, wicked plot! You know about the smuggling along the coast? Men came from outside the village to Beachy Hill, bribing the villagers to use their fishing boats to carry smuggled goods. It was dreadful—good, honest fishermen we'd known all our lives—filled with greed, corrupted! Papa began speaking against it from the pulpit and organizing the villagers to stand firm against the bribery. I think he might have won, too, only the smugglers' leader, whom they call 'the Blue Specter,' organized a false charge against Papa."

Sophia had been searching for a likely grape in the dish held up by a bone china shepherd at her elbow. She found one, and said, while taking a bite:

"What'd they do?"

"They hid a hogshead of smuggled brandy in the pulpit."

Aunt Sophia chortled, nearly choking on the grape.

"We," said Frances stiffly, "could not find it humorous. It caused the Preventives to arrest Papa."

"Don't bristle at me, child. It's no tragedy. No one could possibly believe such a thing of your father! My advice to you is to go to your Uncle Ambarrow. He'll see to it that your papa is released."

"We've written to Uncle Ambarrow . . . oh, thank you." The maid came bearing tea—and also an enormous platter of sweetcakes, cheese, honey biscuits, and cold meats. Frances stared at the mountain of food. "Aunt, are you expecting company?"

"Dining out. Eat your tea, dear, you're thin as a rail. I never did understand how Richard managed to feed nine children and half the lazy wastrels in the community on the miserable portion he gets from the Church. You were saying about your uncle?"

Frances, selecting a piece of white cheese from the bewildering assortment, continued.

"We wrote to Uncle Ambarrow immediately, and he says he will help, but appeals take time, and we must have patience. But I don't have patience!" Frances leaned forward earnestly. "It would be intolerable to sit idly by while Papa is in prison, especially now that we have learned the identity of the Blue Specter."

Sophia was concentrating on delivering the correct measure of tea leaves to the pot of steaming water so her only response to this dramatic announcement was a placid "Oh?"

"Yes! Thursday last, Joe and I . . ."

"Joe?" Aunt Sophia stretched a needlepoint tea cozy around the pot.

"My brother, the one who is sixteen."

"Doesn't he go to school?" interposed Sophia.

"Yes, Aunt, he goes to Eton," answered Frances, as patiently as she was able. "But he's home, of course, because of Papa. Anyway, Joe managed to discover that there was to be a smuggling run last Thursday night, at the dark of the moon, which is what the smugglers prefer! There's only one good place to land when the tide is in, so Joe and I hid there and watched the men unloading their illegal cargo."

"My, how resourceful of you little dears," said Sophia impassively.

"When one has lived on the coast all one's life . . ."

"Quite, quite. Go on with your story. Did you see the Blue Rascal?"

"The Blue Specter, Aunt. Yes, we did! He appeared from behind a gorse bush as quietly as his name, wearing a dark mask. He talked with the fishermen for a while, perhaps giving them orders. Then they left and he melted into the night, but this time Joe and I were following him! Not so close, mind you, that he would hear us. Not knowing the area so well, he carried a shuttered lantern. We stayed in sight of its glow . . ."

Sophia placed another plump grape carefully in her mouth. "I think I saw this once in a play."

Frances had the grace to smile. "One cannot arrange to remove *every* trace of melodrama from one's life, Aunt Sophie! You mustn't think I'm a hoyden; in times of crisis, one is called to extreme measures!"

"So it would seem. What then?"

"At the hill's crest was the Blue Specter's horse, tethered to a ragged pine! Before the man could mount, he dropped something into the tall weeds and had to unmask and open the lantern cover, the better to find whatever it was. We could see his face clearly through Joe's spyglass!"

Aunt Sophia decided that the tea had steeped long enough. She took off the cozy and poured the piping liquid into the blue Bow teacups; then said, "Did you

34

denounce the fellow to the captain of the Preventives?"

"Certainly we did. The next morning. But he didn't believe us." Frances' beautiful eyes flashed with anger as she remembered the skeptical attitude of the captain. "He said it was a wild story invented to get Papa out of prison. Joe lost his temper and accused the Captain of having a grudge against Papa because Papa had once reproved him for bothering one of the village girls. One thing led to another, and we narrowly escaped being thrown out of the man's office."

"Who did you tell him the Blue Specter was, the Prince Regent?" said Sophia, tossing a lump of sugar into her cup with the tea tongs.

"No, Edward Kennan."

"Edward Kennan!" Sophia cried, nearly upsetting the teapot. "Edward Kennan! My dear child!"

"There, you see; you don't believe it either," said Frances without rancor. She could hardly blame her aunt's incredulity. The man she had named was one of the most famous actors in England—a man of almost legendary stature and artistic excellence. Frances had seen copperplates of that face since her early childhood, but she had never expected to see it on a notorious smuggler. Yet there it had been; she and Joe had both agreed that the man was Edward Kennan.

"Of course I don't believe it," declared her aunt. "The idea is too ridiculous to be considered. You're talking about one of your country's most distinguished citizens. You *must* have been mistaken! He plays a mighty mean Macbeth, but I vow that's the closest he's come to villainy. I hope you haven't gone on telling people this, or you're likely to be sued for libel."

"Other than the captain of the Preventives, Aunt, you're the only one who knows. And that's why I've

35

come to London. If I observe Kennan here in person, and can identify him as the same man, why, we can be sure."

"Then what?"

"I'll do what I can to prove his guilt! The villagers are terrified of him, but after he's been caught, I know they will come forward to testify on Papa's behalf."

"Go stay with your Uncle Ambarrow," Sophia recommended.

"Aunt, you know what *they* are, full of conventions and false propriety. If I told Uncle any of this, he'd be horrified and forbid me to have anything more to do with it. He'd announce that he'd taken the matter into his own hands, and that would mean nothing would get done." Frances directed her most appealing smile toward her aunt. "Dear Aunt Sophie," she said, and put her hand on her aunt's plump forearm. "That's why I came to you. Papa says you are the best of his aunts! He's told me many times that you were the only one he could trust with the secrets of his boyhood pranks."

"Hm'ph. You'll get in trouble and everyone will blame me."

"I won't get in trouble; I'll prove father's innocence and everyone will honor you."

"Don't waste your cajolery on me, my girl. Does your mother know about this?"

"I thought," said Frances, looking a little guilty, "that it might be best not to worry her, so Joe and I haven't told her anything about Edward Kennan. She thinks I'm staying with Aunt and Uncle Ambarrow, to help them with the legal formalities of freeing Papa."

"Oh, does she? And what if your mother writes to Aunt Ambarrow to find out how you are getting along?"

Frances fixed an innocent gaze on the plaster ceiling. "Joe has conceived a plan to alter the letters. 'Twill be easy for him. He's always been the one to handle postings. It *is* for Mama's own good."

Aunt Sophie rolled her eyes. "Thank God *I* never had children. Now that I come to think on it, I recall that you've an older brother. Why doesn't he undertake this business? What's his name—Charles?"

"Yes. We call him Charlie! He's the dearest of brothers and a 'right one,' as Joe says, but he's a missionary in the north of Africa, converting the heathen pirates, you see. He'll return at once when he hears about Papa; but with the mails as they are, who knows how long it will be until he gets our letters?"

Aunt Sophie gave her a wondering glance. "What a family! Pirates and smugglers! What next?"

Frances' cherry lips blossomed into a sudden smile. "Spying, if you'll let me stay! I shan't be any trouble to you, I promise. In fact, I might be a help if you could think of a way I could be obliging."

"Oh, well, I really don't think so, my dear, because Henrietta is a marvel of efficiency and inclined to resent interference so . . ." She stopped as a light dawned behind her eyes. "Except for the parrot! Henrietta detests the parrot!"

Frances raised her eyebrows in lively curiosity. "Have you a real parrot? How wonderful! I've never seen one. Can it talk?"

"More's the pity, yes, because he's belonged in the past to a sea captain, and his language would put a dockhand to the blush. The Lord only knows what's in those foreign phrases he says! My friend Mrs. Pingbodie acquired the bird on her trip to the Orient. She's had him shipped home to me and begs me to take care of him until her return this summer. The problem's been that Henrietta's taken him in dislike. But wait—meet him yourself. His name's Mr. Bilge, and I'm afraid that reflects the quality of his manners."

Aunt Sophie summoned her maid and shouted, "Bring the bird," punctuating her request by flapping her arms like wings. Henrietta was pleased to exit with a grimace but returned bearing a large parrot squatting on a much-chewed wooden perch.

Mr. Bilge was an elegant creature, with feathers dappled in shades of gray, a bright-red tail, and a balding head domed with powdery white. He fixed Frances with a beady eye and squawked in a loud rasp:

"Paltry, paltry. A mere nothing!"

Frances laughed delightedly. "Such a gruff fellow you are! Never mind, we'll be friends, I know." Advancing toward Mr. Bilge, she sang out musically, "Pretty Polly."

"Shut yer ugly mug," answered the parrot. He regarded Frances with a fulminating eye before turning his back and tucking his head under a wing.

Frances directed a chagrined smile to her aunt. "I don't appear to have made an instant hit. But I shall persevere. No doubt Mr. Bilge has been roughly handled in the past and has become wary of strangers."

"Could be. Henrietta is convinced that he hates women. *You* may be able to overcome his prejudice."

"I shall! Mr. Bilge shall be henceforth under my wing," said Frances. "Oh, dear. Forgive me, I'm the most dreadful punner. And thank you from the bottom of my heart for allowing me to stay. My whole dependence was on you! It was in my mind most straitly that you would understand, being of such an independent disposition yourself." Frances returned to the settee and sipped her cooling tea.

"Gammon!" said Aunt Sophie, looking not a bit displeased by this reading of her character. "Well, for better or for worse you're here. What's to be your first step?"

"I'm not sure. I *have* decided that I ought to be as inconspicuous as possible."

Sophie subjected Frances' faded print day dress to a critical survey. "I don't love to be the bearer of bad tidings, my dear, but you're not going to appear inconspicuous in that rig. If I may be frank, you look a turn-of-the-century scullery maid."

Having her clothing denigrated twice in one day did nothing for Frances' self-esteem. Rather meekly, she said, "Surely it's not that bad?"

"Worse," said Aunt Sophia. "Someone's going to catch you and stick you in the wax museum. I suppose you don't have the money to dress. Very well; let me fix you up with a couple of items. I know a nice little dressmaker on Bond Street. . . ."

"Say no more, Aunt. I could not! It's imposition enough for me to . . ."

"Fiddlesticks!" intervened Sophia. "If it's the money you're worried about, I'll be glad to have something to spend my shillings on. Last quarter I had so much investment income that I had three thousand pounds to spare." She shuddered at the recollection. "Thank God my financial man is discreet. People might think I'd been practicing a lot of vulgar economies. 'Sides, doubt if I'd fancy my dinner if I had to eat it looking at that dowdy costume."

Miss Atherton had a strict sense of the respect due to her elders; therefore she restrained herself from pointing out that a certain lack of appetite might cause her great aunt more benefit than harm. Sophia took advantage of her niece's hesitation to announce:

"It's settled then. We'll take the carriage to Madame Dominique in the morning! Mind you, before I set you loose on London, I had better say that it won't do to take the city lightly. If some scoundrel isn't picking your pocket, then he's breaking into your house. Have a care what you're about! And watch out for the libertines. Being a parson's daughter, I'm not sure what you know about it, but . . ."

"I know only too well!" acknowledged Frances grimly. She had, for a short time, forgotten her earlier affront. It came flooding back with a vengeance. "I was horribly insulted on my way here. A man (for I won't call 'him a gentleman!) made a suggestion to me of a nature so degraded, so debauched . . ." A trembling anger grew so strong within her that she stood, fists clenched, and would have paced the room were it not so constricted by clutter.

"Was he handsome?" asked her aunt, with some interest.

"Yes," affirmed Frances forcefully. "Very!" She stood staring for a brief time into the roaring fire before adding, "He said he was a relative of the young man living downstairs."

"Downstairs? The Rivington boy lives below me. Hell-for-leather young daredevil, though pleasantly spoken as you please." Aunt Sophie made a small adjustment to her impressively plunging bodice. "Not acquainted with him myself, besides a civil 'how d'ye do' in passing. Above *my* touch! Young Rivington comes from quite a clan—one of Lord Tresten's nephews. Aristocrats rich as kings, smart as whips, and wild as the north wind! I wouldn't call it an insult if a colt from *that* herd made suggestions to me." She chuckled. "Whichever cousin it was, I'll bet he doesn't often get a turndown! You *did* give him a turndown?"

"Aunt!"

Miss Sophie Isles advised her grandniece to avoid

squawking at her in the style of Mr. Bilge and ordered Henrietta to make up the guest bedchamber.

After her aunt left for her dinner engagement, Frances unpacked her dressing case, dutifully filled her bed warmer and inserted it between the muslin sheets, and then sat cross-legged on the well-fluffed feather bed. She twisted her hair into a pair of long braids and tucked these under her knitted nightcap. The familiar chore reminded her of her home. She could see the little ones giggling at their own sweet nonsense as they sat near the hearth on tiny chairs lovingly made by her brother Charlie. The older boys and girls would be gathered to chatter happily around the trestle table. Grandmother would be comfortable in her rocking chair, knotting a fringe to replace the one from the parlor drape that little Edward's greyhound pup had beheaded Wednesday last. "The Bean" (everyone's pet name for the baby) would sit on Mother's lap, bouncing and slapping the table with her tiny fat palms. Just before prayers, fifteen-year-old Pamela, fresh from her job watching the Squire's twins, would burst laughing through the door, late as usual but with her arms filled with Mama's favorite spring flowers. Everyone would be together tonight except for Charlie and Frances— and Father. Father would be alone as well . . . no, best not to think of that. Think instead of something pleasant. Unbidden, before she could stop it, came the memory of the wonderful green eyes, the fresh blond hair, the remarkably attractive features of the man she knew only as Mr. David.

Chapter Three

Whatever criticisms of Miss Atherton's attire it might have been possible to make on the afternoon of her arrival in London, by eleven of the clock the next morning Aunt Sophie and Mme. Dominique created for her a wardrobe that would have satisfied the most persnickety young woman and quite flattened Miss Atherton with a sense of obligation. She arrived at Mme. Dominique's with the firm determination to buy one simple and modestly priced walking dress and an inexpensive bonnet.

Inside Mme. Dominique's intriguing establishment, however, Aunt Sophie had shown rare deviousness by convincing Frances to try on a stunning assortment of gowns under the plausible motive of deciding which would be the best. Once this was done, Aunt Sophie bought them all. Frances was scandalized when she became aware of her great-aunt's treachery, but her stern rejection of so excessive a gift had been answered by her aunt's blunt statement that if Frances didn't like it, then Frances could return to her nasty little village and wallow about with the smelly fishes; if Frances wanted to stay in London, she'd better dress in a manner that didn't disgust her fashionable Aunt Sophie. Miss Atherton was not so easily defeated, and for a full half hour the apprentice seamstresses peeking through the dressing-room curtain were entertained by a fierce battle of wills. They recognized in Miss Atherton a game contender with plenty of pluck, but well they knew that Miss Sophie Isles was a lady who could take on all comers and then some. They were right. Frances was never sure afterward how she had let her aunt bully her into taking home the indecently large collection of dresses; then Sophie rubbed salt into the wounds by directing Mme. Dominique to add matching bonnets, scarves, stockings, and reticules to the order.

This done, Miss Isles sallied off to lunch with her friend Miss Bolton, secure in the conviction that whatever her niece did to disgrace the family while in London, at least she would not do so by her appearance. Frances was left to ride home accompanied on one hand by a mortifying reflection of defeat by Aunt Sophie and on the other by visions of satin half-dresses, velvet plumed hats, and fur-trimmed mantles. It was a bewildering array of finery for a village-bred parson's daughter, and Frances could only trust that the heady emotion she had experienced when seeing herself in the looking glass in the lovely dresses was due to the overpowering perfume Mme. Dominique was wont to sprinkle in her fitting room and not to a previously undiscovered attraction to the Hollowness of Fashion. How could she have let dear, determined Aunt Sophie convince her that she *must* be a monster of selfishness to refuse these clothes, that her plan to appear inconspicuous stood no chance without them. No sop for her conscience there. What lady would appear inconspicuous in a high-waisted gown of lilac-pink satin with deep-pink ribbon accents? Frances hoped earnestly that she had been right to accept the dresses because it was certain that she would never be able to resist the temptation to wear them!

Frances arrived home to find a note from Henrietta saying that she had gone to carry the dinner roast to the public bake oven. Mr. Bilge was shifting guiltily on his perch; a claw-shredded copy of *The Whole Duty of Man* lay at the base of the bookshelves. Frances set the book on a table, casting a look of misgiving at the parrot.

"There, now, that wasn't the right thing to have done. I suppose, though, that you were only bored. Poor Mr. Bilge, was that it? I wonder how parrots like to be entertained. Pretty Polly?" she suggested.

"Bah!" said the parrot.

"If you find my conversation too insipid, perhaps you'd like a breath of fresh air!" Frances went to the window and worked open the sash. There was a rustle behind her, and a flap. As Frances turned back toward the parrot, he leaped from his perch and swooped airborne past her and out the window.

"Mr. Bilge! Come back!" cried Frances. As fast as she spoke, the parrot disappeared from sight.

Frances leaned out of the window, looking frantically up and down the street at the stone block of houses opposite, at the shifting kaleidoscope of traffic in the street beneath. An elderly blind man was strolling under her window, escorted by a pretty girl in a scarlet spencer jacket. There was a resonant thunder as a wagon heavy with newly minted bricks lumbered past, the smocked driver giving an idle pat to a long gray dog at his side. Next door, three workmen were trying valiantly to deliver a pianoforte through the narrow doorway of the house. London was preening itself outside her window; but the parrot was not. For all Frances knew, Mr. Bilge might already be winging his way back toward the Orient! Throwing open the wardrobe door, Frances grabbed her old cloak, let herself out of the apartment and ran down the open stair.

As she was reaching for the front door handle, the door to her right opened and the man her aunt had described as "young Rivington" stepped into the hallway.

In the more detailing light of day, Frances saw the shapely mass of brown curls, the cornflower-blue eyes. The red dressing gown was gone; a white linen shirt lay open at the neck; tan breeches were drape-molded to his narrow hips. A silk kerchief was knotted carelessly about his exposed throat, and Mr. Bilge, looking ridiculously smug, was perched high on one of his wide shoulders.

Rivington gave Frances a quick, teasing smile.

"Looking for someone?" he asked.

Memories of last night's shame lent a light rose cast to Miss Atherton's cheeks, much to her discomfort. She wondered what whimsy of sentiment should cause her to blush; *she* was the injured party!

In the easy intellect of Rivington's glance and in his athletic unselfconscious posture she found his family resemblance to Mr. David, rather than in any similarity of features. It was only to be hoped that Mr. Rivington did not share his cousin's want of principle. Intolerable to think that Mr. David might have repeated the tale of the offer he had made her to Rivington; perhaps they had laughed about it together. Intolerable, indeed! And how in the world had he come by the parrot?

Civility forced her to say, "Yes. I had opened the window and he swooped out before I had a chance to as much as take a breath. Thank you."

45

The blue eyes shot her a glance. "For what, returning him? Henrietta won't thank me, I promise you.
When I returned him yesterday, she said that this time
she'd hoped he'd met his end in some vagabond's stew-
pot."

Frances found no satire in the vivacious blue gaze.
She relaxed slightly.

"This time?" she queried.

"Mr. Bilge has made more escapes than the Merry
Men of Sherwood Forest. He sits on my ledge peck-
ing at the pane until I let him in." Sliding his wrist
to the parrot's feet, Rivington allowed the bird to step
stiffly onto the soft white fabric of his cuff. He stroked
the parrot's head lightly with the back of his hand.
"A funny fellow. Seems not to care for women." The
grin was wicked. "Too much time at sea. Sometimes
these old sailors get a little odd."

Frances permitted herself a responsive smile. "Henrietta did say that she thought Mr. Bilge something of
a misogynist."

"A virtual Simon Grump," agreed Rivington. "When
Henrietta tried to take him from me yesterday, the
Honorable Bilge commanded me to throw her in the
brig." Rivington lifted one tan-trimmed boot to the
bottom step. "I'll carry him upstairs for you, if you
like. He may be content with that."

Frances began to follow Rivington up the stairs.
"That's very kind of you. In the future you might find
Mr. Bilge a reformed character. I intend to teach him
some more civil expressions; last night before bed I
spent the better part of one half hour repeating 'pretty
boy' to him."

"And did he say it?"

"No," admitted Frances, opening the door to her
aunt's apartment. She led the way to a small sitting

room that housed the parrot's perch. "And he didn't relish me saying it to him much either. I'm afraid he has a shockingly irascible temper." Frances watched Rivington settle Mr. Bilge and then said, hesitantly, "A fault for which I am in the greatest sympathy, being something of a tinderbox myself. I don't know what you must have thought last night. . . ."

"I thought you were magnificent. And I thought you must have had a very good reason for being in a temper." He gave Frances a playful shrug. "No, don't bother to show me out, I know the way! Good afternoon!"

He had not quite reached the door when Frances called out, "Mr. Rivington?"

Whatever Mr. David's reason (for Frances was unwilling to credit him with a shred of gentlemanly reserve) he seemed not to have shared what had passed between them with his cousin. If Mr. Rivington knew about the insult she had received, surely there would have been the vestige of strain in his manner toward her, at least a hint of sympathy, or amusement, or disgust—depending on his disposition. Miss Atherton assured herself that whatever curiosity she felt about what had been said between Mr. David and his cousin concerning her was due only to a very natural dislike of becoming the subject for crude jesting between two young men of fashion.

She gave herself a mental shake and determined to push the whole episode from her mind. Her paramount consideration must remain with her pursuit of Edward Kennan. Let Mr. Rivington become her first source of inquiry!

"If you have a moment?" asked Frances, trying to keep her tone casual. "I should like to know . . ." No, that wouldn't do, much too direct. She had better

47

offer some sort of explanation first. It would sound more natural. "This is my first visit to London and there are so many things that I'd like to see! For instance, the world of the theater has always fascinated me." Never in her life had she felt more awkward. Frances could only hope that, in time, lying would come more easily. "One hears so much of the great Edward Kennan. Where would I be able to see him?" There. It was out. A little too abruptly, perhaps, but there was nothing she could do about that now. Still, Rivington seemed to find nothing odd in her wish.

"That's easy enough to do," he replied promptly. "Kennan's company is at the Drury Lane Theatre— they'll open a new play in a fortnight with Kennan in a leading role."

A fortnight! Each day's delay marked one day longer of her father's confinement. "I can't wait that long," said Frances with dismay. "That is," she added quickly, "I can't wait because I may have to leave London by then!"

A smile returned to his crisp blue eyes. "If it's so urgent then, I could introduce you."

"You could?" gasped Frances, horrified that she might have gabbed her interest in Kennan to one of his friends. She mustn't take the chance, not the slightest chance, that Kennan would be put on his guard. "Do you know Mr. Kennan well?"

Frances was not a swooner, but so intense was her relief, she felt something approaching one when Rivington said:

"No. I see him at parties once in a while. He's not someone I'd care to spend a lot of time with. His head's more swollen than a goose belly on the day before Christmas. I do know him well enough to introduce you."

"An introduction is not quite what I would like, Mr. Rivington," said Frances, after mulling the idea in her mind. "What I need is to meet Mr. Kennan without his becoming aware that I want to meet him."

The blue eyes shone with laughter. "I think that David was right about you."

Miss Atherton froze. "Indeed?" she inquired, her back poker-stiff. "In what way, may I ask?"

Observing without comment the effect David's name had on her, he strolled to Frances and gave one long brown curl a gentle tweak. "Merely that you are a very unusual girl." He studied her for a moment and then said, "This is important to you, isn't it? Very important? Not just a fascination with the theater, either, is it?"

"That's all true," admitted Miss Atherton, vexed at being so easily seen through. "I *hope* I can trust you, because this is a matter of the utmost gravity."

Grinning, he said, "The *ut*most?"

"Yes, the utmost," returned Miss Atherton, nettled. "If you can't help me, it's all very well—but I wish you would not stand there making fun of me. I am quite aware that the more seriously I take myself, the more people like to tease me. I can't help that, because I've had a great many things on my mind lately. Under more normal circumstances, I'm as ready to enjoy a joke as the next person."

He heard her out with an appreciative smile. "Why is it that I'm getting the notion that whatever it is you're planning, you're in over your head? Tell me, how far are you willing to go to implement this scheme of yours?"

Frances considered this. "I'd do almost anything." After a moment she added, "Except murder someone. I wouldn't do anything like *that*, of course."

"My, my, you are determined, aren't you? Very well. Let's see if this appeals to you. Tomorrow afternoon the Drury Lane Company will audition for a new cast member—they need a female to fill their ingenue roles since Jeannie Milford eloped last week with Baron de Borchgrave. Kennan *may* come. It's worth a try. Do you think you'd be able to pretend you wanted to audition?"

Miss Atherton's eyes sparkled with enthusiasm. She brought her fist against her palm with a decisive smack. "Easily! Because I wouldn't be pretending! I do want to audition. It would be the very thing! If I joined the company, I'd be able to see Kennan every day, would I not?"

"Most days. All cast members are required to attend every rehearsal. But will it do you any good to join the company when you have to leave London so soon?"

Frances looked at Rivington from under serious brows. "That, I'm afraid, was a lie."

Frances found a promising ally in Mr. Rivington; sufficiently interested to offer some salient suggestions, sufficiently disinterested (or perhaps too well mannered) to demand explanations. She had taken the precaution of swearing him to silence. He had responded with the cordial proclamation that ravens were welcome to pluck out his eyes if he should utter a syllable of Frances' interest in Kennan. Despite her reassurance on this head, however, it was inevitable that the weeds of doubt would begin to grow in Frances' hastily cultivated plot, especially after Aunt Sophie's forceful representations against it. Certainly there were respectable people connected with the theater! Aunt Sophie would not deny it, but she didn't hesitate to add that by and large they were a *fast* group, immoderate in their use of laudanum and hard spirits. It was not the atmosphere for an impressionable young lady! Ignoring Frances' protest that she was *not* impressionable, Aunt Sophie went on to say that, still worse, the theater was the hunting ground for the wolfish bucks of the aristocracy, who could be depended upon to evoke temptation in the most virtuous of feminine breasts. Since it was Frances' considered opinion that if she could resist the temptation of a man as captivating as Mr. David, she was hardly likely to yield to what would surely be the inferior attractions of any other male that Fate should throw her way, Frances was able to dismiss this objective to her plans, telling her aunt simply that forewarned was forearmed. When Aunt Sophie pointed out that no upright youth was likely to take to wife a young woman who had mixed freely in so degraded a circle, Frances wondered aloud that her great-aunt could think so self-interested a consideration could inhibit her from her duty to dear Papa.

That was enough for Aunt Sophie! She said cordially that she guessed she'd done what she could to dissuade Frances from exposing herself to the Corrupting Influence of the stage and offered to drop her niece by the Drury Lane Theatre the next afternoon on her way to the corsetier.

The next day, when Frances arrived at the theater, she discovered the spare neoclassical façade that Mr. Wyatt had designed not many years ago in the wake of a disastrous fire, to be rather disappointingly covered in the layer of dark chimney soot that disfigured the other public buildings she had seen in London. Aunt Sophie told her that the parish had the perilous task of scrubbing down St. Paul's on an annual basis;

51

most other architectural monuments, no matter the time and expense spent on their construction, were allowed to grow blacker and blacker. It was the way of a great city.

Frances dodged a brewer's dray as she followed a tight side alley to the back door through which Rivington had advised her to enter.

She was admitted by a husky youth in knee breeches, who directed her up a wide circular staircase to the stage. Once at the top, a landing rank with the odor of tallow candles led to a large pair of open doors. Stepping through them, Frances found herself in the cramped stretch of the wings looking out toward the stage. To her right was the heavy iron curtain, widely touted as the latest in fire prevention. To her left and at the rear of the stage, a trio of carpenters were building a high scaffold, hammering and sawing thunderously under the direction of a harassed-looking man who was staring stark-eyed at an unrolled sheet of stage direction.

A group of some ten young women stood just outside the wing. They were a willowy, animated group, talking to each other with vivid sweeping gestures and affected voices, pointedly indifferent to a lively girl with auburn hair who was auditioning on the stage apron, giving a cheerful rendition of the popular ditty "Birds Can't Fall and Fishes Don't Drown."

The other young women on the stage must be auditioners also, decided Frances. Their poise bespoke The Professional. And their appearance? It bespoke a word Frances was much too inhibited to have ever uttered. Red-tipped toenails peeped from the glittered thongs of their sandals, though the theater was cold and haunted by sucking drafts. Rouge was smeared gaudily

52

across the young women's cheeks and their eyelashes were suspiciously profuse.

Mme. Dominique—ignorant that Frances would wear one of her creations to audition for London's most prominent theatrical company—had dressed Frances more *à la jeune fille* than *femme fatale*. Frances' own gown of lemon India muslin with a skirt embroidered in white was pretty in its way, but it was neither so startlingly low cut nor so gracefully clinging as the gowns of the women before her. Some of the young women had gone so far toward the display of their charms that they appeared to have worn nothing at all beneath their gowns! Frances was forced to avert shocked eyes. The young actresses had carefully fashionable coiffures that were styled with crimped curls stacked high at the crown, testimonials to the talents of their hairdressers. Frances knew her own long soft brown hair tied neatly with a yellow satin ribbon must look dowdy and childish in comparison.

It was not surprising that Frances began to wonder what naïve confidence had encouraged her to hope that she could gain admittance to so rarefied and alien a world as the London theater. A few of the actresses had turned to direct curious hostile glances at her, and well they might! Who was she? A parson's daughter from a fishing village whose most outstanding public appearance had been caroling on Christmas Eve. She had nothing to offer this intense breed of artistic sophisticates. In over her head, Mr. Rivington had said, and he had been right.

A loose-limbed man in his early thirties crossed the stage from the opposite wing. He talked to one of the actresses, bending forward to hear her replies and nervously stroking his lank dark hair off his forehead.

After a moment, he gave the girl a familiar pat on an area objectionably low on her back and walked over to Frances.

"Everyone I expected to come has already come," he said. "So. I'm Charles Scott, assistant manager. Who are you?"

In yesterday's unmerited spirit of optimism, Frances had planned to use a false name on the theory that if it somehow came to pass that she was introduced to Edward Kennan, he wouldn't (if he were, in fact, the Blue Specter) be able to connect her with the man that he had caused to be falsely imprisoned. Brightcastle was the name she had chosen, Miss Brightcastle being the maudlin heroine in the serialized romance from *Lady's Monthly Museum* that Pam read to keep her sisters amused during Tuesday evening mending. Easy enough to think of a pseudonym yesterday. Today under the skeptical gray eyes of Charles Scott, Frances felt like a fool and an imposter to give it utterance. Still, she screwed her courage to the sticking point and said:

"Frances Brightcastle."

"Well, well. Brightcastle. Never heard of you, my dear," he said shortly.

"John Rawson sent me." John Rawson was the theater manager who had been, according to Mr. Rivington, recuperating from influenza at his country home in Surrey. It was safe enough, surely, to give his name.

Scott raised his eyebrows cynically. "I had a letter from him this morning and he didn't mention you." His tone made the words a challenge.

Rivington, predicting some variant of this reaction, had advised her to shrug. She did so, feeling awkward.

"Little liar," observed Scott. "But I don't care. It's nothing to me, if you want to parade your stuff on the boards. You can go on last. Don't get your hopes up, though. We've about made up our minds to give the part to Theresa Sea—the redheaded piece who's singing."

He left her abruptly. Frances took several steps forward along the curtain edge until she could see into the sunken area in front of the stage. The singer had been playing toward a group of men and women seated there. Frances could see no one among them who might have been Edward Kennan, but her attention was momentarily caught by a beautiful woman standing at the end of the row. The woman was reed-slender with gypsy-black curls lifted off a high, proud neck. A gown colored the tone of a pale alexandrite was draped off her sloping shoulders and molded carefully over her shapely form on its way to the floor. She was standing behind a seated man, her elbows resting lightly on his shoulders, her long hands loosely clasped. Even at the distance, Frances saw the sparkle of the diamonds that adorned her fingers. The man in front of her had golden hair, a uniquely rich color that caught the light from a taper burning at the stage corner. As Frances watched, the woman leaned forward and blew gently on the golden hair, sending it rippling like a rye field kissed by the summer breeze. Turning so that Frances saw his face, he shared a lover's smile with the woman behind him. David, thought Frances, almost gasping the name aloud. David, David, Mr. David. There was no mistake. He was the man who had helped her find her way to Aunt Sophie's house.

Frances felt a sharp internal constriction, as though a small earthquake had lodged its epicenter in her middle. Again, as with the first time she had seen the man, Frances was forced to confront the rather frightening revelation that she, that paragon of self-command, could be susceptible to a powerful physical attraction. No one, not her silly sweet-tempered Mama, nor her dedicated, intellectual Papa, had prepared her for the possibility that a young lady of hitherto unassailable virtue could be affected in that way by a gentleman she barely knew and who, moreover, had proven himself to be undeserving of her trust and friendship. Somehow, it could be no comfort that the beautiful woman behind him was obviously a victim of the same ailment.

The "redheaded piece" finished singing, and after exchanging a few words with Scott, came to stand near the iron fire curtain, tapping her foot impatiently as the next hopeful took the stage.

"I beg your pardon," Frances said to her, "I wonder if you know who that man is there, in the pit? The blond man?"

The actress regarded Frances with an expression that Frances' brother Joe would not have hesitated to characterize as snooty.

"That," she said, in a voice that informed Frances that she found it painful to have to converse with so ignorant a hayseed, "is Lord Landry. I trust you recognize the name?"

Frances did of course. Lord Landry was the premier playwright of the modern theater. One saw his name in columns of literary review, where he was hailed as the new Molière, the new Sheridan. He was an aristocrat, a man so wealthy that it was unnecessary for him to set his hand to work to command life's every luxury; he wrote for the sheer joy of it and donated what he earned from his writing to a charitable foundation for retired actors and actresses. It had always sounded so good, in the shallow and fawning news coverage. Frances found herself staring at Lord Landry in blank astonishment.

"I would have thought," she said, "that a famous playwright would be an older man."

"Stately, with a touch of gray at the temples?" responded the actress. Her smile was a sneer, but as she turned from Frances to look at Lord Landry, her smile became wider and more natural. "Beautiful, isn't he?"

Useless to deny it, Lord Landry was beautiful, or whatever its male equivalent.

"And the lady he's talking to?" asked Frances, promising herself this was the *last* question she would ask about Lord Landry. "That's not—good heavens—that's not his *wife*?"

"You are green, aren't you? He hasn't got a wife. That's Sheila Grant. Yes, *that* Sheila Grant, Drury Lane's leading lady. She and Landry have been lovers for years. She adores him, but so many other women do, too. No one's been able to hold him exclusively."

"A reprehensible history," said Frances with some heat. She could connect them now—the man who had helped her find her aunt's home and Lord Landry. A playwright? Yes, she could believe it. The lively mind, the ready wit . . . she reflected bitterly that he was probably cataloguing her in his artist's mind for some future satire. Prudence Sweetsteeple, the village bumpkin. And she would have to audition in front of him. It was no good to hope that he had forgotten her. Frances did not flatter herself that she would long hold a place in his memory, but only two days had passed. His clever mind, no matter how promiscuous, would retain her image for that long at least. She could leave the theater, nothing prevented her, yet she had not seen Kennan. Surely that was, must always be, her

57

primary objective. The longer she could make an excuse to remain at the Drury Lane, the greater the chance she could see Kennan.

But displaying her meager talents before Lord Landry would be a severe trial. Frances had come to London with the resolve to do whatever was necessary to restore her father's freedom. Never had she suspected, however, that her courage would be challenged in quite so personal or humiliating a manner. Anything for Papa's sake—but oh, how Landry's brilliant green eyes would sparkle with laughter at her expense.

She waited behind the veiling fire curtain, hoping Kennan would arrive, hoping she would be able to have a look at him, before she botched her audition and had no further excuse to remain at the theater. The girls before her went one by one through their paces, with each depressingly adept at comedy, tragedy, the opera. It was not easy for Frances to mount the stage when Charles Scott called her name. She had brought Juliet's dying speech to read, the morose mood of which was well suited to her current humor. This, unfortunately, didn't seem to help her speak the part with anything approaching realism. Perhaps it was the effort she had to make to avoid looking in Lord Landry's direction; her voice sounded artificial and nervous, even to herself, and her emphasis seemed to fall on the wrong words.

It came as no surprise fifteen minutes later when the name Scott announced as having won the part was not her own; it went to Theresa Sea, as he had predicted earlier.

There was a chattering commotion. A spindle-legged buck dressed with foppish extravagance left his seat in the pit and came to give Theresa a congratulatory toss in the air. Disappointed hopefuls donned redingotes and bonnets, leaving the stage in groups of twos and threes. Taking what she prayed was an inconspicuous glance at the pit, Frances saw no Kennan. She was careful to take no interest in the fact that Lord Landry was no longer there.

She took as much time as she dared putting on her cape, tying the ribbons of her new pink and pine-green Breath o' Life bonnet, watching the pit, hoping that Kennan would come. Soon though, even the group in the pit began to break up, its occupants drifting away chatting. It was apparent that Kennan was not coming to the theater today.

Theresa, standing with her waist cuddled by her skinny beau, finished a consultation with Charles Scott, who strode off to a portable desk in the opposite wing. A woolly-haired boy in his early teens appeared with a cup of steaming coffee. Scott flipped the boy a coin and stood sipping at the contents of the cup while thumbing moodily through the small mountain of papers strewn about on his desk. Hard coffee smell mixed with the odor of fresh wood shavings that were falling beneath the saw of a stage carpenter as Frances approached Scott.

"I beg your pardon, Mr. Scott," said Frances, at once wishing that she thought of another way than that prissily correct formality to begin the conversation. "I know that I didn't read well this afternoon, but I'm positive that there must be something that I could do in your company. I've had experience in the theater . . ."

"My eye and Betty Martin!" flashed Scott, recognizing the lie. "Frankly, I don't get the feeling that you've had experience at much of anything—you've been looking around like a barn mouse in a cat's nest. Take my advice and go home to your mama."

59

Frances indulged in some very unchristian thoughts about her attitude toward clever men before saying, "I would be happy for even a tiny part." She held up her thumb and forefinger close together, demonstrating the insignificance of the role she had in mind.

"Miss Brightcastle," Scott whispered in an attitude of lending a helpful hint, "even a tiny part takes talent. In the bit you chose, Juliet was dying; you read it as though she were already a ten-hour corpse."

Frances bore the snub as well as she was able. "Perhaps you could use someone to do mending? I would be willing to work for very little money."

"This city reeks with chits who are willing to do mending for very little money. I can't help you."

Scott turned from her to his cup and his pile of papers. While Frances might be Dogged Determination incarnate, she could recognize a lost cause when she saw one. Knowing herself to be dismissed, she turned to leave, and bumped suddenly and distressingly into Lord Landry. Her recall was quick and clumsy; she bounced back against Scott's arm and heard him swear as hot coffee splashed on his hand.

"Miss Brightcastle," said Lord Landry, laying an emphasis on her surname that told her clearly that he had not forgotten she had given him a different one not two days earlier. His knowing eyes enfolded her in their warm green glow. "How charming to stumble into you again."

Frances saw Scott glance at her with some surprise and a dawning interest. He looked toward Landry to study the famous playwright's expression with academic curiosity. Then Scott said:

"Friend of yours, Landry?"

A slow, sensual smile curled on Lord Landry's lips.

His gaze never left Frances' face. "She might be," his voice was gentle, "if she wanted."

Fresh hot color swam to Miss Atherton's cheeks. She almost choked on her fury, and when the words did come, they tumbled out in shaky haste. "It was bad enough that you made that offer to me in private! It's nothing short of infamous that you should repeat it in public!"

Frances could see that her words had contained a misleading emphasis when Scott responded with barely lifted brows and drawled:

"Oh, I'm deaf, don't worry; just like talking to a peach pit." He gave Frances' shoulder a squeeze with one wide, raw-boned hand. "You didn't tell me you were Lord Landry's friend, Miss Brightcastle. Naturally, that changes your situation."

"I am not Lord Landry's friend!" declared Frances, her tone arctic. She turned on Landry, glaring at him as his iniquities massed in her mind like charging cavalrymen. And the first thought to break into words was:

"You told me your name was David!"

"My first name," acknowledged Landry, with a little smile. "I didn't suppose that knowing my title would have made a difference to you. Would it have?"

Frances made an about-face and marched from the theater without a word.

Chapter Four

A cold rain battered London from dirty gray skies and pedestrians took to their heels, seeking shelter in street-side shops. But Frances was so angry when she left the Drury Lane Theatre that she walked more than half a block before she realized that she was in the midst of a spring downpour. The shops were brimming with a rough company of porters, draggle-tailed vendors, and crossing sweepers. After looking in vain for a hack or a sedan chair that might be rented, Frances decided regretfully that she would have to walk home through the wet. In the rainstorm, a beggar may find himself the most envied man on the street, be he the possessor of a well-oiled umbrella, and Frances could only admire the perspicacity of those fellow citizens who had thought to equip themselves thus when they had ventured from their homes earlier that day. As she walked, Frances had to jockey constantly to stay in the middle of the pavement. The rain gutters on the roof overhung the walkway, sending a sheeting waterfall onto anyone walking too near the walls; near the street one risked stepping into the greasy rainbow-colored filth that was puddling up from the overflowing open sewers.

By the time Frances had reached Aunt Sophie's building, her pine velvet carriage dress was sticky wet and clung like a moist sheet, and the cardboard lining under her bonnet brim hung down, hound-ear style. Mme. Dominique had assured her that the bonnet's plume was "genuine ostrich"; maybe so, but it stank like a damp chicken and its pink dye had bled a messy smear on the bonnet's green satin trim.

Stepping gratefully into the dry hallway, she was forced by a sneeze to take refuge in her soggy linen handkerchief. Not looking down, she almost tripped over a long braided rope that stretched from the stair-foot through the open door of Mr. Rivington's apartment. An abrupt, friendly voice told Frances, "Watch yourself there!"

The speaker of this kindly warning was crouched on the brown hall carpet beside a tangle of rope bigger than a bushel basket. He was a tall man with narrow shoulders and a bristle of wiry graying hair sprouting from his weather-beaten pate and, unfashionably, his upper lip. Swathed neck to top boots in a massive gray cape, he gave the appearance of a big barn spider hunched in exhaustion over a newly mummified fly.

Concern that her nose might be running prevented Frances from immediately lowering her handkerchief so her voice was rather muffled, if perfectly civil, as she said:

"Thank you, sir! I'm afraid I wasn't watching where I stepped."

"And no wonder," offered the barn spider, glaring at her with gruffly paternal solicitude, "with that hat dangling in your eyes." He stood and bellowed toward the open door of Mr. Rivington's apartment. "Richard! Have you got a blanket? There's a poor lass here, and if she were any wetter, she'd have to have gills!"

Rivington appeared in his doorway to look Frances over with astonished empathy. "My dear girl, you're

63

soaked to the skin! You don't want to go upstairs; Henrietta left about half an hour ago to take a basket of old shoes to the cobbler for heel-piecing, and Mr. Pike, the landlord, is upstairs with a sweep doing the chimneys. There won't be a fire in the place. Come into my parlor and warm up."

The disheartening prospect of changing her sodden garments in front of a cold hearth from which a chimney sweep might burst at any minute was enough to cause Frances to make only the most token protest as Richard Rivington propelled her into his parlor, established her in a winged armchair before the fire, and cocooned her in a blanket of Irish frizz. Loose snakes of steam began to rise from Frances' hem as she apologetically pointed out to Mr. Rivington that she was dripping on his carpet.

Rivington gave Frances an ironic grin and denied caring about the carpet, and indeed, its condition lent color to his assurance. The rug's faded red-and-blue pattern bore the scars of being repeatedly hacked by someone who hadn't troubled to remove his spurs after riding. The whole parlor, in fact, was in a state of cheerful disarray and more nearly resembled a tack room. A bureau against the inner wall was littered with and surrounded by knotted ropes, grapnels, telescopes, sextants, and a wonderful variety of brass tools. The opposite wall was covered with a vast bookcase stuffed with a library of volumes that reflected the eclectic taste of their owner. *The History of Aerostation* rubbed shoulders with a cheaply bound copy of *Fanny Hill*. *Steam Power Practicum* suffered in offended silence beside *Ben Varney's Body Verse*.

The man in the gray cape had followed Frances and Rivington inside, and as Rivington began to unlace Frances' mud-limp kid boots, the man made the comment that Richard was getting so many fillies that there was no keeping track of them, and asked with vague interest if he'd met Miss Atherton before.

Frances couldn't detect the slightest trace of embarrassment in Rivington's face as he looked over his shoulder and told the man, "She's not *mine*—hand me that towel, will you please, sir." Rivington accepted the huckaback towel from the man and started to rub Frances' feet. "Frances, your toes are like ice! Oh, and this is my esteemed sire." He gestured behind him with the towel. "No one uses his real name—he goes by Captain Zephyr. A little conceit of his."

Rivington's lack of filial deference seemed to please rather than annoy his father. Zephyr gave his son a playful nudge with the toe of one boot and smiled in the way of a besotted parent who finds a choice witticism in any chance utterance of his offspring. Captain Zephyr's smile widened as Frances exclaimed:

"Not *The* Captain Zephyr?"

Captain Zephyr acknowledged it.

"The Captain Zephyr who ascended eight thousand feet in a gas balloon at Frankfurt-am-Main?" asked Frances with awe.

Again, Captain Zephyr nodded, looking at Frances in a particularly approving fashion.

"The most *daring* of all British aeronauts?"

Captain Zephyr beamed at Frances, modestly disclaimed being the *most* daring, and asked her if she was a student of aeronautics.

"No, sir, I have only a small understanding of what I know to be a complex subject, but my elder brother, Charles, takes a great interest in all branches of the science, and before he left for the mission in North Africa he used to talk of it for hours at a stretch! Once, when Charles was at Oxford, he saw you make

65

an ascension from Hyde Park and he said ever after that it was one of the high points of his education." Since Frances had forgotten that the context of her brother's remark had been a condemnation of the quality of university instruction, and not in praise of the ascension, she had been able to speak with what Captain Zephyr found the most satisfying enthusiasm. Frances continued: "And the ropes in the hallway, sir. Are they—could they be the ropes from your balloon?"

The tone of Frances' voice injected a respect for the ropes that, if it didn't elevate them to a holy relic, at least placed them on par with the Stone of Scone. Captain Zephyr had by now decided that Frances was the most charming and intelligent of the many young women he had seen in his very attractive son's company.

"They are!" confirmed Zephyr. "Last time I went up with Richard here and my nephew, Giles, we took a rip in the balloon fabric and were forced down in a pigpen."

"Enveloping a herd of squealing porkers," added Rivington with a grin. "If you think the rope's a shambles, you ought to have seen our balloon! What a way to travel!"

Captain's Zephyr's right eyebrow quirked into a right angle at the heretical tenor of this opinion, but his voice was perfectly affectionate as he advised his son not to be an impudent chaw-bacon. "In twenty years, Miss Atherton," Captain Zephyr informed her, "balloons will change the way we live. On the corners where you see hackney carriages for hire, there will be balloon stands, ready to ferry people wherever they wish. And at a nominal sum—nominal, Miss Atherton! No need to worry any longer about carriages overturning, or a horse with a strained tendon. No more jolting coach rides over rutted roads! The smoothness of balloon travel is unimaginable. Tell me, Miss Atherton, have you been up in one? No? We'll take you then!"

However thrilled Frances might be by the Romance of Balloons, those who ascended in them were considered the most dashing and reckless of adventurers. Such were the dangers that one heard of whole balloons and their crews vanishing forever in some fearful accident. Therefore, Frances was more alarmed than gratified by Captain Zephyr's stern invitation and was grateful that Mr. Rivington created a diversion by loosening her bonnet and subjecting its waterlogged and misshapen form to a critical inspection.

"My new Breath o' Life bonnet," gasped Frances.

"I don't know much about ladies' hats," said Rivington doubtfully, "but it looks to me like whatever breath of life it did have has been extinguished. Shall I toss it out?"

"Yes!" declared Frances, fervently. "I never want to see it again. I'm convinced it made me look too . . . too *young ladyish* today. What I needed was the Jezebel, or a Bonnet à la Borgia."

However limited might be his knowledge of feminine apparel, Rivington was nevertheless able to interpret this to mean that Frances' trip to the Lane had not met with success. "You didn't get a part? I'm sorry! Did you see Kennan?"

Frances shook her head and stretched her bare toes closer to the fire. "He wasn't there . . ." she said, wiggling her toes. "But I saw your cousin."

"Which? David? I thought he was in Brighton this week, with the Prince."

"Oh, no," interpolated Captain Zephyr, helpfully. "The Prince's party came back yesterday. I saw David at Sefton's rout last night—the young dog! Damned if Caroline Lamb wasn't hanging on his arm, too. There's a connection I wouldn't care to encourage! That's a gal who don't have a notion how to manage an affair of the heart, and you know how crazy women get over David. I remember last year when that Russian princess chained herself to his bed! Took us half the night to chop her free." He stopped, noticing the pink band that was beginning to spread across Frances' satin-skinned cheeks. The healthy glow pleased him immensely, since he mistook its cause, and he said, "There you go, young 'un! A spot before the fire will take the trick every time. The color's begun to return to your face! What's this Richard says about not getting a part? Are you an actress?"

"Not exactly, sir, but I would have liked to join the company at Drury Lane. I was quickly shown the error of my pretension! I don't even look like an actress, and as for being able to act, why, I had no more idea of how to go about it than a cat raising puppies. I looked precisely what I was: an amateur and an outsider."

Having disposed of her bonnet, Rivington came to stand before the hearth; he swung the towel gently as he encompassed Frances in a speculative gaze. "You might," he suggested carefully, gauging her response, "ask David to help you. He can get what he likes at the Lane and you can depend on him not to interfere with your ulterior plans. He's a natural for noninvolvement."

His words weren't phrased as a warning. Was it his expression that made them seem like one? Was Rivington trying to tell her that whatever his cousin offered her, it wouldn't be his heart? Perhaps Mr. Rivington felt that she needed to be cautioned but he was quite, quite wrong. There was no danger, Miss Atherton told herself, that she would fall in love with the shameless Lord Landry!

"There are no circumstances under which I shall request or require Lord Landry's aid," said Frances firmly. "No matter how influential he may be!" she added, remembering Lord Landry's hateful inference that her knowledge of his title might cause her to repent her initial rejection of his advances. "I shall find some other way."

Nearly a week passed before Frances was able to continue her pursuit of Edward Kennan. Her sneeze became a cough, and the cough heralded the arrival of a sore throat. Miss Sophie's maid, Henrietta, an ardent adherent to such time-tested maxims as "Feed a Cold" and "Cold in Head, Stay in Bed," gave Frances three slices of baked beef rump with mincemeat fritters, peas in cream sauce, a compote of Siberian crab, and a currant tart, and encouraged her to take a nap that afternoon. When Miss Isles returned later that afternoon, she took one look at the feverish countenance of her sleeping niece, and, as she had already taken that young lady's measure, Miss Isles seized her chance to stow every item of Frances' clothing in the satinwood-veneered spare wardrobe, lock the door, and remove the key to some mysterious location that she refused to divulge to Frances. Thus persuaded, Frances had no choice but to remain abed, using up stacks of Aunt Sophie's tatting-edged handkerchiefs, writing a long and fictitious account of her activities to her mother and a longer yet and more truthful account to her brother Joe, and trying in vain to teach Mr. Bilge to say "pretty boy" and "you're a sweetie."

Unfortunately, these activities left Frances with more unoccupied time than she was used to, and because a large portion of that time seemed, despite her best efforts, to be filled with unwanted memories of Lord Landry, she was only too glad when Aunt Sophie was satisfied that Frances had coughed her last cough and gave her niece the wardrobe key, decorated with a bow of shiny gold ribbon to suit the occasion. Miss Sophie Isles was not a heartless woman. To be sure, she announced herself to be most pleased to see Frances well, but she added in a complacently disapproving tone that she supposed that this would mean that Frances would be up and trailing after Kennan like a hunt hound after a rabbit.

"Kennan is a fox, not a rabbit!" protested Frances with a smile. "And this time I shall go right to his lair. I'm going to wait outside his house until I can see him and be sure that he *is* the man Joe and I saw on the hill and then . . ."

"Don't tell me!" said Aunt Sophie, holding up her hand to protest her niece's confidences. "What you will do next is more than I can bear to know. Acting in a public theater, indeed!" Aunt Sophie's chubby frame was wrenched by a frugal shudder of revulsion. "I live in dread that next I shall hear you had dressed up as a page and followed Kennan into a Pall Mall gambling hell. You'll ruin yourself yet, missie, see if you won't. And that is my *last*, absolutely my last, word on the subject!"

Edward Kennan, as everyone knew, lived in the Duke of Fowleby's enormous town mansion. Frances had seen the Duke's name mentioned several times of late in the newspapers as a Raphael Madonna had recently been stolen from his fabulous collection of paintings. In addition to being an admirer of the fine art, the Duke was a great theater patron and had acclaimed Kennan as the finest actor of the day.

Besides providing Kennan with a modest stipend, Fowleby granted the actor rent-free use of the east wing in Fowleby Place. There was even a separate gateway with twenty-four-hour guard maintained for Kennan's use. It was to this entrance that Frances directed the driver of the hackney carriage, after negotiating the hire of this vehicle on a street corner near her aunt's residence.

Frances had waited for the cover of darkness to approach Fowleby Place. It was through a black-velvet London sparkling with the flares of a hundred thousand candles that Frances traveled. The hack moved west across the city to Mayfair, where the grand homes of the rich and powerful lay in neat, wide avenues like enormous building blocks left by giant children called away to tea. As she rode, Frances wondered how she would contrive to watch for Kennan with any semblance of discretion. A hack and pair were not to be concealed behind a streetlamp. When at last the Kennan gate to Fowleby Place was reached, however, the problem appeared to be not so much how to hide the hack, but rather, how to stop close enough to have *any* view of that famous gate! Frances was not the only lady to have come by carriage hoping for a glimpse of Kennan! Every available spot lining the pavement was occupied by not only rented carriages, but old family landaulets, jaunty barouches, and even an elegant dress chariot crested with the insignia of a royal princess. As Frances' hack made a slow trot through the long aisle of carriages, Frances could see in their windows the graceful outline of a silk glove drawing back the curtain; the shadowed glint of a jewel.

It was a popular fancy, it seemed, for London ladies to bide waiting to sight that idol of the stage Edward Kennan.

Miss Atherton's hack had to take four separate turns around the block before another carriage pulled away, leaving room for them to stand. They were some thirty feet up the street from the gateway, but its heavily rusticated entrance arch was well lit by a quartet of the first gas lamps Frances had ever seen.

The evening passed slowly. Frances sat with her back to the horses, watching the entrance through the passing traffic. Chinks in the hack's floorboards exposed the pavement, and cold drafts stole inside to chill Frances' toes. Once, the hack driver left his perch and made Frances raise her ankles so he could take the horse's nose bag from under her seat.

As the night elapsed without any sign of Kennan, the fair occupants of the other carriages began to give up and leave. It was ten of the clock before Frances found her hack alone on the nearly deserted street and the driver poked his head through the window for the seventh time to advise her that if she wanted to wait any longer he would be forced to raise the fare another sixpence. Frances lightened her purse of the coin and bestowed it on the man.

It was ten minutes later that her patience won its reward. A small closed carriage driven by a liveried coachman came up a side street that led from the mews. The carriage stopped in front of Kennan's entrance. A moment passed before a man in a voluminous cloak and carrying a gold-tipped cane stepped from inside the Fowleby mansion and glanced up and down the length of the breeze-swept street. Kennan—the Blue Specter. From the shaded interior of the hack Frances could see the black crow's-wing brows, the close-

72

that framed his face. Below
...eks were dramatic hollows, ac-
...ul application of walnut juice,
...eer orange cast under the telltale
...was hooked like a bird of prey; his
...bright. The face of a man born for
...t a spell on the eye. Playing Lady Mac-
...Kennan, Sheila Grant had been widely
...have said, "When first he came to me on
...er the murder of MacDuff and uttered, 'I
...ne the thing,' I smelt blood! I swear I smelt
..." Frances shivered as Kennan climbed into his
...iage. There was no doubt he *was* the man she had
...en on that lonely cliff.

Kennan's carriage broke off at a smart trot, and
without wasting time on lengthy ifs and buts, Frances
lifted the trapdoor in her hack's roof and shouted to
her driver to "follow that carriage." The driver gave
her a look to indicate that he felt she was carrying
the thing entirely too far; but when Frances desperately handed him another shilling he shrugged and
slapped the reins. They kept pace with Kennan's carriage—the poor old hackney horse was almost frisky
after the long wait.

The pursuing and pursued carriages went north, then
east, into the heart of town. Kennan's carriage nearly
eluded them twice; once in a section of heavy traffic,
and once when it took an unexpected dive down a
side street and through an alley. When his carriage
finally stopped on a quiet residential side street, Frances hadn't the slightest idea where they were.

Kennan's destination was a four-story house of
brown stock brick with small, heavily curtained windows facing the street. As they passed, Frances saw
Kennan alight from his carriage, drawing his cloak

collar high to disguise his features. The doo
which he gave two sharp raps was suspiciousl
with the understated dignity of polished mahog
square of light shot out from a small peeker's
and Kennan was inspected by a dark face before
admitted. The heavy door closed behind him, shu
out the curious, shutting out the night.

The lateness of the hour and Kennan's own secret
conduct combined to convince Frances that she h
come upon a rendezvous of some sinister nature. Sh
pulled the check-strap. The hack rounded the next cor
ner and drew in to the curbstone. Without waiting
for the driver to let down the steps, Frances jumped
to the pavement and began to examine the contents
of her purse under the yellow glow of the hack's flam-
beau. The result of her investigation was not promising, yielding only three hairpins, one handkerchief,
the key to Aunt Sophie's front door, and two penny
pieces.

"That'll be another sixpence if you'll be wanting me
to wait," said the hack driver.

She felt a brief spurt of panic. "I don't have it," she
said, beginning a dignified plea. "But if you will allow
me credit, I will write my address for you so you
can come tomorrow morning and collect whatever
monies I may have outstanding to you."

Frances directed her final words to the silent night
air. The hack had driven on before her sentence was
finished.

"Very well," said Frances quietly. Her throat felt
dry and her limbs trembled from nervous excitement.
She was as determined as she had ever been to pursue
Kennan until she could expose him for the evil man
he was, and though nothing in the adventure so far
had been easy, standing lost and penniless (or at least

74

tuppence from penniless), in this curiously nondescript street, placed new strains on her courage.

She took a deep, reviving breath and walked to the street corner. Kennan's coach had vanished and another carriage arrived in its stead, disgorging two male passengers, who signaled their coachman on his way and went into the building next to the one Kennan had entered. One of the men threw back his head and gave a hearty laugh as they climbed the steps. Warm, human sound made the place seem less desolate. It was only a street like any other, and no matter what skullduggery she found Kennan engaged in, help was surely only a shout away.

Emboldened by that thought, Frances began to stroll toward the brown brick house, with what purpose in mind she was not sure. She meant to get in if she could, though she had no idea how. There was a back way perhaps, but as all the houses on the block were connected one to the next by party walls, she wasn't sure how one found their back. Perhaps there was an alley further on. The windows she could see were too high and small to climb through. She gave a quick smile at the idea of very proper Miss Frances Atherton gaining illegal entry to a building by climbing through a window. What a time they would have together when Frances told her brothers and sisters the tale of this adventure! For Mama and Papa there would be a watered-down version, naturally. Frances shuddered to think what those two dear and unworldly people would say if they were ever to hear about Lord Landry and the offer he made!

Her steps slowed as she approached the door that Kennan had entered. Then, as though the inhabitants of that house had sensed her presence, the peeker's window flew open and a voice said:

"So there you are."

There was no place to hide. She poised to flee.

The door opened and a man appeared, a bulky black silhouette against a curtain of candlelight within.

"Well, come on then, we've been waiting for you," said the man. As he stepped toward Frances, the copper blush of the streetlamp covered him. His aspect emerged like a phantom of the last century. On his head, a low sausage-curled wig was heavily powdered with chalk dust. The phantom's coat was long, of an old-fashioned "sloping away" cut. His neck and wrists foamed with lace frills—this on a man as wide as a barge, with pox-pitted skin, and a nose so misshapen by repeated breaks that his nostrils lay nearly flat to the surface of his face.

And this ghoulish apparition appeared to have been expecting her.

"Waiting for me?" repeated Frances weakly. Curiosity stayed her flight—curiosity and ice-cold common sense. No matter how unanticipated, he was, after all, a man, not a ghost. A prizefighter, perhaps. His face bore the look of it. His clothing? There were a thousand explanations. He was an actor, or was going to a masquerade, or was a servant. In homes of the wealthy, Frances knew, the footmen were dressed so.

The man was glaring at Frances. "Aye," he said, "and well you know it! We sent the money to Mother Blanchard more than an hour ago, and finally here you be. We asked for three extra girls; why is it that you're the only one 'at came? Blanchard had a busy house herself, eh? Never mind that, come along in with ye, we've waited long enough for the help, and so says Jem Beamer!"

As Jem Beamer spoke, he approached Frances with surprising swiftness and drew her along with an arm thick in muscle and fat. Frances meekly allowed herself to be pulled inside, hardly able to believe she had been graced with the rather frightening good fortune to have been mistaken for an extra domestic servant, in this house, of all houses, that she wanted to enter. Beamer dragged her quickly through a wide foyer and hall. The walls were hung in baby-blue velvet accented with stripes of gold. Everywhere one looked there were chandeliers of carved gilded wood, twinkling with teardrops of cut glass. Niches lined the hallway housing life-sized Italianate marble Venuses postured in the coy confusion of goddesses, not unhappy to have been interrupted in their baths. The effect of the place was extravagant to Frances' fastidious eyes and preposterous after the conservative exterior.

Beamer turned the handle of a door decorated with a panel of painted greenery.

"Wait in here," he said. "Madame la Princesse will be along in a minute."

Frances had never heard of Madame la Princesse, nor did she know what that lady's connection to Kennan might be, but Frances began to entertain the suspicion that if this was the site of some criminal parlay, it was taking place under quite convivial circumstances. Unmistakable sounds of jollity filtered from the inner distances of the house. There was the energetic rumble of spirited chatter that must belong to a gathering of some size. Laughter came frequently and there was the sweet undertone of a chamber orchestra.

The room Frances was in appeared to be a dressing parlor. In one corner was a screen of shoulder height covered in a soiled dimity print. Beside it was a dressing table smothered in a much-picked-over array of cheap cosmetics. A corner cupboard, a free-standing wardrobe, and an oak kneehole desk with locked drawers were arranged for efficiency only against the dirty orange walls. Here, of a certainty, was a contrast to the foyer and hall. In this room, Frances was sure, Madame la Princesse did not receive her guests. Before this reflection had time to lead to any other, Madame la Princesse herself, or so it must be, had entered the room.

"Good thing you're here—I can use you!" cried the woman, shutting the door behind her. It was incredible! Only moments ago, Frances had thought she might have to resort to stealth to enter the house, and now she found her arrival to be considered a godsend! It was not the rapid reordering of her plans, however, that caused Frances to stare at Madame la Princesse in a manner that, once Frances realized that she was doing it, Frances ceased under the dictates of good manners. It might have been the brassy gold of Madame's potash-water-bleached hair. It might even have been that lady's more than lavish application of scarlet cheek-rouge, but as she was an honest young lady, Frances confessed to herself that it was the garment that Madame la Princesse was wearing, or perhaps it would be more accurate to say, it was the garments that Madame la Princesse was *not* wearing that had been responsible for Frances' having forgotten the respectful deference owed one's elders. Madame's body was in a state of remarkably good preservation for a woman her age. Every night since infancy when Frances went to bed, she had worn a nightgown that went from neck to wrist to toe, kerseymere in the winter, cotton in the summer, and if they had a ruffle she considered herself lucky. This was the first time Frances had seen that exotic and deliciously sinful apparel known as the negligee, hitherto experienced only on

78

the pages of the more daring ladies' fashion magazines that Pamela smuggled home from the Squire's. Madame was wearing a knot of ribbon at her throat, a ruffle at her hem, one diaphanous layer of material, and not much else. Obviously Frances' arrival had disturbed the lady before she had dressed for her company.

"There's no time to lose, because I have to get right back and—" Madame made a disapproving pout. "But you haven't done your hair or your face! And that pelisse—take it off. Hurry, my girl! What are you wearing under? Well! That won't do, won't do at all! Pale-blue chintz, and with that prissy little tucker at the neck, too. What can Blanchard have been thinking of? You can tell her for me that after this, we will look elsewhere when we need additional help! Shockingly unreliable—the two times before this the girls we sent for never arrived, and you come alone, late, and unprepared! That's not the way to run a business, no indeed!"

Feeling that she had done the absent Mrs. Blanchard an accidental disservice, Frances began to apologize. Madame waved her words away with a blue-veined hand that carried a gemstone ring of questionable authenticity on every finger.

"No time for that!" declared Madame. She unlocked the wardrobe and began to search impatiently through its contents. "How big is your bust? Never mind! This will have to do. Put it on! And be quick about it!"

"This" was a soft gown of angelically white gauze so fine that Frances would not have been surprised to discover that it could have passed through the proverbial wedding ring. It was not transparent like Madame's, but so sheer that it would reveal clearly the shadows and curves beneath its surface. Madame began briskly to unfasten the back of Frances' gown, making short work of the tiny hooks and eyes Mme. Dominique had sewn in with such painstaking care.

"Why Mother Blanchard has dressed you like Miss Chastely Goody-grapes is beyond me," continued Madame, tugging Frances' own satin gown off over her shoulders. "Nothing could be more passé. If you cater to sophisticated tastes, you build a sophisticated clientele! No, no. You can't put the gauze on over your underclothes. What's the matter with you? Your zona will show straight through and so will your drawers. Heavens! Everything must come off, everything!" She took a step back and glared suspiciously at Frances. "Come to think of it, I've never seen you before." Madame's hard blue eyes grew harder and bluer. "Are you *sure* that you know what you're about?"

This was Frances'—and perhaps it would be her only—chance for contact with Edward Kennan. Modesty and an alarmed bewilderment about the nature of an establishment (which Frances was beginning to think must be some kind of club rather than a private home) that dressed its domestic servants in attire better suited for a Turkish harem—these things must be thought points of trifling insignificance when compared with the chance of bringing Kennan to book.

"I'm very experienced," said Frances lamely, hoping Madame la Princesse would not question her far enough to discover that Frances didn't know what it was at which she ought to be experienced.

"You had better be!" Madame yanked poor Frances' drawers down past her knees. "I told Mother Blanchard in my note that I wanted only the best! Good Lord, wench, do you know who I've got in my salon tonight?"

Frances shook her head miserably as Madame began stuffing the gauze gown over Frances' bare shoulders.

"Edward Kennan, that's who!" announced Madame triumphantly. "And half the fashionable bucks in town, that's who! Lord Nascole is having a party for his nephew's twenty-fifth birthday and he's invited the cream of the aristocratic cream to drop by here to celebrate after My Lady Jersey's drum." Tsking fussily, Madame arranged the dainty puffed sleeves and corrected the gown's drape. She found a wide silver ribbon in the corner cupboard, and setting it high under Frances' breasts, she developed an artistic bow at the back of the gown. "There, it looks very well. You've got all your twelves and sixes, I'll say that for you. Ay! What are you doing? Stop fussing with that bodice—it's not meant to be worn any higher. Just when I had it laying right, too. Stand still! There. Come!"

None too lightly, Frances was shoved onto the stool before the cosmetic-cluttered dressing table. In the wide arched mirror, she saw the confirmation of her worst fears about the gauze's translucency. The color that rose to her cheeks was covered over almost before its arrival by the artificial coat of rouge supplied by Madame la Princesse. A sparkling powder crushed in a mortar and pestle was added to Frances' eyelids and a brown paint to her lashes.

"Don't shut your eyes 'til that dries," warned Madame. "I once knew a wench that blinked like a wood owl when the paint was wet. Ran into her eyes and turned her blind, it did. And what am I supposed to do with your hair, may I ask? It's too long to put up and there's no short bits in the front to curl around your face. We'll have to brush it into long curls, pin a white rose behind your ear, and call it done." As she worked, Madame la Princesse continued her discourse on the presence of Lord Nascole's party, which she seemed to regard as a tribute to her shrewd and imaginative theories of management and a major coup over all rival hostesses, who, if Madame was to be believed, would currently be found in their boudoirs gnashing their teeth and wringing their hands in envy.

Madame completed her work, looked at Frances in the mirror, and said, "Beautiful."

Frances regarded her very showy image in the mirror and closed her eyes as if in pain, but Madame was already dragging her toward the door. Once there, Madame bent from the waist and pulled off Frances' dainty velvet slippers.

"You'll look better barefoot,". declared Madame.

"Barefoot!" squeaked Frances, quite unfamiliar with this scandalous hypothesis. Madame put a hand to the small of her back and whisked her from the room.

Chapter Five

There was a hallway, a right-angle turn, another hallway, more blue-and-gold walls, more coquettish Venuses. Suddenly, the hall dodged left and burst open
into a spacious chamber filled with what could be no
less than fifty elegantly dressed males and a smaller
number of elegantly undressed females. Frances gave
a horrified gasp as she realized that Madame la Princesse had the bald intention of entering the mixed
company in her current dishabille and another gasp
when she realized that Madame's lack of attire was
the standard garb of the female company present. In
contrast, her own gauze seemed almost modest. She
made a spirited attempt to convince herself that these
ladies were probably actresses. Perhaps it was merely
the mode of the elite to practice such sparing use of
undergarments—so she tried, and failed, to convince
herself. In her heart of hearts, Frances came wretchedly to the correct conclusion of just what sort of establishment this was.

Madame la Princesse bent to whisper in Frances'
ear. "Do you know Lawrence St. Pips? No? It doesn't
matter. You can entertain him."

After her first miserably enlightening glance around
the room, Frances had fastened her gaze relentlessly

to the floor. She saw no reason to remove it from thence as she whispered back:

"Can't I entertain Edward Kennan?"

"Certainly not! The nerve of you!" Madame's voice hissed indignantly. "Listen: St. Pips has been drinking since nine. He's three sheets to the wind by now. He gets clumsy when he's boozy, so you're going to have to be careful how you handle him. Last time this happened, he gave Carolina a bruise that showed for two months. You'll have to entertain at least three or four other gentlemen tonight, so I don't want you to get roughed around. Any damage to that dress comes off your wages! And mind, St. Pips has already paid his shot. If he hands you so much as a penny gift, you're to turn it over directly to Jem Beamer. I don't tolerate my girls holding anything out on me, you can count on that, you hear?"

On which dismal note they arrived before a young man slumped into a lolling tête-à-tête upholstered in raspberry-colored mohair.

"Ah, Miss-sewer St. Peeps!" purred Madame, who had suddenly acquired a French accent. "I have here a young girl who has been beg-ging to meet you. Per-mit me to introduce to you . . ." Her words were forced to a halt under the realization that she had never bothered to learn Frances' name. ". . . A lady we call 'the mysterious white rose.' "

Frances wished she were small enough to sink be-tween the blue orchid petals splendidly adorning the yellow carpet beneath her bare toes.

Mr. St. Pips said something that might have been, "Likes me, does she? Well, well, well, well . . ." The "wells" trailed off and he reached unsteadily for Fran-ces' arm, bringing her down with a jolt to sit beside him on the tête-à-tête. St. Pips was on the youthful side of thirty, and the possessor of a nose that looked as if it might have been borrowed from a camel. This large and distinguished member was the focal point of a small and squint-eyed head encumbered by nothing more than a sparse and sandy fringe of hair that poked out sideways over his ears. His very expensive suit of clothing gave the appearance of having started out the evening in prime twig, but now his cravat was askew, his stockings bagged at the knees, and his white shirtfront wore wine spots from the excess of spirits that had dribbled down his chin.

The speed with which her situation had gone from bad to worse to disastrous had stunned Frances, but Mr. St. Pips' drunken attempt to cement the foundation for their future friendship by slipping an arm around her shoulders left her no time to sit agonizing. As Madame moved off through the crowd, Frances shot to the far side of the tête-à-tête. In St. Pips' right hand was a full glass of wine. Frances gave that vulnerable hand a hardy, slap, dumping half the contents of that glass onto the seat cushion between them.

"How awkward of you!" exclaimed Frances. "Last week Madame paid twenty-five guineas to have this piece reupholstered. How angry she'll be! And send you a bill for the whole, no doubt!" Poor Mr. St. Pips was too intoxicated to realize that it was Frances who had caused the spill. He stared at her with drunken dismay. "But never mind," continued Frances, forcing herself to pat his fuzz-covered hand. She gave him a stiff conspiratorial smile. "We won't tell her you did it."

Beaming his relief, St. Pips lunged to give Frances a physical demonstration of his gratitude and she shoved him back in his seat, saying, "No, no, stay on that side of the couch, you'll sit in the wet, and how will that look when you stand up? Tell me about your horses."

It had been the oft-expressed opinion of the Squire's good wife at home that, "Introduce the topic of politics or horses and you'll have a man talking for hours." St. Pips was clearly in no state to discuss politics. How fortunate for Frances that Mr. St. Pips had a filly running in Derby next month and had bored his friends and family so with the subject that they had refused to discuss it further. Nothing could have pleased him more than a willing listener.

St. Pips embarked upon a largely incoherent lecture regarding the training of thoroughbreds that was based in its entirety on misquoted comments from his jockey and *The Gentlemen's Sporting Monthly*. An occasional "Is that truly so?" or "A sound point, Mr. St. Pips!" were the only role Frances need play in the conversation; the greater part of her mind was free to take stock of her situation.

Tonight, Frances knew, there would be no opportunity to probe the secrets of Kennan's knavery. Mischief, indeed, might explain his presence here, but it would be mischief of quite another order than smuggling! Tomorrow she must plan a scheme for Kennan's undoing; now all that Frances desired was a swift and safe retreat to Aunt Sophie's. She must put aside how she was to find her way home in the dark (for it was the city fathers' stingy policy to provide oil for the streetlamps only from sunset to midnight); her immediate problem was to show a light pair of heels to the domain of Madame la Princesse. But caution must be the byword. Something in Madame's hardened expression had warned Frances that any attempt to leave might be construed as desertion and dealt with harshly. And Beamer, with the monster arms—would he try forcefully to prevent her from going? If she created a tumult and Kennan should notice her, he might be wary of her in the future. It would be folly to attract attention! She must sneak away quietly.

Jem Beamer stood by the hallway from which she had entered. If only he were called elsewhere, she might be able to disguise her departure among the general comings and goings.

Beamer's glinting survey began to swing in her direction, so Frances shifted her gaze.

The rest of the room, she found, was decorated with a feverish opulence and without the best of craftsmanship, a matter that did *not* seem to be exercising the concern of the gentlemen present. To the right lay a wide curving stair, its balusters adorned with gilt cherubs shooting tiny pointed arrows. Ready to be grateful for each small kindness of Fate, Frances was relieved to see the walls decorated with a series of unobjectionable, if bland, landscapes and not, as she had feared, by murals of couples locked in the Marriage Act, which was the impression Frances had mistakenly gathered from the dire hints of journals seeking to reform the nation's moral clime. And whatever orgiastic revels might be taking place elsewhere in the building, within this room at least, the entertainment consisted of sprightly conversation groups, hard drinking, and a great deal of flirtation. Kennan was at the far end of the room surrounded by a sizable clique of prestigious gentlemen, if one was to judge from the attention paid them by Madame la Princesse and her compatriots. A royal duke was there; Frances recognized that stout noble from the thousands of lampoons that pilloried his extravagance. It must be Lord

Nascole's nephew beside the Duke, receiving a hearty round of birthday salutes. Frances knew none of the other men but their demeanor, their bearing, the cut and fit of their evening wear, marked them as gentlemen of the highest caliber—the cream of the aristocratic cream.

There was a stir by the door. A man entered, but Frances had been watching Kennan, so by the time she turned to see the new arrival, he was already surrounded by a large group of friends, which obstructed her view. Obviously a popular gentleman, he was at once borne to Kennan's crowd, where he received another round of exultant greetings. A very popular gentleman! His back was to Frances. She could see his sunny golden hair trap the candlelight. The man turned, and two of the prettiest negligeed beauties slid beneath the branch of his arms and kissed his laughing countenance with obvious sincerity. Lord Landry! If he sees me, thought Frances, I shall die of shame. She whipped her face toward St. Pips.

As the night progressed, Beamer stuck to the entrance as if he'd been glued there. The company grew drunker, the conversation more ribald, and the flirtations into fondling. Couples began to break from the group and ascend the staircase, accompanied by merry encouragement from those remaining below. It was almost more than poor Miss Atherton could bear.

Frances was so intent upon both keeping her head, her profile even, from Landry's direction and peeking to see if Beamer left his post, that she was caught unaware by a shift in St. Pips' mood. True, his monologue about horses had distracted him, but it had also had the unfortunate effect of sobering him enough to realize that he was in no way tapping Frances for her full potential. Suddenly, he thrust a strong arm around her waist and drew Frances roughly to his lap. Her instinct was to slap him, and she did. St. Pips gaped at Frances, then shouted with beery laughter.

"By God, don't I love a naughty wench! What a time we'll have together!" He poked his fingers gleefully into her ribs. "The slap and tickle, eh? You slap me, and I'll tickle you!"

"I'll do a lot more than slap you if you don't remove your hands this instant," muttered Frances, fighting to disengage herself from his bullish clinch.

"Oh, you're a good one, you are. Tell you what . . ." St. Pips made a suggestion to her that made Lord Landry's proposal of last week seem the pinnacle of delicacy. "So let's go upstairs."

Covered with a full body blush, frightened that Madame or Jem Beamer would observe their struggle, frightened of St. Pips' beefy strength, Frances felt her poise beginning to waver.

She demanded to be released, but St. Pips persisted in his belief that they were having a grand time of it. Catching her wrists in one hand, St. Pips used the other to continue tickling at her waist. It was in the midst of this miserable tussle that Frances heard Lord Landry speak.

"My friend St. Pips!" Yes, it was Landry's voice, untroubled by temperament, unmoved by pity; the same easy, friendly tones that promised much and nothing. "How are you?"

St. Pips stopped wrestling with Frances and stared up, blinking in befuddlement.

"Landry!" he blurted, "but you never talk to me! . . . Oh! Wait! Didn't mean that. What I mean is—Hullo!"

Frances sat frozen on St. Pips' lap, cringing, filled with the most vile humiliation, her gaze fixed on the clinging fabric of her gown.

"Introduce me to your friend?" suggested Landry.

"This one's the Mysterious White Rose," guffawed St. Pips, and gave her a jovial swat on the back. "Make no mistake about it, she's a game one." He gave a suggestive wink. "Likes a spirited play."

"What rare discernment, my dear St. Pips." Frances didn't have to see Lord Landry's face to know that he was smiling. "But how is it that you're not drinking? Here's your glass, and full, too! Give me your opinion. The burgundy is tolerable stuff, don't you think?"

Flattered beyond words to have his views solicited by so elevated a connoisseur, St. Pips began a rambling attempt to prove that he was in exact agreement with Lord Landry's pronouncement. Landry, meanwhile, was able to introduce the wineglass into one of St. Pips' hands, and at the same time free Frances' wrist from the others. Frances felt the cool, steady pressure of Landry's hands high on her sides as he whisked her from St. Pips' lap and sat her carefully in a nearby chair.

"What a lot of names you have, Miss Atherton," he whispered, his breath soft among her curls.

Frances' quickly accomplished removal left St. Pips staring with hazy bewilderment into the space where she had been. He frowned up at Landry, who returned the look with an encouraging smile. It spoke volumes for the intimidating ease of Landry's self-assurance that the moment passed without St. Pips making an objection.

"You have a horse running next month at the Derby?" inquired Landry suavely, who was nothing if not well informed. Delighted with this show of interest, St. Pips launched once more into his favorite topic.

Never before had so many conflicting emotions raged in Frances' breast: resentment, trepidation, awful embarrassment, and a niggardly sum of gratitude that pricked her like a nettle. How she would have liked to know what Landry was thinking. The worst, no doubt. Frances stole her first nervous glance toward Landry, who was conducting an amused and thoughtful study of St. Pips. Landry was dressed in a gray evening coat, which contrasted admirably with his glinting green eyes and his shining, impeccably cut blond hair. His legs, finely muscled and long, were stretched casually before him, encased in tight-fitting breeches, as he leaned back in a chair next to Frances. He reached out an elegant hand to her and played gently, absentmindedly, in her curls with his tapered fingers. She shivered involuntarily and was about to bat his hand away when she saw Madame la Princesse bearing down on them.

Madame had made a point to keep her eye on Frances throughout the evening. How she hated to use girls she had not personally trained! One never knew what gaucherie they might exhibit before a client. And tonight of all nights she wanted no slipups. She had seen Landry's show of interest in the girl—his possessive sequester of her. Almost it had made her laugh —the foolish St. Pips gulled by the most beautiful man in the ton. These minor rivalries over girls were frequent in her house and they added spice to the business; but the White Rose was an unknown quantity. Could Madame trust her to keep the situation from getting out of hand? From the tight, unhappy look of her, it seemed as if the girl was going to exercise no conciliatory charm on either man. Perhaps she had already been handled too roughly by that stupid St. Pips. Or perhaps . . . the thought sprang to Madame's mind—Mother Blanchard might have treacherously sent the girl with the villainous purpose of deliberately causing an incident to bring unfavorable publicity to Madame's rival establishment? Madame's heels took wing toward the trouble spot.

"Ah, Lord Landry. Do you enjoy yourself? And Miss-sewer St. Pips, you are happy, oui?"

St. Pips gave her a lushy grin and raised his glass. "Tolerable burgundy, Madame," he said thickly.

"And the little mademoiselle, she is fond of you?"

"Slapped me right across the face," he said proudly.

"She is original, la petite mademoiselle," replied Madame la Princesse, and darted a look that bode ill toward the Mysterious White Rose. "I know Mademoiselle the White Rose is eager for you to take her upstairs to continue your game in private, n'est-ce pas? I shall have Miss-sewer Beamer show you to a room."

Landry lifted his graceful body from the chair. As he did so, Frances saw him send a deft signal across the room to a young, strikingly handsome man standing by Kennan. The young man set down his wine, gave a wry smile, and came toward them. Landry made a subtle gesture, indicating St. Pips. The young man's grin widened, and he gave a tiny affirmative nod. As the young man reached them, Landry said:

"Mr. St. Pips, you know my cousin, Sir Giles? No? Giles, I know you'll recognize the significance of St. Pips' views on horseracing."

The young man rolled his eyes comically, murmured, "Only for you, David," and came around the tête-à-tête to sit by St. Pips, inviting him with an air of solicitous interest, to talk. Satisfied, Landry draped an affectionate arm around Madame and walked her to a spot a few feet away, engaging her in a quiet discussion. Frances couldn't make out Landry's words, but after a moment of listening, Madame exclaimed:

"Please, my dear Lordship, I cannot! Instead, I shall let you have Nanette. She's my best girl and I was saving her for His Highness, the Royal Duke. Only for your satisfaction will I make this concession."

Frances couldn't hear Landry's reply.

"I beg you, Your Lordship," cried Madame, "to be reasonable. I've already promised the White Rose to St. Pips. How can I tell him that she's not for him, when he's so obviously so happy with her?"

Landry laughed, and replied in a low voice.

Madame wrung her hands in distress. "How can I choose between you? St. Pips is a regular *paying* client. You have come to the Chez la Princesse but twice before, on the occasion of parties given by your acquaintances—and neither time did you stay to delight any of my girls with your attention."

Landry's quiet answer must have been persuasive, because when he was finished speaking, Madame threw up her arms in submission.

"As you will have it," she declared, "but not a word of this to a soul, My Lord, or you will ruin me. Only for you . . ."

It was with difficulty that Frances hid her agitation as Madame discreetly summoned Jem Beamer, then leaned down to dig her red-tipped fingers into Frances' arm.

"If Landry's not happy when he's done with you," Madame hissed in Frances' ear, "Beamer will personally make you wish you were never born!" But nothing could have been more genial than Madame's expression as she turned to smile at Lord Landry.

"So, I will take you to a room, Miss-sewer."

Madame drew Frances to her feet and began to pro-
pel her toward the stairs, then up them. Behind her,
Frances heard Beamer talking to St. Pips, explaining
blandly that the White Rose had been called away to
care for her sick mother. St. Pips' bellow of rage
boomed to hit Frances as she came to the top step,
and as she looked back she saw heads throughout the
room turn curiously in St. Pips' direction. Kennan was
among the interested.

"See what trouble you cause me," chided Madame,
turning back with a come-hitherish smile to Lord Landry as they walked down a narrow corridor. "But here
is your love nest! Au revoir!"

Madame threw open the heavy oak door with a dramatic sweep of her hand. Some instinct must have
caused her to sense reluctance in Frances' hesitation;
Madame put two hands below Frances' shoulder blades
and gave her an inconspicuous shove. Frances stumbled
into a square chamber with a thick wool carpet, a
black marble fireplace, and a grandiose ornamented
bedstead hung with crimson drapery. There was the
neat click of a well-made lock as Lord Landry closed
the door behind them. The only light came from red
coals that glowed from the hearth's dark maw.

"Touch me," announced Frances, "and I'll scratch
your eyes out."

"Oh, yes, the spirited play that so enchanted Mr.
St. Pips," said Lord Landry, amicably. He bent to re-
animate the sullen fire with a poker. "Tell me, are
you drugged?"

"I? Drugged? I should hope not!" gasped Frances,
shocked from her fierce distress.

Landry took a candle from the bronze athénienne
by the bed, held it in the fire to light it, and replaced
it on its stand. As he spoke to her, the new flame

flickered and grew. "I'm hoping not, as well. But if you've had anything to eat or drink here, it's always a possibility."

"I haven't," said Frances tightly.

"That's good." He gave her a clinically approving smile. "According to Giles, creative apothecary is one of Beamer's specialties. I wouldn't be surprised if there was a little poppy dust in St. Pips' next goblet."

Frances' eyes grew wide. "Horrible!"

"Don't worry," he said casually, shrugging out of his jacket. "They'll be careful not to kill him; only think of the scandal."

"This is a terrible place," she whispered shakily.

"There are a lot worse." There was no sentimentality in his smile. He draped his jacket over a convex girandole mirror that hung beside the hearth. "To broaden your horizons, Miss Atherton, that's what you do with a two-way mirror. Are you going to faint?"

Miss Atherton's voice was high and thin as she said, "Certainly not."

"Very sensible. God knows what's been spilled on this carpet." He leaned against the wall by the fireplace, long legs braced apart, and watched her, smiling with sparkling eyes. "Would it cheer you if I told you that I looked on this more as a rescue than a purchase?"

The color began to return to Frances' face, and the resentment to her breast. Her chin went up.

"I didn't need," she said in a brittle voice, "to be rescued."

He laughed, unoffended. "Then I can look upon this as a purchase?"

"Certainly not." Her reply and his mimic of it were spoken simultaneously.

"Poor mysterious Miss Atherton." He smiled into

her arctic glare. His voice was warm with sympathy. "Do you know what *kind* of a terrible place it is?"

"My horizons," she snapped, "are sufficiently broad for me to know that, even though I was not aware of it when I first came in. This is, Lord Landry—and I shall not mince words—it's an . . . abode of wrong-doing!"

"Miss Atherton, you minced words," he said reproachfully. "A euphemism for a euphemism."

"Very well, if you will have it! This is a bawdy house!"

"Wherever," he asked good-humoredly, "did you learn all this plain speaking?"

"My father is a parson," she said with dignity.

"Ah!" The green eyes were bright as emeralds. "Prudence Sweetsteeple, parson's brat. It explains much. Are you here to save those poor sinners downstairs from themselves or to raise money for the missions?"

As the scattered shards of her self-confidence began to reunite, the desire to justify her presence to him began to war with a strong conviction that she ought to show him how little she cared for his good opinion. It took her a moment to devise a retort that would satisfy both requirements.

"I suppose that means that you think I owe you an explanation for being here," she asked.

Reaching out his hand, he traced a slow path with one finger across the pale skin above her gown. He watched her tremble, and smiled. "My sweet Prudence," he murmured, "how are we going to get around this excess virtue of yours? It doesn't feel the same as when St. Pips touched you, does it?"

Frances felt the skin heat under her cheeks. Backing away, she said chokingly, "I think you're odious."

"No, you don't, too bad for you. You've got a lot

to learn, parson's brat." He stepped forward as though to touch her again and she retreated quickly. "Careful, Miss Atherton, you're getting closer to the bed." He gave her a lazy smile and leaned back against the wall, crossing his legs. "Relax, dear. You don't have to skitter from me like a fawn. I'm not going to chase you around the room. Do you know this is the first time I've made your bosom heave with indignation in such a skimpy gown? It's quite an effect. And I ought to point out that yanking the neckline higher is not achieving what you want it to, because that draws the material tighter over you . . ."

"Stop this instant!" flashed Frances, hardly knowing whether to cover her ears or her bodice. "If you had a shred of decency, you would disdain to take advantage of my predicament by behaving in this hateful, insulting fashion."

"Which is my cue to point out that I don't view my attentions to you in the nature of an insult, to which you reply, with a great deal more heaving of the bosom, that it *is* an insult unless preceded by an offer of marriage. Do you want a husband, Miss Atherton? Look downstairs; half the men there are husbands."

"I don't want a husband!" she shouted.

"You don't want a husband, you don't want a lover . . ." His eyes took on a wintergreen tinge, the firelight gave his skin and hair a clean gold glow. "Do you want to tell me what you *do* want? And you don't owe me anything, least of all explanations. Tell me why you're here if you want to; don't, if you don't want to. It's entirely up to you."

After eying him resentfully for a moment, Frances said, "I've never met anyone like you."

He smiled. "Prudence Sweetsteeple meets Lord Rakehell."

Frances wasn't sure quite why, but somehow she found she was unable to resist that irresistible smile. Against not only her will but her better judgment as well, she smiled back. Some of the tension that had haunted her body flowed from her like a fleeing ghost.

"You really are incorrigible, you know," she said.

"So they tell me."

"You're wasting your time."

"I'll take my chances," he said serenely.

"You're very difficult," she told him, "and I don't know what I'm going to do about you yet, *but* the reason I'm here is that I'm conducting what might be termed a . . . private investigation."

Lord Landry appeared to find great charm in her confession. "Whose privates do you want to investigate?" he asked cheerfully. "This is certainly the place to do it."

"Don't be vulgar. I followed Edward Kennan here."

A slight surprise registered on Landry's handsome features. He raised a mobile eyebrow. "Kennan? Is one permitted to ask why?"

"I can't tell you. And come to think of it, I wish you would not tell anyone my name is Atherton, either."

"Ahh. Hence Frances Brightcastle. The pieces begin to fall together—except, of course, for the enormous gaps. Does this have anything to do with why you wanted to join the Drury Lane Company?"

"Yes, but I didn't get a part, so . . ."

"So you came here? I hate to disappoint you, but Kennan doesn't visit this place very often."

She frowned as she paced the carpet, rubbing her toes in the pile, her hands behind her back. "I didn't plan to stay. And when Kennan got out of his carriage and came in so stealthily, I thought he must be here for no good purpose. As I was looking for a way to sneak inside, Jem Beamer came to the door and mistook me for an extra girl from a Mrs. Blanchard. Naturally, it seemed like a heaven-sent opportunity."

He burst out laughing. "For a preacher's daughter you have a singular notion of heaven."

"How was I to know?" said Frances defensively. "There's no sign over the door saying 'Brothel, Keep Out.' Madame dressed me like this and said I had to entertain Mr. St. Pips. The rest you know."

He stared at her, then said slowly, "And you say *you've* never met anyone like *me* before." The white rose behind her ear had come loose and he put it back in place, anchoring it firmly among the rich brown locks. "Do you want a very sound piece of advice, Miss Atherton? You ought to get out of here as quickly as possible."

"I shall." Frances gave a decisive nod. Lord Landry's tolerant acceptance of her adventure made its terrors shrink; her earlier fear of Jem Beamer seemed the product of an overwrought conscience. What a departure from her usual self-reliance to have allowed herself to be meekly shepherded about by Madame la Princesse! "I ought to have left as soon as it became clear there was nothing to be gained by remaining. It was the height of melodrama to have been so intimidated by Madame la Princesse! I shall find her and demand the return of my clothing."

Thankful to at last have a strategy, Frances began to walk toward the door, intent on implementing it without delay. She was brought up short by Lord Landry.

"Whoa!" he said, catching her shoulders from behind.

Frances twisted her head to look indignantly at him. "Why 'whoa,' Lord Landry?"

Landry had made a careful effort to revive the white-faced and stricken girl he had found in St. Pips' arms into the endearingly plucky creature he had met twice before, but he saw that he had been too successful.

"I admire your determination," he said in a measured tone, "but your approach leaves a little to be desired. Wait for me here, and I'll return in a few minutes to take you home. Leave Madame to me." Even a man with half Lord Landry's perception could not have mistaken her expression. "Oh, God, I know that look. I'm about to receive a 'certainly not.' Miss Atherton, what possible objection could you have to what I've suggested?"

"Your intervention is quite, quite gratuitous," said Frances mulishly. "And if I may be frank? I'm getting a little weary of your smug rescues."

"Are you?" inquired Landry dispassionately. He gave her a level smile, as free from rancor as it was from charity, then walked around her to open the door, motioning with his hand that she was free to leave. "Very well, my White Rose, do it your way. You'll soon be sadder but wiser."

"I doubt it, My Lord," Frances sniffed, and marched out of the room, almost colliding with Jem Beamer in the front corridor.

"Where are you going?" exclaimed that worthy in his bluff way. "You wasn't with his lordship long."

"That's no concern of yours," she said, looking Beamer straight in the eye in an effort to compensate for her earlier weakness. "I'm going to get my clothes and leave."

Beamer stared at her as if she'd claimed the Tower

of London was made of cheesecake. "Have you gone mad, girl?" He stuck his face so close to hers that she could see the intricate pattern of tiny red veins in his yellow eyeballs.

"No," she said firmly. "But I must have been mad before, to have flinched from asserting my rights. This country is governed by laws. And if I want to leave, I *can* leave! Let me pass, or I'll . . ." Her threat was reduced to a helpless mumble as he clapped a huge hand over her mouth.

"You little Bedlamite," he growled in her ear. "We've got four clients already paid for you. You hold your sauce or I'll pump so much opium into you that you'll think you're walking on the ceiling. Going to behave yourself?" He pulled his hand off her mouth.

"Unhand me, sir," she demanded stormily, "or I'll report you to the magistrates."

"Magistrates!" thundered Beamer. "Magistrates, is it?" He socked his hand back over her mouth. "By God, you'll rue the day you said 'magistrates' to Jem Beamer. How are you going to get the magistrates if I break both your legs?" He dragged her toward a nearby room; she bit into his hand and tried to scream, and he squeezed her so tightly as to cut off her air. She was ready to lose her breath entirely when she saw Landry leaning against the doorframe of her vacated "love nest," swinging his jacket from side to side.

Beamer saw Landry at the same time. "Your Lordship! Has she done ought to displease you? By God, if she has, I'll settle her hash. So says Jem Beamer!"

"No," he said placidly, a sardonic smile playing on his lips. "She was delightful. In fact, I'd like to take her home with me."

101

"H-home?" stammered Beamer, his grip on Frances loosening. "This one? I—we couldn't have that, sir. I'm sorry, sir, but it wouldn't do."

Landry produced a hundred-guinea note from an inside jacket pocket, exposing it in slow rotation to the light from the sconce.

"Trade?" he said.

Beamer looked greedily at the enormous sum being handled so negligently by His Lordship. "I want to oblige you, My Lord, but she's a troublemaker. Been talking about going to the magistrates."

"I guarantee that she won't." Landry walked to Beamer and tucked the note into Beamer's ample waistband. "My word as a gentleman."

Beamer hesitated another second, then released her. "The clothes she came in is in the room at the back. I'll summon your lordship a hack, if you please. Enjoy yourself, My Lord."

Chapter Six

It was a mere matter of minutes before Frances was changed and being handed into the damp interior of a hackney cab by Lord Landry. Landry joined her inside and the cab lurched forward; the bright tattoo of the hired horses' hooves came muffled through the hack's grease-filmed windows. Frances stared at the footbath of foul straw covering the floor.

"One hundred guineas," she said as though she couldn't believe that he had spent so great a sum on her behalf.

Lord Landry stretched his arm lazily across the cracked leather seat behind Frances. "Don't let it distress you; I regard it as an investment."

"How could it not distress me?" asked Frances. "I shall pay you back every penny if it takes me forever! What do you mean, an investment?"

The hand that he had stretched in back of her lifted unobtrusively to stroke her cheek. "Frances. Is that your real name? Yes? Look at me, Frances."

She had too much pride to refuse. His fingers lowered to brush the sensitive skin on the side of her neck.

"I still want you. But I didn't want it to happen there." He smiled. "It's probably been a month since they changed the sheets. Come home with me."

Frances swallowed convulsively, and shifted to avoid his hand. "I can't think it possible"—Frances' voice was grave and nervous—"that even *you*, Lord Landry, would expect me to make good my debt to you by becoming your . . ." She couldn't say it.

"Mincing words again, Frances?"

"Your mistress," she snapped explosively. "And I didn't give you permission to use my first name."

He laughed softly and pulled her close against his chest; his lips touched the top of her head. Then he released her completely and sat up, away from her. "Forget the one hundred guineas and come home with me anyway."

"No!"

He touched her chin with the curve of his finger. "All right. Fear not, Miss Atherton, I'm not going to abduct you." His green eyes were like a soft summer mist as he gazed peacefully at Frances. "I can wait."

Frances had met his gaze bravely as long as she was able. When she could do it no longer, she turned her head as though to look out of the window at the passing night scene. Unfortunately, the window had been broken and replaced with a wooden shutter. She felt ridiculous staring at it, and the acid silence burned her nerves.

"You make it very difficult for me to say thank you," she said in a suffocated tone.

"I know," he said. "Is it so important to you, saying thank you, or is it another thing you think you ought to do? Your hand's trembling. What's the matter?"

"I'm tired, and you make me feel uncomfortable."

"I can't help that, dear." His voice was soft. "Unless you'll let me."

His hand slid through the front of her coral bro-

104

cade pelisse and made a warm cup over the thin chintz gown that covered her shoulders. Quickly, fearfully, she braced her small mittened hands on his chest, resisting him.

"Frances, lovely Frances, you know what happens between a man and a woman, don't you? I couldn't possibly do that to you here; there's not enough room. You can stop fighting for a moment."

"Tricks," she said, trying to free herself, "and more tricks!"

His expert grip held her easily. "Very astute," he said with a dangerous sparkle. "I wouldn't like you so much if you were stupid. Besides, you've got a fighting chance. I've been honest with you—I told you what I wanted within an hour of meeting you."

If only she were not so keenly aware of his closeness. "You won't be able to seduce me."

It was his most attractive smile—tender, faintly amused. "If I'm not going to be able to seduce you, then what are you so worried about?"

He coaxed her closer with the light urging of one hand. "You can then let me do this with perfect safety." He rested the other hand against the back of her head, bringing her face up to his own. Then his lips were at the side of her face, nestled in the thick dark hair; she felt his soft breath and the warm, living texture of his skin. He touched his lips in a slow, circular motion over her smooth brow, down her small, perfectly shaped nose. "And this," he said, "shouldn't disturb you at all."

He moved her in his arms and then brought his lips down on hers. She made a sudden startled motion to pull herself free, but he was ready for it, and ruthlessly held her still. Landry was careful to cause her no pain. His grip was all steel but lined with velvet. He wanted nothing to distract Frances from her slow and frightened meeting with aching, unexplored needs of her body. Cool and dry on her quivering softness, his searching lips taught her the lesson nature had intended her to learn. The delinquent scorch of passion began to burn away her rebellion, and as he felt it, he drew from her and studied her face. Her eyes were closed, the lovely dark lashes outlined against the blushing cream of her cheeks; her cheekbones stood out rigidly, yet delicately, the curving sculptured contours leading up from the small round chin. Frances' hands were clasped before her in an attitude of fervent supplication, her lips slightly parted and full. As he watched, her eyes fluttered open, gazing at him in raptured inquiry.

"It feels sweet when you don't resist, doesn't it?" he asked gently.

She shivered, and shook her head weakly in denial. Landry laughed under his breath, and pulled her mouth once more to his, this time letting her feel some of the warmth of his desire, not enough to scare her, but only to feed her fledgling pleasure. He framed her face in his hands, dragging his lips back and forth across hers, then moved his mouth to the soft curve of her throat. Her response was a sharp, catching gasp. He covered her opened lips again, and gathered her close. Whispering her name against her softness, letting his fingers part and filter her curls, he shifted the slim girl tenderly against his body. He kissed her lips a last time and put her from him. His fingers spread on her cheek, caressed her dulcet and pliant lips with his thumb, feeling her shaky breath. Breaking contact, he opened the door of the still carriage, and escorted her silently to her aunt's house.

"You don't know half my tricks, preacher's brat," Landry whispered to her before taking his leave.

The bells of St. Peter's had rung in the dawn before Frances drifted into an uneasy, exhausted slumber. Her reflections had been no lullaby, and regret that she had entered the bawdy house struck repeatedly with the force of a brick heaved through a window. There seemed to be no end to the evil consequences! If she should be recognized by anyone who had seen her there, she knew she would achieve a notoriety that would stain her name as long as she lived. But paint had hidden her features, even if the white gauze had done the opposite for her body. Who had seen her closely? Madame and Beamer, she discounted. She wasn't likely to see them again, and if she did, their treatment of her rendered them vulnerable for prosecution. They would never claim her acquaintance. There remained St. Pips, with whom she had sat with more than an hour, and Lord Landry's cousin Giles, whose assessing gaze had been shrewd and thorough. Never, never must they find out her real identity!

Oddly, not for a moment of her gnawing anxiety, did it occur to her that Lord Landry would betray her. All thoughts of Landry she suppressed with a near-fanatic vigor. When that frenzied effort failed, she could only twist wretchedly in her bed, trying to find a cool spot on her pillow to soothe her hot cheeks and stinging lips. Why, oh why, had she not screamed or shoved him from her with quelling revulsion? So much for her fine talk of virtue and resolve! He must have thought her the veriest straw damsel! Tomorrow, without a doubt, she must find a way to discover more of Kennan; the sooner it was done, the sooner

107

she could return to the protective wing of her family. The thought was a poor little solace to her misery, but it was her only one.

At last she shut her eyes and awoke with a headache a painfully few hours later to see the parrot, Mr. Bilge, perched on the footboard of her bed, flapping his wings and emitting ear-piercing screams. Frances brought herself, on stiff arms and elbows, to a semi-sitting position, and stared at the bird. To her fuzzy morning eyes, he looked like a large gray blob.

"Hello there," said Mr. Bilge in a soft feminine voice.

Frances felt her wounded pride swell; she had spent hours trying to teach the bird that phrase. Finally, he was repeating something she had taught him.

"Hello there," she answered with sleepy enthusiasm, rubbing her scratchy eyes. "Hello there."

Mr. Bilge beamed at her with hook-billed benevolence, then suddenly stiffened, spread his wings, and shrieked:

"Move yer arse, ye swab."

Frances lay back and pulled the cover over her head. Mr. Bilge hopped down from the footboard, landing with a *flump* on the bed, and walked his way up her legs, his large talons digging fiercely into her, screaming, "Open the gunports! Fire!"

She rolled to escape the bite of his claws. His footing disturbed, Mr. Bilge flapped over to sit on the wardrobe and gave her a knowing look with one beady eye. Frances sighed, slid from her bed, and began to dress.

The parrot watched with approval as Frances covered her arm with the protective glove of heavy leather that she wore when carrying him. She attached a braided leash to one of his scrawny legs.

"Pretty Polly," she said. "Do you want to go for a walk, Mr. Bilge?"

The city air was heavy with soot and stank from the yeast house near the river, making Frances pine for the stark salt breezes of her coastal home. In spite of that, the exercise did succeed in clearing her headache, and mingling with the animated crowds did something to dispel her melancholy. She bought her baby sister a penny jack-in-the-box that emitted a high-pitched squeal as it leaped from its box, and she chatted with a street hawker selling "lily-white vinegar" who had stopped to admire Mr. Bilge. Meeting Mr. Rivington in the hallway on her return, she was able to greet him with a measure of her customary equanimity.

"Well! Frances Atherton!" he said when he saw her. He had been maneuvering a giant wicker basket through his apartment doorway, but he stood upright to smile at her, flex his shoulders, and run a hand through his crisp brown curls. "Good morning! An important purchase?" he said, indicating the box she carried.

She flipped the catch on the jack-in-the-box, which snapped silently open to expel its nodding, grimacing prisoner. Mr. Bilge dived from Frances' arm and flew as far as the reach of his leash to the stair handrail with a noisy flurry of wings. He cocked his head sideways and looked at Rivington.

"It didn't squeak!" exclaimed Frances. "When the vendor showed it to me, it made the most charming cry."

The corners of Rivington's blue eyes crinkled in amusement. "A hoodwink, Miss Atherton. The sellers make that sound themselves without moving their lips."

"A fine swindle," said Frances, returning his smile. "I shall have to learn the squeak myself before giving my sister the toy."

"Or teach Mr. Bilge," he said. "Has he learned to speak like a gentleman yet?"

"Not in the least! Yesterday he hopped on the tea tray and told Henrietta that rats had fouled her flour store. And she so neat! It was the greatest injustice, and Henrietta vows she'll cook the creature yet. Aunt Sophie only says that if Mr. Bilge *is* cooked, she hopes he may not be served to her! Did you and your father finish the untangling of your balloon lines?"

"Yes. There are some rents in the balloon skin, though, that must be dealt with before we'll be able to make another flight. While I have you here talking, I'd better mention that David . . ."

From outside the building door came the sound of a boot toe banging against the unyielding threshold, accompanied by the coarser sort of oath occasionally applied by gentlemen freed from the civilizing presence of the Fair Sex. Rivington met the interruption with a gesture that begged Miss Atherton's pardon and opened the heavy door to admit Captain Zephyr, who came into the hallway bearing a greasy armload of machinery fittings. Captain Zephyr dropped them in a clanking heap on the hall carpet when he saw Frances, wiped his arms with an oily hand rag, and shook Frances' hand.

"Charming to see you again! Looking bright as a cherry, too. Over your head cold, are you? Good. Good! What's that you've got? Richard, isn't that the parrot that comes flying sometimes through your window? A fine fellow! Do you have the keeping of him, Miss Atherton?"

"Yes, sir," said Frances, looking at Mr. Bilge with

110

more fondness than he probably deserved. "Though I have the feeling that he resents me for it. His disposition is remarkably independent."

"Is it?" Captain Zephyr gave the parrot his smiling approbation. "Must be the nature of flyers. Tell you what, Miss Atherton, come over here. I'd like you to have a look at something." Zephyr walked to the wicker basket and snapped up the lid to expose a handsome mass of folded silk richly dyed in red, blue, and gold. "Ever seen a deflated balloon? It's a lovely creature. Not half the glory it is in the air, though." He grinned as he added, "Been laundered since we had it in the pigpen, of course."

Frances exclaimed delightedly as she stroked the colorful silk.

"I can imagine it floating in a sky blue as cornflower, passing a soft, white sun. . . ."

Rivington raised his eyebrows and pointed out unromantically that any balloon that floated past the sun would be in a very sober predicament.

"Hush!" admonished his father. "The child has a poet's heart!"

Frances appeared surprised and disconcerted. A poet's heart? It didn't sound quite respectable. She was about to deny possessing so frivolous an organ when Captain Zephyr continued:

"It's those with large ideas who recognize the potential of flight! Bonaparte for one. He planned to invade England, carrying his army over on balloons. Did you know that, Miss Atherton?"

"I believe that I did hear that it was perhaps under consideration at one time but that it was abandoned as hardly feasible. . . ."

"Hardly feasible! That's what his generals said, the damned chuckleheads. Not a scrap of imagination

111

among 'em. The military's the same in this country. March around like stickmen and blow each other's heads off with a cannon, that's all they know. Times out of mind I've proposed to General Wellington that we establish our own Air Navy of ballooncraft. We'd better have a fleet of balloons for defense, before someone else builds one. Now you take the Germans . . ."

Mr. Bilge had not the slightest intention of taking the Germans, at least not until after he had breakfasted. Clamping his powerful black bill on his leash, he began to tug with brutal insistence and an angry moan. Captain Zephyr was startled into a chuckle, and Frances decided that she had best take Mr. Bilge upstairs to be fed. She excused herself and made her good-byes. As she mounted the stairs, she turned back to look over her shoulder at Mr. Rivington.

"Oh. I seem to recall that you were going to mention something to me about your cousin. . . ." She contrived to instill an indifference in her voice.

"Lord, yes! David was around before you came in from your walk and asked me to pass on a message from the Drury Lane. It seems Scott's changed his mind. If you come to the theater this afternoon, he'll place you in the company."

It might have been only Frances' sensitive imagination, but it seemed to her that Rivington's tone smacked of irony. Bristling, she said:

"Scott changed his mind—or did Lord Landry change it for him?"

Rivington's shrug was carefully noncommittal. He turned toward his apartment, but stopped before reaching his door. He hesitated, then returned to the stair-floor and looked up steadily at Frances.

"You'll have to ask David that yourself," he said, with a trace of impatience. "This whole business is—"

He seemed to alter his choice of words. "—is between you and David. You weren't here when he called, I'm only repeating what he told me. That's *it*. Full stop. I'm not interested in becoming a . . ."

"Panderer?" suggested Frances, glaring at him.

"Go-between!" snapped Rivington.

Captain Zephyr had at first been confused by the flash-flood suddenness of the quarrel, but at his son's words a light dawned. Into the silence, he said gloomily:

"I see what it is. David's been bothering Miss Atherton."

"No!" exclaimed Frances, flushed with embarrassment and wishing she had not let her temper get the better of her.

"Don't have to douse cane sugar over the thing on my account," said Captain Zephyr, looking comfortingly paternal. "I know how these young bucks are. More females than they know what to do with, but forever thinking they must have one more. I've seen Richard here, and Giles go that same route times out of mind."

A certain glint in Rivington's blue eyes informed Frances that he in no way relished the fatherly strictures. Concern that she might have inadvertently provoked an argument between the two men led Frances to intervene hastily.

"I wouldn't like you to think that Lord Landry has been brutal or . . . or coercive. It's just that I shouldn't care to be in his debt." The one hundred guineas he had expended to remove her from Chez La Princesse swept unpleasantly into her mind. Her voice was uncomfortable as she amended, "Anymore than I am already."

Captain Zephyr shook his head, tsking while he sat

113

on the bottom step, and still looking at Frances, patted the space beside him invitingly. She joined him with a pretty air of uncertainty and he removed the irritable Mr. Bilge from her arm and consigned the grumbling bird once more to the handrail with the words:

"You stay there!" To Frances he said, "You want to act at the Drury Lane Theatre, am I correct?"

"It's not exactly that I want to . . ."

"Yes or no?" interrupted Captain Zephyr sternly.

"Yes."

"Very well then! Don't stand-muffit fretting about a lot of false obstacles. This thing with David; I love the boy like he was one of my own. Does the family proud! Aye, he's a good lad, but mind you—with the ladies, that's another sonnet. Pretty filly like yourself has got to watch her step, I know! I'm not saying that it would have been a good idea for you to *ask* David to help you out, not with him pestering to make you one of his light o' loves. Cat's on a different cot entirely, if *he's* gone and talked to Scott without consulting you. All you do is to write out David a note going something like this, see: Miss Atherton chooses to inform Lord Landry that she is willing to accept the Drury Lane role with the understanding that her gratitude shall be expressed in no other form than the thank-you herein."

"Would that really serve, sir?" asked Frances, doubtful but impressed by this unexpected stroke of savoir faire. The question was directed at Captain Zephyr, but it was his son who answered.

"That might deal with David." Rivington braced his shoulders against the hallway wall and folded his arms in front of him. "But the more I come to know you, Frances, the more I regret having suggested trying the

Lane. You should never have so much as set your little slippered foot in the back door. Won't you consider giving up the idea?"

Frances swallowed her misgivings and stood with what looked like a lot of determination. "Certainly not! It can't be so bad if your father approves."

"My father," said Rivington sardonically, "approved when my sister wore red lamé to her come-out ball and kicked her shoes off for the waltz. Every tabby in the place had a spasm."

Richard Rivington's friendship with his older cousin David had been one of unmixed harmony. There was trust and affection on both sides, and because they never interfered in each other's lives, they never clashed. Since Richard would have loathed to so much as pass judgment of Lord Landry's snuff sort without being invited to do so, the past was void of any precedent that would have allowed Rivington to condemn his cousin's attentions toward Frances. When Rivington had first met Frances, it had not occurred to him that he might ever want to do so. What was she? Pretty, yes, and stuffy in an appealingly droll fashion. Her obsession with Kennan had seemed a schoolgirl intrigue that she would soon be forced to abandon by some parental authority. When no such intervention came about, Richard found, in his growing fondness, a nagging sense of being somehow responsible for Miss Atherton. He had no right to tell her what to do, of course, and no right to protect her; undoubtedly she would have erupted like an Italian volcano if he tried. He wished he knew what to do with the girl!

Rivington was not without experience with the female sex, as his father had bluntly pointed out, but his associations had been with women of quite a different order. Young ladies of his own class were invariably presented to him with careful prior advice from their mamas; he was a brilliant matrimonial catch and on no account was Miss X to say or do anything that might prejudice her chances. The fruit of these strictures was that in Richard's company the youthful damsels would find themselves covered with awkward blushes, able only to stammer inarticulate agreement with any overtures Mr. Rivington might choose to make. Being himself unselfconscious and direct, it was not surprising that Rivington found such behavior irritating. Thus, he had attained the interesting age of twenty-three with a remarkably untouched heart. Or so it had been until he befriended Frances. Not that he was in love with her; instinctively he knew that if he had been, his feelings toward David would have been closer to a blue-bright rage than the rational exasperation he possessed now. Dammit, why must Landry callously play off his tricks on a girl who was so obviously naïve? Rivington had never seen him doing anything like it before. He could only conclude that the attraction David felt toward her must be unusually powerful—the worse for Frances!

To top it off, here was his father cheering Frances on about a return to the Lane. It *had* seemed safe to repeat David's message. Richard was sure that she would have said no if it had not been for his father's unfortunate, if well-meaning, interference. Useless to explain anything to Captain Zephyr—Rivington's father had long held revolutionary views on the encouragement of women's participation in the arts. The excellent mind of Hannah More! Mary Shelley's imagination! Richard's own mother was a noted satirical essayist and his sister's poetry had earned a congratulatory word of praise from Lord Byron himself. It was one thing, though, Richard knew, to pursue intellectual interests from the pedestal of Wealth and Rank; it was another to take a bit role on the public stage. Nor was it likely that Frances' *mind* would be the section of her nubile anatomy to cause the most excitement among her audience.

Rivington tried gently to probe for the reason that compelled Frances to risk herself in pursuit of Kennan. She looked uncertain, as though she might confide in him, then announced with an air of apologetic bravura that this was nothing to do with Edward Kennan. In fact, she had decided that she would really like to become an actress. It was such a poor excuse for a lie that Rivington warned her tartly that he had grave doubts about her ability to carry off such an extended charade. Still, he did what he could for her. Frances received a frank and pithy lecture on what sections of the theater she must not enter to avoid contact with the bucks in search of comely actresses willing to make an after-hours appearance in their bedchambers. He wished that he were able to convey her safely back and forth from the theater, but to be seen in his company would have given rise to exactly the kind of speculation about her character that he wished her to be spared. Instead, he saw to the hire of a reputably operated sedan chair and warned Frances to ride with no one else.

Chapter Seven

Before the elapse of her first afternoon at the Lane, Frances discovered that she had no latent flair for the drama. It was fortunate that her assigned part was a small, undemanding role as the daughter of the house in the one-act comical farce coyly styled *A New Way to Get Married, or Give a Man Luck and Throw Him in the Sea*, which, so the bill of play claimed, would stir the audience to "right merrie mirth." Her lines were three: "Papa, I did *not* see Baron Ogle kiss Mama," "Watch out, Lord Wineflesh, the chandelier is falling!" and "It must have got in when I forgot to close the door." After her first walk-through of the part, Charles Scott had no eulogies. Her language was stilted, her stage manner self-conscious, her sense of dramatic timing—atrocious. It had taken her more than forty-five seconds to enter the scene after she'd received her cue. Very well! thought Frances, determined to do better. At her next entrance, she rushed onstage with such sincere eagerness that she collided by accident with a catapult left on the wings from last Wednesday's performance of *Zadoc the Sorcerer, or The Princes of Persia*. The misstep caused the release of a large basketful of paper bats, which rained vengefully upon the actor who had just delivered Frances' cue: "And here is our beautiful daughter now."

Frances found that if she was looking up to avoid a piece of flying scenery that was being changed by handrope and pulley, she risked an unplanned exit through one of the stage trapdoors. When she was watching for the swinging platform at her right, its counterbalance was swerving around to smack her from the left. On her third day of rehearsal, it was Frances' misfortune to provide the company with a free afternoon by brushing against a stack of precariously stored flats, which promptly fell and knocked over a pot of chemicals, creating an artificial smoke that hung over the theater like a pall. Scott said not a word, though his stare was baleful indeed.

Frances was assigned to spending the greater part of her offstage time prompting Sheila Grant for her leading role in the featured attraction that was to precede the farce. This play, proclaimed a "masterpiece" by everyone in the company who had read the whole of it, was a tragedy written by Lord Landry concerning the last sad year in the life of the late French queen. It had been titled simply *Marie*. The most challenging moments of the role came in a speech some fifteen minutes in length to be delivered by Marie Antoinette before her execution. It was a moving declaration; subtle, and ingeniously wrought, about the fear of death. Written with sympathy, insight, maturity, and even a gentle touch of humor, it bore the hallmark of genius. Frances came to know each beautifully sculptured passage by heart as she worked with Miss Grant in one of the small rehearsal rooms below the stage. It struck Frances that the nobility and grace of the play squared ill with the ignobility of its author!

Frances saw nothing of Lord Landry. She had braced herself for their next meeting, so when several days passed without its occurring, she experienced an emotion that bore an unpleasant similarity to disappointment. No doubt he had found his pursuit of her boring, casual and intermittent though it had been. Frances was genuinely shocked to find that reflection accompanied by a definite melancholy. Even more disturbing was the suppressed but real elation Frances felt when she learned that Landry was *not* consciously avoiding her, but had gone out of town. She was obliged to Captain Zephyr for the information; he paid a morning visit to Frances and told her that David had been summoned to his home in Buckinghamshire, where his younger brother (an irresistible scamp of nine years) was stricken with a mild case of the measles. Nothing would cheer the lad save a visit from his idolized older brother! Landry had gone at once. If this threw Landry's character into kinder relief, it did nothing to mitigate his behavior to Frances, with its alarming mixture of kindness, callous seduction, and mockery. Frances was exceedingly grateful to have so many things to occupy her mind.

The theater was a small, self-involved world where petty jealousies, gossip, and rivalries were conducted with passionate energy. The ascent to the pinnacle of the profession was arduous, the public favor fickle. Success could destroy a character as quickly and totally as failure. Frances soon learned that Landry had more friends here than a dairy has cats, while Edward Kennan was universally hated. A distant and reverent public held Kennan in the highest esteem. Kennan's associates knew him better. He was a man who spent a fortune and more on his own comfort but paid his servants the meanest of wages. Every attention must be given to Kennan's consequence; he might imagine himself slighted at a triviality. Last month, it was said, he had nearly caused the firing of an elderly and much loved actor, an injustice prevented only by the diplomatic intervention of Lord Landry. The unfortunate man's offense: he had begun to speak his lines before the applause occasioned by Kennan's entrance to the stage had ceased.

Frances wasn't sure whether to credit Landry's discretion or Charles Scott's, but she found that though Scott would direct a disagreeably knowing glance toward her at the mention of Landry's name, she had been granted the happy anonymity of having no one else at the Lane aware of her connection with Landry. As a minor cast member with limited responsibilities, Frances had opportunity and time to engage in conversation with the scenemen, the ticket sellers, and the other bit players who worked at the Lane. It wasn't hard to get anyone to talk about Kennan. Everyone was glad of a fresh audience before whom to display his or her grievances. There was hardly a person at the Lane who had not, at one time or another, been the recipient of some petty cruelty of Kennan's. A portrait emerged that fit the Blue Specter character— that of a ruthless and self-involved man. Most significant to Frances were the stories she heard of his high-living ways; it seemed he lived on a scale befitting someone with a key to the Crown Jewels. It was not unusual to hear of his having dropped a thousand pounds at faro in one sitting. He maintained not one, but two, elegant town carriages, with full matching teams for both and a complement of grooms and coachmen. His clothes outshone the beaux of the dandy set and were of the finest cut and fabric (there was a rumor that he never wore the same shirt twice).

Frances knew his salary from the Lane, and while he was the highest-paid actor in the British Isles and had an allowance from the Duke of Fowleby to boot,

Frances was willing to bet that the two combined could never have supported the half of his luxuries. Discreet questioning of other company members showed that none of them much cared about Kennan's finances. It was widely supposed that he derived income from unknown investments, but it was Frances' opinion that Kennan lived too high to have a penny to invest. She became convinced that Kennan's "investments" were a mythology that he had carefully evolved to disguise the ill-gotten profits from his career as the Blue Specter, and she grew daily more confident that she would eventually discover his Achilles heel.

It was with this goal in mind that Frances sat in the cavernous basement storeroom, eagerly encouraging Miss Freelove, the wardrobe mistress, to declaim on the subject of Edward Kennan. Miss Freelove belied the rather lurid implications of her name by leading a life of irreproachable middle-aged spinsterhood and holding the male sex in utter abhorrence. The two ladies had been sitting on low three-legged stools making an inventory of costumes used three years ago in a production of *Midsummer Night's Dream*. Miss Freelove was folding Puck's green shirt into a neat pillow as she said:

"There's never been another actor in the theater to match his conceit! Believe me, I have less trouble with Sheila Grant. You take his costume in Landry's newest, *Marie*. Kennan is to play Robespierre—very well. What happens when I finished his coat? He says the tails are too long—but as soon as I had them hemmed, he said they were too short! Then he complained that the waist was too tight. I let it out a mere half inch, and you know what he said? The fit was too loose!" Miss Freelove bent close to Frances, took a careful glance around the obviously deserted room, and whispered in a confidential tone, "I know something about Kennan unbeknownst to another living soul! Can I *trust* you, Miss Brightcastle?"

Frances felt her hopeful heart skip a beat as she nodded vigorously.

"Kennan is not what he appears to be!" whispered Miss Freelove. "I have to pad his shoulders and chest with buckram to plump out his scrawny figure. Like a plucked chicken he is, without his jacket!"

Disappointed, Frances forced herself to smile wanly as a sceneman appeared with the news that Miss Freelove was wanted onstage to repair a ripped flounce. Frances finished the inventory task alone, then gave herself liberty to wander for a few minutes through the fascinating chamber.

It was a room filled with a thousand dreams. To her right was a temple of ancient Greece, its plaster columns finished only on one side; to her left, a forest of sketchy trees which had never seen the sun. A huge screen painting of a sea battle leaned against the wall. King Arthur's round table—nicked, scratched, and piled high with debris—was standing in the corner. There was a maze of age-darkened wardrobes filled with costumes for wood nymphs, Chinese princesses, and nuns. One could find a gown for Marie de Medici, Joan of Arc, Isabel of Navarre, or the Fair Maid of Perth. Frances drew a silver-painted wooden sword from its scabbard and made a brave flourish in the air, imagining herself the martyred warrior saint leading the French armies at Patay. Feint, thrust, a bit of fancy footwork, and she retired the blade. Then she picked up a gilded chalice. Placing a hand on her forehead, she became Socrates drinking the fatal cup. In her death throes, she collapsed against an old chest, dislodging an object which clanked to the floor.

Giggling at her own clumsiness, she bent to find she had knocked over an iron lantern, the wick encased in a glass globe of a particularly acid shade of blue. Memory stirred within Frances—the lantern was exactly like the one she had seen in the Blue Specter's hand the night on the beach! She examined the chest the lantern had been resting on. Though it was in a particularly dusty and abandoned corner of the storeroom, the top looked as if it had recently been cleaned. With Pandora's trembling fingers, she opened the lid. There, lying neatly folded on a costume pile, lay the cloak and mask of the Blue Specter. She stared in amazement at her unexpected discovery, holding the cloak to the light that filtered through a small street-level window.

"What are you doing?" The voice came from the doorway. She whirled, to confront the viciously scowling aspect of Edward Kennan.

"I—I . . ." she choked out as he strode across the room. Upon reaching her, he clamped a hand on the wrist holding the cloak, lifting it with a steady twist. His eyes looked like stones.

Into this ghastly tension came Lord Landry's voice, light, affable, and impervious to the hostile undertones.

"Hello, Miss Brightcastle. I see you've met Edward Kennan."

"Do you know this girl?" said Kennan.

"Scott introduced us upstairs," lied Landry smoothly, and received a grateful look from Frances. "Miss Brightcastle wanted to see the headdress and jewelry Sheila wore in *Cleopatra.* I'm afraid I misdirected her

124

—they're in that chest at the other end, I believe."
Landry's casual tone did much to allay Kennan's suspicions. The actor let go of Frances' wrist and bowed slightly, as if in apology. The madness left his face, and he said testily:

"Very well, but these are valuable props and we can't have them mulled by inexperienced hands."

"Isn't Miss Brightcastle holding the costume you wore in *Sorcery*, Edward?" said Landry. "You needn't worry that she'll mistreat any costume you've worn, Edward. She's one of your most fervent . . . followers."

This promptly reminded Frances that Landry's sense of humor made him, at best, a capricious ally. She managed a simulated smile as Kennan extended his hand to her, apparently soothed by the reflected credit of Landry's acceptance of Frances and by the playwright's agile flattery.

"Ah," said Kennan, "I have seen you about . . . in the farce, are you not? A new face! And you take an interest in my career, do you?"

"Closer than you imagine," murmured Landry.

Frances hoped her hand was steady as she received Kennan's. "I feel you are the most interesting actor in the theater."

There were footsteps in the hall, and then Sheila Grant appeared in the doorway.

"David! Scott said I should find you down here. I'm delighted to see you back in London!"

Frances stood with cold hands clasped loosely before her, a tightness building in her chest, as she watched Miss Grant give herself into Landry's arms for a kiss of greeting. Insanity for the parson's daughter from Beachy Hill to care who the renowned Lord Landry chose to kiss!

Miss Grant gave a shiver of pleasure and danced coyly out of Landry's arms. "Have the measles been put to rout?"

"The measles," said Landry, "never had a chance. We're a healthy lot. But I hear you're to be beheaded."

Sheila made a pretense of fussing with his cravat. "There's no bearing it! Could you not have talked Scott out of the idea?"

"My dear Sheila, I only write the words. Scott does as he likes with the production. He was very enthusiastic about the new touch. He fancies himself as catering to the popular taste, so it seems." Landry gave Kennan his effortless, winning smile. "I hear it was your idea, Edward."

Kennan smiled back—a canine smile, the lips rolling over his teeth. "The appropriate flourish to end *Marie*. When Marie Antoinette finishes her monologue on death, she will turn, walk toward the back of the stage as though in a trance, and drop to her knees before . . ." He pointed dramatically to a tall, shrouded object at the back of the room and strode over to it. With both hands he pulled a dust cover away to reveal—a guillotine! It was apparently in operating order, still surrounded by wood shavings at its base, the serviceable blade poised for its assigned task. Kennan basked proudly in the little shriek given by Miss Grant at the sight of the machine.

"It's hideous," exclaimed Frances involuntarily.

"But so effective, don't you think?" Kennan grinned at her and ran a finger carefully across the length of the blade. "Sheila will lay her head here"—he indicated the stock below the blade—"the apron lights darken, and then the blade falls, appearing to decapitate the pitiful Marie. We bring down the curtain as the blade emits a satisfying clang. A brilliant ending!"

"A smarmy ending," retorted Sheila, and studied the contraption with a disdainful eye. She threaded her slender arm through Landry's and smiled enticingly at him. "And after all your beautiful lines . . ."

Landry disengaged himself with deadly friendliness, pinched her chin, and gave her a kind smile before resuming his study of Kennan's dreadful brainchild. "You designed the monster, Edward? Is it safe?"

Kennan's face showed clearly that he relished not at all the implied doubt of his engineering ability. "Of course it's safe! You see the pipe sections here? They'll catch the blade before it comes close to Sheila's pretty neck."

Frances said daringly, "Would you put your own head in it, Mr. Kennan?"

Arrogance and cruel enjoyment of the grotesquerie before them were in Kennan's face. "If my part called for it, yes. But, as I play Robespierre in *Marie* . . ." He shrugged.

"Robespierre followed Marie Antoinette to the guillotine, don't forget," said Landry smoothly, with amusement. "Perhaps I'll write a sequel to accommodate you."

"You're too kind," said Kennan sardonically. "Which calls to mind that I promised Her Grace the Duchess to entreat you to attend her masquerade ball on Sunday evening. No occasion could be a success without your . . . so charming presence! The Duchess has spent thousands preparing Fowleby Place for this event."

"I've already thanked the Duchess for her kind invitation and told her of my previous engagement that evening." Landry's gaze focused with unconscious volition on Frances, and she stared back. She had no intention of spending that evening or any other with

127

Landry, nor, she was sure, had he meant the accidental linking of their gazes as an invitation; yet Frances felt some desperate undertow of emotion tugging her toward him. She was sure Sheila Grant had seen the attraction in her eyes, for the actress gave Frances a look of suppressed hatred. Too clever to show jealousy, Miss Grant attached herself once more to Landry's arm and spoke sharply, as though to cut through any budding connection between Frances and the golden playwright by her side.

"I'm surprised the Duchess has continued with the idea of a masked ball after the dreadful thievery of His Grace's art collection. Four masterpieces stolen in as many months; the Fra Angelico, two canvases from Filippo Lippi, and then the El Greco. Is he not worried for another attempt?"

"He worries about it day and night." Faint contempt seasoned Kennan's voice. "He's done what he can. There are guards watching the door into the gallery and anyone entering who is not a member of the household is stopped instantly. Fowleby grieves over his lost paintings as if they were lost children! The Duchess feels it best to go ahead with the ball to divert His Grace's mind."

Landry was as relaxed as ever, but it seemed to Frances that he was studying Kennan closely during this last speech. "They still have no clues, then?" asked Landry.

"None," answered Kennan. "The canvases were slit from their frames, the last three practically under the noses of the guards. The only sign of the thief's presence was a window left open downstairs after the first theft. The mansion has been searched from tip to toe but not a single piece of evidence has been turned out."

A search! The word sparked in Frances' mind. She

had regretfully acknowledged that her discovery of the Blue Specter's costume was useless. It was impossible to prove that Kennan was the man who had worn it to Beachy Hill. If, though, she could find an opportunity to search Kennan's apartments at Fowleby Place, she might find positive evidence to link Kennan with his crime. If she could find one incriminating letter, one list of names, perhaps it might be enough! And Sunday night's masked ball would be exactly the chance she needed to enter the Duke of Fowleby's guarded mansion.

Chapter Eight

By Saturday morning Frances' plan to gate-crash the masked ball at Fowleby Place had so far advanced that she had obtained the necessary disguise from Miss Freelove, who, Frances had discovered, made a generous addendum to her otherwise modest salary by arranging illicit loans of theater wardrobing upon request and the presentation of two pounds, six shillings.

That left the problem of how to get into the party. No one in the Drury Lane company was invited, save Kennan, in his privileged position as Fowleby's grantee. It was an affair open only to the first stare of fashion. The gentlemen of that lofty breed might choose to pass their leisure time with dramatis personae, but ladies of birth, except for an infamous few, would have as soon enjoyed an evening with a tribe of wild nomads. Even Aunt Sophie, a lady of quite respectable birth and reasonable fortune, could not aspire to the Duke's ball. So Frances discovered at Saturday tea, politely interrupting Miss Isles' fervent condemnation of her friend Mrs. Lairlarge's cook, who had possessed the temerity to have served Miss Isles red mullet *boiled*.

"Baked, broiled, or roasted!" exclaimed Miss Isles with an emphatic rattle of her teacup. "But on no occasion boiled! Of course I'm not invited to the Duke's. I don't know the man. And If I did, he probably wouldn't invite me anyway. That's the castle and ten-thousand-acre crowd."

"You're a bishop's aunt," suggested Frances hopefully.

"It wouldn't make any difference if I was the Pope's aunt. Religion's been out of fashion since George I. Mark my words, child, nothing below an earl will nose through those gates Sunday night. And if you think to sneaking in masked, it won't serve. You'll have to show an invitation at the door. You'd think you had learned your lesson the last time—Chez la Princesse indeed."

Frances eyed her aunt with mild reproach. "You promised if I told you, you wouldn't lecture me."

"You made me promise, *then* you told me. Is that your notion of *summum jus*? Your mother would have fits."

"My mother," said Frances seriously, "never has fits, though of course it wouldn't do to tell her. I shall tell my brother Joe, and Charles, too, as soon as he returns to England. But my mother—never."

Miss Isles treated herself to a chocolate drop from the Wedgwood comfit dish before her. "And what if Lord Landry starts talking? You've no idea how many people you've never met in your life would be fascinated to hear the whole story."

Frances stared at her aunt with puckered brows. "Lord Landry wouldn't gossip about it."

"Ho. Wouldn't he? I thought he was Herod, Caligula, and Machiavelli rolled into one! So you've led me to believe. And now I hear he won't gossip."

"What I said," replied Frances carefully, "was that Lord Landry was a dissolute, obnoxious, cunning, and thoroughly selfish man; I didn't say he was a blathermouth."

"I had wondered," Aunt Sophie said dryly as she dabbed a smear of melting chocolate from her forefinger with an embroidered handkerchief, "when you would begin to notice his redeeming qualities."

Frances looked self-conscious. "I hope, Aunt Sophie, that I am not so *judging* as to blind myself to the full value of a fellow being. There are reasons, though, that compel me to . . . in short, dear ma'am, I find it more comfortable to dwell on his shortcomings."

"That's why I don't worry *so* much about you." Aunt Sophie's lips twitched into a conspirator's smile. "You've got half an iota of common sense—which is more than I can say for most girls at nineteen! I'll warrant, though, that when your mama finds out that you've trod the boards at a public theater, she won't like it a bit better than your scuttley-tup at a bawdy house. Or do you intend swearing the audience to silence?"

"They'll know me only as Frances Brightcastle," she reminded her aunt.

"All you need is one, just one, soul to recognize you and . . ."

"Oh, I know, Aunt Sophie, and I worry, but what's to be done? If only I could gain entrance to Fowleby Place tomorrow night; and then, while everyone was occupied at the ball, I could search Kennan's apartment. If I could bring him to book before Tuesday's opening, then I need never appear in public!" The mahogany long case clock in the corner gave a mechanical sigh and ponderously chimed the hour while Frances mulled over the possibilities. "I wonder . . . Aunt, do you think I might be able to induce Mr. Rivington to help me enter Fowleby Place?"

Aunt Sophie threw up her hands. "I shouldn't be surprised at anything you could induce some poor harried

132

male to accomplish. Just don't tell me your plot. I find it harrowing enough to hear about them after! Come into my bedroom instead and give me your opinion on my new redingote. Canterbury blue, they call the color! Unless I miss my guess, it's just the thing to wear tomorrow morning when I ride out to Westminster with Pris Bolton. Don't have rehearsals, do you? Why not join us?"

"Thank you. But I've already promised Captain Zephyr that I would assist him tomorrow with his balloon."

"Bless my soul, child, you haven't agreed to ascend in it, have you?"

"Oh, no, nothing like that! Captain Zephyr is preparing a paper for the Academy of Science pertaining to altitude and animal temperament. *Next* month he will ascend in Surrey with a pair of sheep. Tomorrow he will only inflate the balloon to test its airworthiness and try the sheep in the gondola. And I'm sure Mr. Rivington will be there, so I shall be able to talk with him about Fowleby Place without resorting to anything as improper as knocking on his door to ask him. Aunt! Why are you laughing?"

Rising with the assistance of the chair arm, Miss Isles gave her newly discovered favorite niece a friendly pat on the shoulder. "Because, my dear, you have the *oddest* scruples of any female to pass through my acquaintance!"

Frances rode beside Captain Zephyr to a field outside the city in a bright-red Essex wagon filled with hydrogen casks and the gondola, which overlapped the end of the cart by a foot and threatened to abandon them after a particularly hard bump. Mr. Bilge had joined the expedition at Captain Zephyr's invitation. Frances had agreed to bring him, deciding that a day in the country would do the parrot good, as well as provide a respite from his presence to the long-suffering Henrietta. So Mr. Bilge sat, an exotic accent on the wagon shaft, where he was attached by a long leather thong, and enlivened their ride by whistling, waving his wings, and startling the docile carriage horses with an occasional shout of "Avast abast a beam!"

The Sunday afternoon air was light and soft, with dry clouds that soaked in the sunlight and sent it to the warm earth in pale yellow streams. Leaves were delicate with new green and the roads damp from the spring rains. It was too early in the year for the dust to rise in the choking white mists that would later coat a drab layer on the thick growth in the laneside hedgerows. Blue violets were in bloom, and the flowering peach. Daisies cut a dash under the hazel's spreading branches. Brooks gurgled, orange-brown butterflies skimmed over the tender grass; the thrush sang from her nest in a young, ivy-laced elm. It was a pleasure to breathe in the fresh spring, a pleasure to sit upon the cozily bumping wagon bench listening to Captain Zephyr rattle away about the beauty of ballooning. Frances was glad Henrietta had talked her into the Prussian-blue Witchoura mantle with fur trim at the hem and high-standing collar. It wasn't too warm, as Frances had earlier feared, and her matching satin bonnet with its curving fur brim was no more and no less than was needed to fend off the slow, clean breeze.

They arrived at the daffodil-dotted meadow shortly after Richard Rivington and a company of four companions began to spread the balloon. It's bold red, blue, and gold silk was a vivid streak of color against the sweet-smelling green clover carpet where two thick, woolly sheep were munching contentedly.

134

As they drew closer, Frances saw with a start, Lord Landry among the men working on the balloon. He was dressed casually in buckskins, and was hatless like the others, his golden hair lightly disheveled by the wind. He looked up, saw Frances, and smiled. She hadn't expected to see him and felt a tightening in her throat. How odd it was that in the first snap of recognition, the surprise should seem a happy one.

Captain Zephyr, who had followed the line of her gaze, surprised her by saying:

"Does that worry you still, my dear? I will say something to him, if you like. Not that I can guarantee that he'll listen to me."

"No, no. No, thank you. In fact, I'm used to him now. Almost. I shall just go on in a natural way."

Captain Zephyr gave her an enigmatic smile.

"You'll do," he said as he drew in the rein and locked in the gilt-oak brake handle.

The wagon's jerky halt disturbed Mr. Bilge, who screamed a protest and flew to the handbar beside Frances, stretching his leash to its farthest extension. As Captain Zephyr clambered down his side of the wagon, Frances saw Lord Landry rise with negligent grace from his position beside Rivington and come toward her. As Landry reached the wagon, Mr. Bilge cocked his powder-white head and cased the man with an inquisitive stare.

"Pretty boy," observed Mr. Bilge, in a particularly accurate copy of Frances' voice.

Lord Landry laughed and stroked the parrot's chest feathers with the back of one finger. "Thank you, sir," he said, "but I'm afraid you're a flatterer." Eyes green as a fairy's coat smiled at Frances. "Lord, what a pleasant surprise to see you! Has Uncle Zeph kidnapped you for the day?"

135

Unaccountably, and rather bewilderingly, Frances felt shy. "I've never seen the balloon inflated. I'd not considered, of course . . . that is, I didn't know you'd be here."

"I don't spend all my time at Chez la Princesse." Landry's eyes sparkled wickedly as he put his hands on her waist and lifted her to the ground.

Captain Zephyr walked around the carriage, in front of the horses, and clapped Landry on the shoulder. "Ah, David, you made it. Good boy! Yes, take Frances over to the balloon. And Frances, don't worry about Mr. Bilge—he'll be quite comfortable here! I'm going to unhitch the team and hobble them so they can graze. But mind, David—give Frances a hand. There might be rabbit holes."

Frances' lips curved reluctantly into a smile. "I beg your pardon, sir, but I'm not so fragile. Have a care what you say or Mr. Bilge will lose all respect for me. He takes pleasure already in telling me that I am paltry."

"He doesn't know you the way I do," said Landry, taking her elbow with easy gallantry.

Lifting the skirts of her mantle with tan leather gloves, Frances set off toward the balloon beside Lord Landry. She could feel the softness of the ground through the soles of her kid half-boots—it was earth beginning to feel the touch of spring but not yet sobbing from it; the clover greens were crisp and sweet. One of the sheep regarded them curiously and then returned to its munching. Rivington, who had been kneeling beside the balloon straightening the inevitably tangled lines, rose to his feet to greet her.

"Frances, how lovely you look!" he said. He took her hand. "Were you glad to wave good-bye to the city for a day?"

"Immensely! As we cleared the last house of the last outlying district, I turned back and saw the veil of chimney smoke that huddles over London like a shroud. I don't know how we breathe there."

Rivington smiled. "Don't raise the issue to my father or he'll invent a fearsome face mask and expect us to wear it in defense of our lungs. I'm going to unload the gas. David, why don't you introduce Frances?"

A fair-haired man had been stretching the netted guide ropes over the far end of the balloon bag. He looped a rope through a final knot, tested its strength, then stood and came toward Frances and Lord Landry, bending to test an occasional binding on his way. There was a painful snap in Frances' chest as she recognized the tall, slim man as Sir Giles, the cousin of Lord Landry's that she had encountered at Chez la Princesse. In vain had been her prayers that she might never see anyone who could recognize her from that dreadful place! The hope that he might not remember her died instantly; as he looked at her, she saw recognition and a rather incredulous curiosity.

Frances was unable to raise her gaze from the ground as Lord Landry introduced Sir Giles to her with what she felt was the most heartlessly cheerful nonchalance.

Sir Giles' first words were not, as she had feared, to question the advocacy of bringing a doxy to a balloon ascension. Instead, he said merely: "Hello, Miss Atherton."

Since Frances was worried that any voice she might produce to return his greeting would be high and squeaky with embarrassment, she didn't answer him immediately. Sir Giles gave her a moment and then bent his knees, bringing his face level with hers. Tapping up her chin with an index finger, he repeated:

"Miss Atherton. Hello."

Sir Giles gave her that particular burning smile that Frances was beginning to recognize as a family trademark, the smile that reached such a seductive brilliance in Lord Landry's wanton green eyes.

"Hello," said Frances, in what she felt was perilously close to a croak.

"My God, I must be intimidating today!" Sir Giles laughed gently. "Please look at me, Miss Atherton. I won't eat you."

"That," said Lord Landry, a good deal amused, "is patent. She's more likely to eat *you*. Miss Atherton's timid demeanor is no more than a temporary aberration. Mostly, she spends her time threatening to haul hell-born knaves before the magistrates."

Recovering a little, a becoming color high in her cheeks, Frances said, "Yes, but this is my day off."

Sir Giles let go her chin. She couldn't imagine why, but somehow she seemed to have pleased him. "Are you such a fire-eater, Miss Atherton? Just David's style! Have you met Jean-Pierre Annonay?"

"The second person to make a balloon ascension in Denmark," said Landry, "the second man to cross the English Channel by balloon, the second man to ascend carrying a rooster and two molting hens. You don't want to miss Jean-Pierre. Think nothing of it if he gets in a blistering quarrel with Captain Zephyr—there's a heated scientific rivalry between them."

Frances allowed Lord Landry to escort her around the outside perimeter of the unfurled balloon, at the same time trying to fortify herself with the largely fallacious notion that though Sir Giles might have formed a very poor notion of her character from the locale of their first acquaintance, she cared not a whit what anyone in this rather overpowering family thought of her.

Monsieur Annonay, when they reached him, was

138

pounding furiously with a sledgehammer upon the splintering head of a hooked anchoring peg. A small, dark man with a beaked nose and crooked lips, he hurled the hammer to the ground and spread wide his arms to exclaim:

"Ah, the beauteous mademoiselle! I kiss you hands." He snatched Frances' hands from her sides, and did so with great energy. Then, apparently satisfied, he stood back, hands on his hips, to admire her while Lord Landry effected the introductions. Annonay thrust his forefinger into the air in a mighty spearing gesture and exclaimed, "Ah, the emotion that fills me—what courage for one of the weaker sex to assist in the rearing of a balloon! To brave the dangers of the so-explosive hydrogen . . ."

"The explosive hydrogen!" ejaculated Frances, turning involuntarily to look at the tanks Rivington and Captain Zephyr were unloading from the wagon.

"Not since the death of my dear wife Madeleine have I been one of a ballooning party that included a female. Poor Madeleine—the greatest female pilot of our time! 'Twas ten years ago this April that a sad accident put a period on the sentence of her life. She was making a solo ascension at the Champ de Mars in Paris, delighting the crowd below with a display of fireworks . . ." He fell back a few steps, gesturing toward the heavens as if to conjure up a vision of the fearless Madame Annonay. "Gold and silver rain poured from her basket —a cascade of sparks. Below, the crowd cheered with excitement, thinking it a part of the act. But no, the basket was on fire! The balloon began to plummet earthward. As it reached the level of the rooftops, a current caught the car and flung it against the chimney of a house in Rue de Provence. Madeleine fell to the street and spoke to me her last words: 'Ah ha, I have

broken Monsieur Bibot's record for rapid descent.' "
On Monsieur Annonay's head was a high-crowned
beaver hat with a curious pair of canvas earflaps dangling from the brim to his shoulders. He yanked the hat
from his head and held it soulfully to his breast; poking
out from his head came a mass of short fat braids
trussed with spirals of wildly jiggling copper wire.
Frances gave the kernel of a shriek, and stared agape
at the bizarre coiffure.

"Monsieur, your hair!" she said.

"You noticed, mademoiselle!" said Annonay with
what Frances felt was a rather maniacal grin. "This is
the ceromancy—I have the metal woven into my hair,
the better, Miss Atherton . . ." Annonay lowered his
voice and gestured her closer with a crooked finger, "to
conduct my bodily electricity."

Because Frances' contact with lunatic inventors had
been of the most restricted nature, she most unwisely
made the comment that she didn't think the body had
electricity, and if it did, that it would conduct itself
very well on its own accord. Thus Frances exposed
herself to a full half hour of a stern and enthusiastically
delivered essay pertaining, but not limited, to bodily
electricity, acupuncture, and Hindu levitation, and was
preparing for an alarming plunge into the diagnostic
values of examination of the tongue, when he was called
away by Captain Zephyr to participate in transferring
the gas into the balloon bag.

Frances turned to Lord Landry, who had been, so it
seemed to her, deriving enormous enjoyment from listening to Annonay's discourse. Had she been told that
Landry's approbation stemmed instead from watching
her response to Annonay, she would have been amazed,
even though Landry had demonstrated a certain interest in debauching her. She had been reared to habits of

140

self-confidence, but also modesty; no one had ever told her how delicate and beguiling was the perplexed curve of her lip, how bright her well-opened hazel eyes, or how entrancing was that expression that designed her features when something happened to flabbergast or fascinate her.

She delighted Landry further by saying to him:

"Do you think it's true what Monsieur Annonay said about holy men in India being able to float in the air? I'm sure my father is as holy as any men in India and *he* never did so."

"Great as my respect is for the British imagination, I don't think we're a nation that would tolerate much floating on the part of our clergy," offered Landry. "Don't brood over Annonay. He's quite non compos mentis. Last summer he designed a parachute shaped like an inverted umbrella, and has tried times out of number to talk someone into piloting a balloon from which he can jump."

"An inverted umbrella? I've a very small understanding of physics, but I shouldn't think that would work," said Frances.

Landry grinned. "It would best Madeleine's record for rapid descent. Come by the wagon; I'll put down a blanket and you can sit to watch the balloon inflate."

Frances was situated in time to see Captain Zephyr attach a hydrogen cask to the balloon bag with a snaky leather hosepipe, which began a mechanical monotone hissing. The puddle of blue, red, and gold that lay on the ground began to take form and rise, first in waving bulges, then taut and full, transformed into a live, beautiful semicircle that sat on the clover like an uncanny dome. Suddenly, it lifted from the ground to bob slowly, persuasively, at the tethered gondola beneath. The sun shimmered and broke like a wave on the rounded sides of the fully inflated balloon, casting a long, fanciful shadow on the soft sea of clover.

The peace was broken by M. Annonay and Captain Zephyr, who had been engaged in a terse disagreement about the proper adjustment of the bag's valve. Zephyr shouted that M. Annonay was a jackass and was over-filling the balloon. M. Annonay retorted with a string of French expletives so graphic that Lord Landry asked Frances if she spoke French. When she said no, Rivington raised his eyebrows at Landry and laughed and said, "Good thing, too!" Before the combatants could go to again, Lord Landry draped an arm around his uncle's shoulders and showed a blithe disregard for the truth by telling him that Miss Atherton had been be-moaning her lack of opportunity to closely inspect the finished balloon.

Frances was pulled to her feet by Captain Zephyr and brought to admire the neat arrangement he and Rivington had made of the basket suspension cables. Not to be outdone, Annonay interrupted to draw atten-tion to the difficulties of his share of the experiment, which had been to prepare in his workshop the hydro-gen gas. To a ton of iron shavings and water, M. An-nonay and his assistants had added a half ton of diluted sulphuric acid to generate the gas. The stench of the sulphuric acid escaping from the barrel! The corrosive fog! A scene of Stygian drama!

The melodrama of Annonay's tone caused Rivington to point out dryly that if they would agree to experi-ment with ordinary illuminating gas, it would render ballooning at once easier and less expensive. With the natural revulsion any innovator must feel to an idea not thought of by himself, M. Annonay frowned at Riving-ton, and even Captain Zephyr looked reproachfully at his much-beloved only son and heir. The older generation was allied to bemoan the fecklessness of the young! Sir Giles tactfully turned the sentiment to good account by asking Annonay if it was true that Tetu-Brissy had ascended while mounted on a horse suspended from a rectangular platform below the balloon.

The conversation flowed to Garnerin's pioneering parachute jump in 1797, and had washed into the scientific balloon ascensions of Bibot and Gay-Lussac when Frances noticed that the grazing sheep had migrated to within ten feet of a spreading bracken bush. Probably they were too smart to chew upon its poisonous branches, but country-bred Frances knew better than to place any dependence on the intelligence of a sheep. Quietly she left Captain Zephyr's side and went to the sheep, where she built a rapport by scratching the sides of their necks through the thick woolly fleece. Then she led them away from the bracken; they trotted happily after her.

Before many minutes passed she was joined by Richard Rivington, who said, "You missed your calling, Miss Atherton. You ought to have been a shepherdess."

She had been weaving the daffodils with rye straw into a spring crown. He dropped to the turf beside her, saying, "I hope you won't ever hereafter feel obliged to stare at the ground when you are around Giles."

Frances looked up quickly from the green sprigs she was manipulating. Her tone was suffocated as she replied, "You can't know! The most mortifying circumstances are connected with our acquaintance."

"But I do know. David gave me an outline of your adventure! Don't worry—I don't think it soils you forever. And you can rest assured that Giles isn't so fallow as to think you belonged at Chez la Princesse. If he seems to take an interest in you, it's because he finds you intriguing."

Frances set down her daffodil crown and stared at Rivington with startled hazel eyes. "Why would he?"

A smile hovered around Rivington's mouth. "How could he not? You are the most *unconventional* conventional girl I, for one, have ever met. While being quite—forgive me!—straightlaced, you make nothing of acting at Drury Lane or of entering a notorious brothel. . . ."

"I don't make nothing of that!" Frances interrupted him to protest.

Rivington's blue eyes were bright with laughter as he begged pardon. "No, well, but *also*, perhaps Giles finds you intriguing because it's obvious David has a *tendre* in your direction."

"*Tendre!* You're quite out there. Nothing like that exists in his attitude toward me, I promise you." She rather spoiled the effect of this brave announcement by adding wistfully, "He doesn't take me that seriously." She stared at the blossoms of a flowering peach tree nearby, then gave a great sigh and prepared to rise.

Rivington stood up, helping Frances to her feet. His face was thoughtful, but he said only, "There are times when I have the thread of a feeling that David is not so case-hardened as he insists." He picked up the daffodil crown and handed it to Frances. "I don't know. No doubt I'm wrong. He's left more lovers than Don Juan. It's just that I have a great deal of affection for him. Don't let him break your heart, will you?"

"No danger of that," said Frances so stoutly as to compensate for a certain want of conviction in her tone. They walked together toward the sheep, and Frances amended in a light way, "I daresay I was only the moment's diversion for him. Already he's probably beginning to lose interest."

Since it was not in Rivington's power to deny that

his favorite cousin's attachments were remarkable for their lack of tenacity, he said nothing.

The clover sent sweet fragrance into the air as it was crushed beneath their feet—a fragrance that was carried away as they walked by a fresh spring breeze that now blew in gusts, setting smaller branches waving, shaking off last autumn's holdout leaves. Frances held the crown of daffodils on her fingertips, swinging it back and forth at her side as she walked, saying diffidently:

"I can't imagine what he would have said to you about—I believe you called it my adventure? You don't wish to tell me, perhaps. I don't care, really, but naturally one wishes to know what is said behind one's back."

"Naturally," agreed Rivington, rising nobly to the occasion. "It wasn't anything much, I can assure you—only that you had followed Kennan there thinking he was on some nefarious errand."

Frances' pink lips curved upward. "So he was! And though it's not the least use for me to know it, I do think that his visit to Chez la Princesse points Kennan up as a very bad character."

Since two of his cousins and any number of his friends had been present as well as Kennan, Rivington was only able to give qualified agreement with her statement. He did say kindly that he didn't think she ought to worry about being recognized by anyone who had been there, since he didn't doubt that the most of them had been foxed.

"Foxed?" Frances gave him a wide-eyed, inquiring look. "Inebriated, do you mean? But Sir Giles recognized me! I could see it instantly in his face."

"He only took note of you because of your connection with David. You can trust Giles to stay mum."

"Then there's Mr. St. Pips," Frances pointed out gloomily.

"Don't worry about St. Pips. Did David not tell you?" questioned Rivington. "He went back to Chez la Princesse that night and engaged St. Pips at faro. I can't remember how much it was that St. Pips lost, but at any rate, he was obliged the next morning to leave London for his Lincolnshire estate, where I suppose he'll have to rusticate for a long, long time. If ever he does return to town, I'm sure *that* will be the memory he retains of that night, and not anything associated with you."

Not unnaturally, Frances was bereft of speech. Staring dazedly at Rivington, she stretched one hand automatically to stroke the small ewe that had come to nuzzle her skirts. Finally, she said:

"Lord Landry did that for me?"

"It seemed like the right thing to do," responded Rivington, with a half smile. "To David, to me, it's not important that you were there. They say we're a lawless family. There are others, however . . ."

"Who will think otherwise!" finished Frances. "I know! I've had to do it all, though. I've *had* to!"

Rivington's bright smile answered her rueful one. "You're quite a heroine, I think."

Frances' expression said clearly that she did not embrace this classification of her character. "No, no! In fact, so far I've made an ignominious botch of things!"

Frances tried to strike Landry's potent image from her thoughts. Now, if ever, was a moment perfectly tailored to ask Rivington's assistance to enter Fowleby Place. She must find exactly the right words, though, or risk a reanimation of the disapproval he had expressed about her acting at Drury Lane. He was much too tolerant to nag. He might even express admiration for

146

her courage, but he had let her see more than once that he bore a latent anxiety about her safety.

The ewe distracted her then as it bumped against her knees, then pressed its cold nose against her wrist. Frances placed her crown of daffodils over its ears and watched with Rivington as the sheep shook its head. The crown slipped to a tipsy angle over one eye and the ewe gazed from underneath it with a particularly wise look, causing Frances to laugh. The sheep, as if attracted by the musical sound and interested by her heightened color and merry eyes, stretched its neck to her and pursed its lips.

Frances gave its cheek a last gentle rub and then turned her face toward Rivington, determined to introduce the topic of entering the Duke's ball. Before the first of her words had time to issue from her lips, however, she was disconcerted to find she had lost her chance. Lord Landry was coming toward them across the clover, his golden hair loose in the sunny breeze. To Rivington he called out:

"Your father has sent me to issue a very civil invitation to Mr. and Mrs. Mutton to view the interior of the gondola."

"They won't like it," said Frances, shaking her head with knowledgeable pessimism.

"You say that because *you* think you wouldn't like it," retorted Lord Landry with a grin as he joined them. "The sheep will love it."

Landry was right, rather to Frances' surprise. The sheep allowed themselves to be led into the gondola as though into a stable, and stood side by side chewing on a bale of fodder as nonchalantly as if they had a barn over their heads instead of the swollen orb of the balloon. The gondola bobbed a few inches off the ground from its tether. Landry leaned over it from inside, talking to Frances and the four men. A gusty breeze pulled the gondola two feet away from under her hand. She pulled back, surprised, with the exclamation that the balloon was tugging at its anchor like a boat tied to a dock during high tide.

"Ah, ha, ha," said Annonay, "it *is* riding on an ocean of air. And the wind is increasing, so it's fortunate that today we only test. It would be too dangerous to make a flight. The balloon might, I estimate, go as much as thirty-five or forty miles an hour."

"Yes, indeed," said Captain Zephyr, looking as though he rather relished the idea. "But I'll tell you what, little Frances. Why don't you climb into the basket beside David? Then you can feel a bit of what it's like to fly."

"No—no, thank you!" Frances backed away from the basket, palms out, as if fending off the suggestion, shaking her head vigorously. "I think not! I've never felt the slightest desire to fly." She saw Rivington, wearing a grin, advance on her purposefully. Quickly she turned to flee, but he caught her around the waist. She laughed and struggled, and demanded that he unhand her as he bore her inexorably toward the balloon.

"Hush! You'll startle the sheep. And if you keep wriggling like that and your skirts fly up, don't blame me," managed Rivington, half choking with mirth. Swinging her in his arms, he set her lightly in the gondola beside Lord Landry, who steadied her with an arm around her shoulders as the balloon dipped and then steadied itself under her slight weight. However, it was not for nothing that she had been raised in a fishing village, and she soon had her sea legs and was standing with a semblance of confidence. Landry, seeing she was capable of supporting herself, stepped back

148

in the gondola and looked at her. There was a lull in the breeze, and the gondola ceased its eddying.

"Now you can say you've been in one at least. How do you like it?" he said.

Her dark-lashed eyes reflected her enjoyment of the strange, weightless sensation. "It *is* exhilarating! As long as this is the farthest I get from the ground." As she spoke, the forgotten Mr. Bilge arrived to perch on the gondola's rim in a rush of gray wings. He had the end of a piece of rope in his black beak, but dropped it to give a loud scream.

"Mr. Bilge, you've escaped your leash!" said Frances. "And you've been chewing on a rope." Her expression was one of comical dismay as she turned to Rivington and Captain Zephyr. "I'm so sorry. I hope he hasn't damaged something important." Frances was expecting only a polite reassurance, so she was much surprised when she saw Zephyr's jaw drop. Before she heard him speak, he seemed to shrink and move away from her. It was an extraordinary feeling; she didn't quite realize that it was she going and not Zephyr, Rivington, Annonay, and Sir Giles, until she heard Landry's pointedly calm voice in her ear, saying:

"I don't want to alarm you, my dear, but it seems the parrot's chewed through our anchoring line. To carry on your nautical analogy, we've been set adrift."

"We're what? Adrift?" she whispered. Zephyr, rapidly diminishing to doll size, was shouting at them through cupped hands, while Rivington and Giles waved their arms and Annonay stared up openmouthed. Frances looked in front of her to see a huge tree branch poking for them and then falling away beneath as the balloon cleared the treetops. She wavered a bit, and closed her eyes; then opened them to see before

149

them, at a distance that was being rapidly closed, the crest of a craggy hill spiked on the top with a lightning-blasted oak tree. She grabbed for a basket suspension cable.

"Oh, Lord! Help!" exclaimed Frances weakly, between shock-numbed lips. Then, "What are you doing?"

Landry was leaning perilously over the side of the gondola. He deftly snapped open a knot and a large sandbag fell from the gondola to the ground, far, far below. "Dropping ballast," he said, his voice strained and muffled.

Frances watched him in a stunned way, grateful merely that *something* was being done. Her relief evaporated as they shot higher into the air with each dropped bag. Confused, staring at Landry, Frances said bemusedly, "But why?"

"To lose weight so we can rise, unless you want to throw out a sheep," he answered her.

"Rise?" said Frances, catching onto the one word, convinced that the altitude had affected his senses. "We want to go down!"

He was working at another knot, his shining hair profiled against the bright-blue sky. "Not just yet, my love. The hill—the forest ahead—you see them? There's not a chance we can land before we get there, so we'll have to pass above them."

"No!" said Frances. "No, steer it back!"

He was leaning out of the basket, nearly doubled, his strong hands working rapidly. The words that came back to her were a little breathless, though there was a laugh in them as he said, "Frances, one can't steer a balloon. It goes with the wind. Don't you listen to anything Captain Zephyr says?"

He let go a string of four sandbags and the balloon took a great leap, giving Frances visions of them rocket-

150

ing into the upper ether. She announced in an ominous tone, "Don't dare lose another of those things. I forbid it; I *refuse* to go higher!"

He bent up to look at her, and she could see that he was laughing. "We're caught in a gust! Did you ever see anything hit a tree at forty miles an hour?"

The author of their predicament had been perched on the edge of the gondola, watching the proceedings with a jaundiced eye. As though he understood the import of Landry's words, Mr. Bilge gave a deafening scream and sailed off to where they had left the ground, which looked like a small patch of open terrain punctuated by four dots.

"That's all very well for you," Frances called to Mr. Bilge. "*I* don't have wings, you odious creature!" She watched the receding stick figures below, realizing there could be no help from them, and turned to Landry. A feeling of unreality swept her; again she must look to this brilliant amoral man for assistance.

The sheep had been peacefully chewing their fodder as though nothing a bit out of the ordinary were taking place. Frances felt a tug on her skirt and looked down to see that her hem had become entangled with, and mistaken for, the proper diet of the sheep. She gently freed her hem from the working mouth of the ewe and knelt to put her arms around its neck.

Landry was leaning far out of the gondola, unknotting the last sandbag. "There!" Frances felt the balloon take another upward leap. "Thank God Annonay was stupid enough to overfill us. We're going to make it over," Landry continued, and straightened and turned to see Frances kneeling, white-faced and clinging to the sheep. Her eyes were squeezed tightly shut; she was therefore unable to see the sympathetic speculation on Landry's clear, sculptured features. A sparkle made a glamorous light in his vivid eyes. How well he knew the quickest way to revive her.

"When Jeffries was making his first Channel crossing, his balloon lost altitude so quickly that he had to dump everything, equipment and all—in fact, they came so close to plunging into the water that he and his assistant began to remove their clothes and jettison them as well. I think you should prepare yourself for the possibility that if we come to another hill we may have to strip!"

Such was her disorientation at finding herself flying in a gas balloon with Lord Landry that she responded to this blatant provocation only by staring up at him in a numb way and saying, "That was a joke, wasn't it?"

"Yes, Miss Atherton," he said, his eyes shining humorously. "It *was* a joke." His back was braced against a suspension cable attached to one corner of the gondola; he reached out his hands to her. "Come and stand up beside me. The best part about this is the view."

Other than to shake her head vigorously, Frances moved not a muscle. "It's too high, we're too high now. All I want is for you to make this thing go back to the earth."

"I can't now; there's the Epping Forest beneath us. There's no clear place to come down. Come beside me; see England as the hunting eagle sees it." She still hesitated, so he said gently, "Don't be afraid—I won't let you fall." He knelt beside her and slipped his arm firmly under her shoulders, slowly helping her to stand. "It's all right, Frances. Do you want to stand by yourself? No? Then settle back against me."

As Frances leaned her back stiffly against the hard length of his body, he shifted his weight slightly to accommodate her and lifted his arm from her for a moment. Suddenly insecure, she cried out:

"Don't, don't, please! Hold me!"

His arm slid quickly around her waist and held her securely, a secret smile playing at the corners of his lips.

"What do you think?" he asked her. "Do you like it?"

"I do," Frances admitted in a shaky voice, "but I try very hard not to. I'd never let you do it, you know, if I wasn't so scared of falling out of this balloon."

Her answer startled him into a delighted laugh. "Frances! I meant the view!" She felt his breath on her cheek as he leaned forward around her to look in her face. "Child, you've got your eyes closed! Open them," he admonished her softly.

She did as he asked. It proved to be a simple motion that revealed to her a perfect England she had never seen before—an England so well formed and appealing, so spotless and pristine, that she could only gasp in amazement.

"How beautiful!" she whispered. A sensation of height was nonexistent, and it looked as though she could bend down and rearrange, if she desired, the scenery beneath, as if it were spread before her on a garden path. The undulating, sensuously curving hills were broken by dark footpaths and frosted with new green grass. Following closely the swirls of topography were forests misted with minty spring buds, and a broad glassy serpent that Landry identified as the Roding River twisted away to meet the horizon. She pointed happily as they slowly passed over a village, a tiny cluster of cottages surrounding a massive, unadorned Norman church tower, which looked sturdy

153

and friendly from the air, rather like a large gray mastiff. Then they were over a country manor looking like a gingerbread dollhouse surrounded by fields, some newly plowed, some yet containing the stubble of last year's planting. The horizon seemed directly in front of them, a curved line of a light, creamy blue like a robin's egg, rising to a deep purple above their heads, marbled occasionally by a gathering of pure white clouds. And to add the final note of utterly impossible beauty, the landscape seemed to sparkle, a diamond flash rising and disappearing almost instantaneously from random points. Landry was aware of her disbelief at this almost gratuitous display of scenic perfection and volunteered:

"Those pinpoints of light you see are caused by the sun reflecting from a window or a pool of water far beneath, and it seems to flash because we are moving past it so rapidly that the angle of reflection is extremely short-lived."

"Are we moving rapidly?" Frances breathed in wonder. The enchantment had so overcome Frances that she lay back, relaxed, dreamy, against Landry, as innocent and unaware as a child. "It seems as though we are suspended and the earth is turning beneath us. It's so still here. Why can't I feel the wind?"

"We are the wind." He settled her languorously closer to him. "As the breeze goes, we go, moving at the same speed and not fighting it, as you would walking on the ground."

The air was pure at this altitude, without taint, and to breathe it was to give a rest to the lungs. Frances breathed through parted lips, and her eyelids grew heavy. She was in a waking dream, and as Landry's arms gathered her, she felt curiously united with him, wind-bound and harmoniously one.

154

Frances' mood was no mystery to her companion, and he knew, even if she did not, how quickly her newly discovered sensuality could shift to another, more adult arousal. She would be as easy for him as the answer to an oft-repeated child's riddle. He wondered briefly what the Academy of Science would make of making love at two thousand feet. Damn the sheep! The humor of it struck him and he laughed quietly.

Frances twisted slightly to turn her hazel eyes inquiringly toward him.

"It's nothing," he told her, not wanting to disturb the unselfconscious happiness of the slender girl who lay against him so trustingly. Women by the dozens had come and gone in Lord Landry's life. His inamoratas ranged from the most gracious of the great London hostesses to the most sought-after actresses of the London theater. He had been with women more beautiful than Frances, certainly, and far more accomplished, far more educated. But Frances, without accomplishments, without social rank, had held his attention long after he might have expected to become bored by a merely pretty provincial. Memorable was the ungainly pride that could lead her into disaster or crumble into honest self-awareness in a moment. There was a freshness about her, a charm free from art under the prudish exterior to which she clung as to a lifeline. Painfully virtuous, at once gullible and skeptical, with a curiosity and a streak of common sense that was as likely as not to manifest itself in the most whimsical manner, the parson's brat had caught Landry's promiscuous interest and held it.

The wisps of water vapor that had added a creamy texture to the sky's blue had begun to coalesce with the few clouds into a gathering gray mass to the north-east, which, although it could not presently be called ominous, gave some indication of becoming so. Storms could come up so quickly. He hoped that, if there was to be a squall, they would be somewhere less exposed by the time it hit. Glancing down at Frances, he realized with amusement that she was so involved in her present euphoria that she had forgotten the dangers of their situation. Or perhaps Captain Zephyr had never told her that the landing was the most hazardous part of any flight. He wondered how to keep her from becoming frightened, and decided he had better make her angry. Landry studied the horizon and then remarked casually:

"We're beginning to drop, I think."

"Are we?" asked Frances, drowsily, turning to look at him.

"The balloon isn't gas-tight and the hydrogen leaks gradually."

"That's good, isn't it? Won't the balloon come gently to land?"

Landry took his arm from her waist and transferred his hands to grip her shoulders. "Yes, indeed! And while I don't have the equipment to make any accurate measurements, judging from the approximate speed of the wind, relative to the velocity of our descent, I estimate that, barring any mishaps, we ought to touch down somewhere in the middle of the English Channel."

Shock exploded her trance into a thousand fragments; the sleepy content was blown back into the recesses of her mind. "Barring any mishaps?" repeated Frances. "You don't consider *that* a mishap? Do you mean to stand there at your ease and tell me that we're going to land *miles* out at sea?"

"I'm not exactly standing at my ease. In fact, it's

all I can do to hold you still enough to keep us from capsizing. If you were a teapot, Frances, I swear you'd be steaming."

"I'd like to know why I shouldn't be! You've had the effrontery to encourage me to gaze at the scenery like a bank clerk on a day excursion when our very lives are in peril!"

"That was bad of me," he conceded soothingly. "I'm sure you would have found it much more satisfying if I had whipped you into a state of hysteria."

Any charity she'd been foolish enough to feel for Lord Landry evaporated on the instant. She recollected suddenly that he was the most odious, hateful man she had ever met. "I suppose," she said bitterly, "you will let me drown as well."

Observing that Frances seemed by now to be quite able to keep her balance in the lightly swaying basket, Landry released her. Then, stepping carefully over a sheep, he reached to a cord that was connected to the neck of the balloon's silk bag and wound around a support rope to a point accessible to passengers in the gondola. He began to disentangle it.

"Good thing for you I'm too gentlemanly to point out that it wasn't *my* parrot that chewed through the tether," he said, not looking at her. "Look there, Frances . . . where this cord leads? That's the valve— a very delicate piece of equipment. If we can find a stretch of bare land between here and the Channel, and if the valve doesn't stick open and release the gas so quickly that we sink like a skyrocket, and *if* we can find something sturdy enough for the grapnel to hold, then we may survive in spite of all."

The entire experience seemed not to have altered Lord Landry's serene good humor so much as one whit.

"Lord Landry," Frances ground out, "there are times when I find you *excessively* amiable. Why is it that you didn't add, 'if we aren't struck down by the lightning storm brewing to the northwest.' Had you not noticed the clouds?"

"I had, but I didn't want to frighten you," said Landry with unabashed cordiality.

Chapter Nine

The forest beneath them became laced with swamp, the reflecting tendrils of water snaking in among huge ancient oaks. Oxlip and orchids provided brilliant splashes of color accenting among the brown and gray. Their hope that the swamp would border an open, grassy area was not borne out, and Frances watched disappointedly as the water disappeared and the swamp changed into thick, dark forest. Then the wind veered and they were sent scudding in a new direction as if by an unseen hand. The sudden switch sent Frances grasping for the side of the gondola.

"The wind's shifted; we're going south," said Lord Landry. He smiled at Frances. "It might be good."

"*If*," said Frances, through gritted teeth, "a woodpecker doesn't drill a hole in the balloon silk and drop us like a shot." She hadn't finished speaking when, in the far distance, a green open chase peeked through a break in the forest line. "There!" she shouted, pointing.

Lord Landry had seen already. He was gazing at it intently, shading his eyes from a shaft of sunlight. "I wish I could see how far the flat stretch reaches." He looked at Frances. "We have to make a decision right away; we'll have to start losing altitude immedi-

159

ately if we want to land in the open area. Do you want to sport canvas?"

"Yes, I do," said Frances, "if you mean, do I want to take a chance. I'm not familiar with a lot of horrid boxing cant."

"So I observed." Landry smiled and added the cordial hope that he could put the thing down without killing them. "Only consider the chagrin of our surviving families should our corpses be discovered entangled with a couple of deceased blackface sheep."

Frances knelt and looked at the approaching landscape, her knuckles white on the gondola's edge. Over her head Landry manipulated the valve, and she heard strange hisses and whistles as the toy trees grew larger and developed distinct and very jagged branches, which reached up to snare them. The gondola began to sway under the balloon as they lost altitude, and the ropes to twist and shimmy.

There was a drop of perhaps a hundred feet that left Frances gasping, and the balloon swung wildly to the side, skipped over a knoll, and dropped rapidly on a collision course with the great ruin of a Palladian manor house, which seemed to erupt from the hill's flank. The balloon dived and swung at the mercy of the wind, and the great walls of the burnt-out manor loomed closer. Frances' heart pounded like a blacksmith's hammer as she waited for the jolt.

The gondola cleared the wall by inches, and Frances found herself looking into a hollow interior filled with sooty flame-blackened timbers. She pressed her palms over her eyes.

"We've cleared the manor!" Landry called to her encouragingly. "I'm going to toss out the grapnel and see if we can anchor."

"What's down there?" she asked, not daring to look.

"An overgrown garden." There was a loud, brittle crash from below. "*That* was a statue of a nymph holding twin bear cubs. We've just lopped off her head. I think we'll catch on this dusty wreck of a fountain. It has a sea serpent in the middle and we may grip on the coils. The force of the snag will bring us to earth in a hurry! So—Frances, what are you doing? Stay down!"

The blind suspense was too much for Frances, and she had braced herself against the side of the gondola for a look at their circumstances. Landry caught her in a steel arm precisely the moment the grapnel caught with a spine-jarring jolt. She surely would have been thrown from the gondola had he not had the presence of mind to grab her. The violent arrest of the balloon's rapid forward motion caused the balloon and gondola to come whipping to the ground through a white wood arbor festooned with dead vines. The gondola made matchsticks of the delicate woodwork, and Frances had a quick impression of splinters of white wood flying everywhere and the mad, flashing colors of red, blue, and gold silk leaping wildly around them. The breath was sucked from her lungs as the gondola collided with the ground, and the rope suspension cables became a thrashing prison. The sheep abandoned the gondola immediately, their little sharp hooves running painfully over Frances' compressed stomach as she lay half on her back; then she was half lifted, half dragged by Lord Landry over a bed of crushed rock, away from the fretting, bounding balloon.

Fighting for breath, Frances collapsed, still wound in his arms, into the sharp, grassy scent of an aged planting of March-come marigolds. Landry was laughing; Frances could feel his hard chest shudder.

"That wasn't bad for practice," he managed between

choked bursts of mirth. "We'll try the real thing to-morrow."

"How can you laugh? How can you?" The words bit as they struggled through her flayed throat. "I've never been so afraid in all my life!" Her heart was banging painfully against her strained lungs, chastising Frances for squandering her drained energy on speech. The jolt she had received from the balloon's landing came cresting over her in a stunning aftershock; she lay for a long time as she had fallen, unable to order movement to her limbs or more than a pittance of breath into her lungs. Landry had cushioned her fall neatly with the warm length of his body, while chance had tucked her cheek into his soft linen shirt and thrown one of her legs across his lean thighs. One of her fragile white arms was curled near his shoulder, with her hand resting beside his head. Frances could see the sky above her, pearl-gray and rolling with black-tipped clouds, forever shed of its mysteries. With the lark and the sparrow, she had sailed there.

The hammering of her excited heart began gradually to lessen, though not slowing to its normal pace. And as her shock wore away, a new and even more powerful weakness came to take its place. Some nagging hum tucked into her mind warned her that she ought to stand up, to move off. Without quite realizing that she was doing so, Frances quieted that wary voice, pleading for just one more minute, I'll only stay one more minute like this, then I shall get up and it will be over.

Landry hadn't spoken since her words, and she wondered what he was thinking and if it might be possible to guess, were she to tilt her head a little and look into his eyes. Her bonnet had fallen loose on its ribbons during their escape from the gondola, so the slight motion of her head brought her deep-brown hair shimmering out to ripple across the upper part of his body.

Landry had recovered much more quickly than Frances. He was able to smile with luxurious charm into her upturned face. She noticed how the brightness of his hair dulled the marigolds and the green of his eyes outshone the leaves framing his countenance. A spray of pollen had flown into the air as they had fallen on the marigolds, and he saw that it had given a fine dusting to her tawny cheeks and dark eyelashes. He put up his little finger, took some of the clinging pollen onto the side of it, and gently brushed it onto the swell of her lower lip, where it lay, a speckled gold luster against the dusky redness.

"Marigold mated," he whispered. She felt a tensing of his arm as he reached out to behead, between his thumb and forefinger, three of the marigold flowers nearest, and her captive gaze followed his hand through the air as he brought them, to slide them ever so gently into the thick wavy hair behind her ear, where they were trapped and firmly held. He shifted her on his arm, turned on his side, and held her close; and reached a hand to arrange her hair in its proper fall across her forehead; then lightly brushed the pollen from her lips with his own.

Frances knew that she ought not to close her eyes, but she did it anyway. She could feel his deft fingers as they sought and loosened the first of four large fabric-covered buttons that held closed her cloak. He spread the collar to bare her throat, saying huskily that she was anointed. She felt petals softly dropping to touch and lie across her throat and his breath skimming her skin as he blew them off. A thrill of enticing fright shook her as he opened the second button; her soul learned the shy rapture, the feared wonder, of a butterfly emerging for the first time into a fresh and freer world. It was as though the balloon had carried her to a magic isle where old rules and problems no longer existed and she was tied not to the rigid standards that had governed all her life before, but to discovery and joy. Her past became a pale, fading mirage against the insistent reality of Landry's warm, vibrant presence. Color, scent, texture, and sound were vivid and exaggerated; she could experience them in a way that she had never done before. No, she had been so once before, on the carriage ride when he had brought her home from Chez la Princesse. With the memory, her conscience weakly threw up the attendant self-censure and regret, jogging her vanishing sense of responsibility, reminding her that she ought to stop him. One more minute. Please. Please. She made a compromise and turned her face away from him, knowing as she did it that it was not enough.

"I wish you would not," she said in a curiously forceless voice.

"Do you?" His tone hadn't changed. She turned her head, opening her eyes to look at him, and saw with a prick of shame that he knew she was lying.

"We should—I think we ought to"— she spoke to distract herself as much as him—"to look for someone to help us." How lame her words sounded. "The big house looked as though it had been burnt. Do you think it has been deserted?"

He gave a light laugh in response, and she felt the thickly bunched head of a marigold as he brushed it against her cheek.

"I can give you all the help you need," he said peacefully. The flower slid around to her chin, and was left to rest on her throat as he slipped the third

164

button of her cloak from its nest. "I know where we are. This is Wrenleigh's estate in southern Suffolk. It's been deserted since the fire seven years ago. When the Earl was forced to the Continent to escape his creditors, he put a torch to the place to keep it out of their hands. The grand gesture. It was the kind of thing that appealed to him."

"What a tragic story! Did you know him?" Her heart still fluttered alarmingly.

"He was a school friend. I spent a month here the summer I was fourteen." His hand had moved to her side, where he laid it broadly, fingers spread, stroking underneath her breast. "The story's not as tragic as you think. Wrenleigh won a fortune at hazard in Naples, and when I visited him last year he was set up in a villa at the edge of town, better fixed than he'd ever been." He freed the last button of her cloak, and she felt cool air on the base of her neck as he parted the heavy garment and tucked it by her sides. Under the cloak was her blossom-pink robe *à l'anglaise,* flaring slightly under the high bodice that had been cut on the cross to cling to her full, soft breasts. It was a perfectly respectable garment, but was made to be worn while standing and the material was such that, in her present position, it fiercely accented the lush contours of her body.

She made a fretful, shaky motion to pull the cloak about her again, but he caught her hand and carried it to his lips.

"Frances. You worry too much," he whispered, gazing steadily into her eyes.

"It would be well for you if I didn't," Frances answered him. Her tone was defensive but she was quaking inside, knowing she was too close to the flame. Frances was reminded once more of the kiss he had given her in the carriage after they had left Chez la Princesse. If he had wanted her then, could she have resisted him? Could she resist him now?

He kissed her fingertips one by one and gently took the tip of her middle finger between his teeth. "It would be well for *you* if you didn't. All this self-denial will give you a migraine."

"What you want is sinful." Her voice shook slightly.

He gently opened the palm of her captured hand and moved his fingernails from her wrist upward, lazily but firmly, leaving white trails on her flesh that changed to red as the blood rushed to the surface once his nails had passed. His fingers seemed to be reaching a destination as they pushed smoothly through her tightly clasped hand and wound them, tendrillike, through. He carried their entwined hands to his lips and gently nibbled her knuckles. His head was tilted to the side, his golden hair falling over her outspread brown curls.

"Does it feel like sin when I kiss you?" he asked.

She was visibly discomposed. "Yes! Yes, it does! It feels too good not to be!"

"And pleasure is wrong?" He dipped their paired hands to her mouth and moved them round the curvature of her lips, which relaxed and parted involuntarily, then snapped closed as she caught herself, biting her lower lip in her small white teeth. "Why do you think you have those feelings? Only to gauge how well you can resist temptation? To punish yourself?"

Her cheeks heated; Frances drooped her long, pretty eyelashes and turned her head. In a voice ruffled with shame, she said, "I shouldn't have those feelings for you."

He was amused again. "It's pitiful what they teach women in this country. Frances, poor child, what do you think it means? Young girls sighing over lending-library romances, or giggling when the squire's handsome son waves at them on the village green? Why do you think men and women dance together, and write love letters, and stand half-naked statues in their gardens? It's a part of the same appetite—of course you should feel it, too; that's the way we're all made."

"That's exactly the kind of thing one would expect a rake to say." Frances tried to prevent her voice from trembling.

Landry grinned. "At least I've taught you something." He trailed a finger down her cheek. "I've never seduced an innocent girl. And I'm glad you're so clever. It keeps me from feeling guilty. But I think I've told you that before."

"Something like that," she agreed, torn with anger, fright, and desire.

A blue-white flash of lightning split the sky to shatter against a high corner of the hulking manor, joined by the crackling scream of a thunderclap. Frances jumped as though she'd been shot.

"It was only lightning," he said, holding her close, his hand straying comfortingly through her curls. Three fat raindrops fell heavily nearby, and a cool wind swept the hills, bringing with it a deluge. He pulled her from the rapidly soddening ground and held her while he peered through the enveloping sheet of water for shelter. There was a path of gray stone nearby, and he led her to it, covering her head with her bonnet. A second lightning bolt struck an elm on the slope behind the manor.

"It's God's reproach for your want of principle," she said with the wavery trace of a smile. Raindrops lay like crystal beads on her skin, leaving her cheeks fresh and dewy.

167

"How do you know it's a reproach? Perhaps it's an endorsement," he answered.

"Of all the base, impious . . ." Doubtless he couldn't hear her words over the drone of the splashing rain and the smack of their feet on the graveled walk. Landry propelled Frances up the lichen-covered steps of broken stone that led to a wide upper terrace collaring the great house. More than a century had passed since the second Countess of Wrenleigh had extravagantly caused the terrace to be bedded in chips of snow-white marble and hired a small army of youngsters from neighboring farms to combat the subversive encroachment of weeds. The democratic hand of time had overthrown the tyranny of the terrace's chaste whiteness; a plebeian assault of scrubby dandelions and groundsel had surged through the stones like a smug family of ragged squatters.

The mansion hung over them, dead and heavy, as they rounded the corner of one charred wing. Landry turned away from the house. Leaving the stones and pulling Frances behind him by one hand, he crossed a rectangle of scraggling, sick greenery to a high brickwork wall. Frances felt her feet sinking into the rich loam of what must once have been an exquisite plantation of expensive annuals. Her toe came up unexpectedly under a sinewy stone arm grotesquely severed from a nearby Heracles, and she cried out and stumbled. There was no slackening of Landry's long strides, and Frances reflected with some umbrage that she would probably be pulled face first in the mud.

"Are we running toward somewhere?" Frances yelled to be heard over the rain. "Or are we just running?"

Through a speech-obliterating clap of thunder, she heard him say something about "the old stable" and "might still have a roof on it." They reached a wicket gate bare of paint and welded shut by rust. Lord Landry tried it unsuccessfully, then drew up his knee and kicked the gate from its hinges. The gate fell hard, nearly disappearing in a thick mat of dried grass.

"You're certainly devil-may-care with other people's property," shouted Frances as they passed through.

He gave her a look of mock reproach. "And I thought you would be so impressed with my swash-buckling heroics." They entered a wide eroded yard, crisscrossed with deep wheel ruts filling with water. Frances saw an old stable mushrooming ahead through a steamy mist thrown into the air by the collision of rain and earth. It was barnlike and timbered, with a sturdy stone-tile roof. Spouts of muddy water sprang from beneath their feet as they headed for the black square of the open doorway.

They stepped inside as a white flash of lightning lit the interior. Visible in eerie relief were two long rows of oak roof-support posts stretching into the darkness like a long church nave and lined with piles of straw stored perhaps by local farmers. The lightning's flicker outlined the narrow eyelets cut at intervals into the wall to admit light and fresh air. The rain drummed with a metallic echo on the stone tiles above them.

Soaked, bedraggled, her cloak a wet slab on her back, and her loose brown hair hanging heavy and cold on her shoulders, Frances' only warmth was in the hand Lord Landry held. He turned to face her, his hair curling from the rain, and raised his free hand to drag off her bonnet and toss it on the straw. His expression was tranquil, and yet to Frances compelling; she could neither speak nor tear her gaze from his face as he slid his hands under the cape covering her shoulders and sent the garment falling around her ankles. A sudden chill took her, and a whisper of fear. Her feet caught in the sticky wet folds of her cloak as she backed from him, wide-eyed, shaking her head.

"No. No." Frances found the sound of her voice jarring in the sweet-smelling serenity of the stable and the lulling thud of the rain. Then there came a damp breeze flooding through the doorway and a fresh clatter of falling water. Frances crossed her arms, hugging herself pathetically. "I'm cold," she said.

"Frances, you're not yourself." He was smiling, but made no move to approach her. "You ought to know better than to give me an opening like that."

"I hope you valued it, because that's the last opening you'll have from me!" she said meaningfully. She stepped back further, desperate to widen the distance between them. Her skirts and petticoats clung like a phantom skin over each graceful curve and swell, hobbling her; she lost her balance and fell to her knees on a pillowing foothill of the straw stack. He came to her, kneeling, and drew her tightly to his body, entwining his arms about her shoulders, pulling aside the damp curls. His lips singed the bare skin on the side of her neck, searing a path to her earlobe.

She tried to pull from him, but the heat of his nearness was overpowering, and the pulling away turned into a helpless throat baring, and the hands that she put up to push him back instead weakly clung to him. His lips worked their way from her ear down her delicate jawline, and when their lips finally touched, she could only drink in his deep kisses as though they were her breath of life. Sweetly they tasted one another; he held her so closely to him that her body ached with the contact and her tense muscles began involuntarily to yield. Her world was damp and warm, shivering with pleasure's fever. In the vast bursts of

170

lightning her gaze found the sensual line of his mouth, the fine eyes gentled with passion, as she lifted her hands to lay them on either side of his face. She heard him say her name and after each kiss whisper the delight she gave him. His lips parted hers farther, tenderly probing her shy mysteries and filling her with an exquisite, anguished longing so potent that she wished to open every pore of her body and have him flow inside until each empty cell overran.

His mouth took hers again and again as he raised her body and with one competent hand brought freedom to the hook-and-eye fastenings at her back. Her gown fell, baring her shoulders, and he laid her back on the straw, carefully spreading her flowing, rain-perfumed hair. Her breasts were soft and swollen beneath the damp fabric of her bodice, and Frances watched his face with fearful wonder as he eased the gown lower. Modesty suddenly intruded. She could look at him no more. A hard shiver ran the length of her spine as she pressed her eyes shut tightly. Beside her she felt him stir, then lift her hand and carry it to her breast. Uncurling her stiff fingers, he touched them gently against the blossom of her own fullness.

"You're soft as a rose petal, sweet," he said in a quiet voice so near and intimate that she might have made the thought herself. His lips found her tingling palms and then brushed feather-light over the tips of her breasts. A half-suppressed moan burned her throat; she arched her throbbing shoulders, fretful and confused. And when his mouth came again to her, she whispered "yes" when she had meant to tell him that he must stop.

With mindless innocence, she pressed against him, wanting to feel every inch of him through the clinging wetness of their clothes. They had been side by side, and she did not stop him as he pushed himself gently on top of her and kneaded her shoulders with strong hands as she fiercely fought him for more . . . deeper . . . wetter . . . her body tortured by the onslaught of new sensation.

Had she been any woman, Landry would have been careful of her needs; it was his nature to be so. But with Frances, he was careful and something more. Fine-tuning to the fragile soul of his virginal lover, he held back with tender patience, deferring his more sophisticated desires to lovemaking consistent with her inexperience. Checking his ardor to her slower pace, he made sure she had the time she needed under the refined luxury of his guiding hands. Later, he would reflect that he could not have gone about it any other way, even if he had fully known the price. If he had taken her at once in the white-hot giddiness of her early passion, she might have been too confused to stop him. Instead, he had waited for the blooming of her participation and the full and knowing maturity of her willingness. While Frances had long passed rational thought, she owned an inhibition stronger than the paradise she found in Landry's arms. Infallible, unquestioned, was the conviction that the intimacy of her love must be given only to the man she would marry. Without triumph, without criticism, she accepted the tenet. The feelings she had for Landry seemed as immense as the heavens, but he had made plain to Frances the quality of his commitment, so that her trust for him was weaker than her faith in the dogmas of her childhood.

He would have loved her there in the warm straw, but as his fingers spread their heady magic beneath her breasts and lower, a gust of agony blew cool against the tide of her flaming blood. Her pulse surged, one beat hot, one cold, one hot, in an awkward chill as she tried with desperate haste to muster her surrendering strength. Her palms left his back to shove his chest and, in a voice she scarcely knew as her own, she whispered:

"You mustn't . . . I don't want . . ."

Landry had seemed to her so involved that she had anticipated a lengthy battle to gain his attention. He responded so rapidly that she felt a start of shock.

"What is it, love? You're afraid?"

Her breath came in tattered gasps, and her eyes pleaded for his compassion. "Yes—but not that only. I can't—you must know I can't. You were wrong— wrong to start this."

"I? Has it been all me, then, Frances?" His voice was gentle, but there was a curious trace of—what? Bitterness? No, it was more temperate than that and more subtle. She couldn't have hurt him; it was impossible that she would have that much power. He was the only man who had brought her to these forbidden twilight realms, but to him she was merely one in many. Other women had shared, would share in the future, the same clever hands, the same expert lips. How small an effort for him to bring her, like all his others, to this silly joyous heaven, the better to plunder their flimsy charms and slake, for the moment, the boredom of his complex, questing intellect. The thought nagged her temper like a biting fly.

His words were too disturbing to be answered directly.

"I should like to get up," she said in a tight, cold voice that reflected nothing of her bruised heart. The hard, hot comfort of his body pressed to hers was still igniting the tempest within her and the hands she had bravely lodged against his chest had caught his shirt and clung. The faint, cloudy light filtering through a high eyelet slash lent silvery highlights to his profile, and as she watched him, instinct was the only sense that warned her of the stronger emotions veiled beneath the seemingly relaxed detachment that had suddenly occupied his features.

His fingers spread slowly over her breast, her erratic, jumping heart. "Your tongue has a language different from your body."

Shame that she was to be had with such ease took hold in her soul and gave her the courage to move sharply, as though to roll away. He stopped her by catching her wrists in a relentless grip and carrying them to the straw on either side of her head. His mouth met hers in a brief, sensuous caress.

"I wonder . . ." he mused dispassionately, "if we might be happier if I took the decision out of your hands."

When Landry picked up arms, he chose his weapons well. Frances cried out piteously, as though she had been struck.

"Would you force me, David?"

If her words moved him, he gave no sign. "We both know, don't we, sweeting, how *little* force you'd need."

Salty tears began to burn in Frances' eyes. "I know I shouldn't have let you believe that I would—" She couldn't say the word. "I—I en-encouraged you, but . . . I couldn't help it."

"Did it occur to you that you might ask yourself why? What we feel together is real, and not your mewling protests!" Odd that such biting words could be spoken so gently.

Virtue and ardor were so garbled in Frances' mind that they began to seem as meaningless as the storm's patternless staccato. It seemed tragic to stop, tragic not to; it was the loss of his half-mocking, effortless affection that hurt her most deeply. Never before had she admitted to herself how dear that had become to her, or that she might be willing to do so much to gain it back. Would the world be forever bleak after "no" and "I can't"? She turned her head to the side, into the cold pile of her hair, rejecting her unhappy choices.

He gave her no time to cower. Shackling both her wrists under one hand, he brought the other to catch her chin, jerking her face toward his. There was no option for her then. She must commit herself to one thing, or to the other; and she had already thrown her lot with chastity.

Landry watched sardonically as she fought his implacable grip. Then he said, "Far be it from me to shatter any of your fondly nourished illusions, but in the interest of fostering an advance in your immature understanding of physical contact, I think I ought to point out that writhing around beneath me like that is *not* doing anything to lessen my desire."

"Oh! How dare you!" Stung by this new injustice, Frances' wildly flailing emotions veered into a bright, healthy anger. "You know I am trying to free myself!"

Frances was released with disconcerting swiftness, a burning cold stinging her where Landry's body had been. His crisp movement was a paradox with his expression, which had become abstracted, almost preoccupied, like a man who has suddenly remembered an appointment he must keep across town in half an hour. Finally he stood and asked her:

"When I'm not touching you, does it make you free?"

She lifted her head to see him moving like a shadow toward the door of the stable.

"David?" The word burst from her.

He stopped, but it was a moment before he spoke.

175

"I'm not deserting you. I have to find a place where we can get warm. Wait here."

Then she was alone in tomb-quiet, save the intermittent drumming of the rain and the tiny flicker of a sound as a mouse scuttled toward its nest in a far corner. As she waited, the last of the light deserted her, and the tall rectangle of the doorway glowed eerily blue, surrounded by black. Ancient horsey smells arose from the cobbled floor beneath her and mingled with the odor of damp and straw. Draughts surrounded her, and desolation, They were the loneliest minutes of her life.

Landry did return as he had promised, but after so long a time that she had begun to fear he had, indeed, left her. He came through the doorway and stood over her, silently extending his hand. She didn't take it, struggling to stand in the clammy wetness of her gown. Her eyes had become accustomed to the dark enough for her to see him find her mantle and bonnet and drape them over his arm as he led the way from the stable. Faint starlight filtered through a break in the clouds as she followed Landry along the outside of the building. Tiny blisters rose on black puddles in the yard as they were struck by the dying rain, but Frances and Landry were protected by the overhanging eave. Over his shoulder, Landry said casually:

"And you were the one who didn't believe in bodily electricity."

They reached an open stairway, which Landry mounted, his boots echoing on the wooden slats as he climbed. She made no move to follow him, and he turned.

"The coachman's quarters. It's not perfectly pristine, mind you, but at least horses haven't been living in it for two hundred years. And I've made a fire."

Frances hung back with her icy hand laid on the stairwell. "Before you left the stable—you said—you threatened . . ."

He clattered back down the stairs toward her, and she felt his hand warm on her own as he embraced her for a quick second and then released her completely. "There—you see? I'm a reformed character. I've made myself busy long enough to erode the nasty wash of temper. Lesson one hundred and thirty-six: Don't take seriously anything a man says when he's lying on top of you. Did you really think I was going to ravish you? Things said in anger . . ." She saw him shrug in the darkness. "Don't let it distress you; no doubt I came by my just deserts. Come up with me."

He began to climb, and when she hesitated still, he turned back and with a note of laughter in his voice said, "Besides, I've seen to it that we're to be adequately chaperoned. I have a very respectable missus and her husband in attendance upstairs. Come up and greet them."

She decided to follow him, with trepidation and curiosity. Once they had reached the top of the stairs, she noticed that the lock to the door had been smashed, but instead of calling Landry to account for his disrespect for the property of others, she peered nervously around the corner.

Before her was a small sitting room with a motley scatter of elderly furnishings much the worse for wear and a broad stone-linteled fireplace bright with a cheerfully crackling blaze. Before it sat the two blackfaced sheep, chewing dreamily on the moth-bitten remains of a green carpet.

What remained of the evening was fortunately not so hideous as Frances had earlier pictured in her imagination, for which Landry's cheerful control was much responsible. Nothing could have been more ingenious than the provisions he had made for her comfort. He had explored the other buildings in the home farm; the local tenant farmers were apparently using the buildings for storage, and he was lucky enough to find a cache of root vegetables, apples, and cider, and made for them a passable meal of boiled potatoes and cider hot in the jug, consumed while kneeling in front of the small homey hearth; the potatoes were eaten with their fingers and the cider drunk from the jug, swapped back and forth in turns. The adventure seemed to appeal to Landry's sense of humor. He took their situation in such good part that a casual bystander would have been pardoned for thinking that the excursion had been deliberately arranged for his entertainment. Here was no citified dandy at a loss without his valet and butler!

To anyone unacquainted with Frances, it might have seemed odd that the kinder Lord Landry was to her, the more withdrawn and monosyllabic she became. His goodness to her began, quite unaccountably, to pile in her mind. Not only had he helped her when she had first arrived in London, he had rescued her from Chez la Princesse and, without a single question, gotten her a part in the Drury Lane Theatre. Perhaps these hadn't entailed any special effort on his part, but what of his timely dispatch of Mr. St. Pips at the card tables? Perhaps his many chivalries had not been devoid of self-interest, but then, he had never made the slightest attempt to deceive her on that score. It was inevitable that Frances should begin to draw parallels with her ungrateful and dishonest conduct in their relationship, in one breath condemning his kisses and in the next responding to them like a tulip trying to cup the dew. A timid self-query as to why his kisses filled her with such heady sensations had only a single, irrefutable answer: Frances Atherton, parson's daughter, was in love with the renowned Lord Landry. It seemed incredible, but there it was. She wasn't sure where she had erred, or how she could have been so stupid as to have let it happen. If only she could go back to her first day in London and avoid any action that might lead to their acquaintance—but what good was hindsight? Two months ago she might have scoffed at the plight of a lovelorn miss languishing over a handsome rake. Now she was wiser. Folly on folly, and it was all hopeless, too. To her, love must only mean marriage, while he had made it clear that it meant the opposite to him.

For a long time after their gypsy's dinner she sat quietly staring into the fire, heartsore. She wasn't sure later when she had closed her eyes. When she opened them again it was later, much later. The fire was low and she was covered by two warm, clean-smelling horse blankets. Under her cheek she felt the soft grain of fine wool cloth. Raising drowsily on her elbow, she found it was Landry's coat, smoothly folded. In the first waking moment she had thought herself in the bed she shared with her sister Pamela on Beachy Hill; then her sleepy, groping mind had recalled her to an unwilling reality. The little ewe lying at her feet gave a snort in its sleep.

Instinct made her sit up and look for Lord Landry. He was standing by the window, one curved hand gracefully resting on the frame, the other at his hip. His stance was so relaxed that it never occurred to her that he was spending the night watchful for her sake. Deserted ruins in these troubled times served often as havens for vagabonds. Some were honest men unable to find employment, but others were of a sort that had left more than one body behind them on the move. Perhaps his acute senses felt her gaze on him. Perhaps he had only turned to see what made her stir. He came across the roof and bent on his knees beside her. A single eyelash had fallen to her cheek, and he brushed it gently away with the soft stroke of a finger. After a moment, he said:

"You called me David."

"I—did I?"

"Yes." The fire crackled and sang peacefully in the hearth, dancing orange and pale-blue flames flickering as a small log burned through to the middle and collapsed in a mound of glowing coals. He turned to look into the fire, the reflection bringing into relief the hollows behind his cheekbones. "Did you ever look at a fire to see shapes in the flames?"

"Yes." Her voice was drowsy. "I'm not very good at it, though. All I ever see are castles and Chinese dragons."

"You must concentrate. That—in the corner"—he leaned slightly, indicating the direction her vision should take—"is a dog. Carrying a parcel. Wearing a top hat. Go back to sleep, Frances."

She chuckled sleepily and made no protest as he laid her down. "Looks like a castle to me."

As he walked back to the window, she said, "Do you think we should go looking for an inn?"

"It's still raining."

"What if it rains forty days and forty nights?" she asked dreamily.

"We'd begin to blanch at the sight of potatoes."

There was a long silence. Just as he was beginning to believe she'd fallen asleep, she said, "Poor Captain Zephyr. He'll be distressed about the balloon."

"He'll be glad we're alive."

She cuddled further under the blankets. "D'you know where I meant to be tonight? Fowleby Place."

"Were you going to tell the butler Mother Blanchard sent you?"

"Climb over the wall with one of Richard's grappling irons." Her voice was faint.

"Good God. Did Richard know about that?"

"No."

"Someday—perhaps—you'll explain to me what all that's about."

"Someday . . . perhaps . . ." Her voice trailed away, and the rhythm of her breathing told him that she had gone to sleep, but it was a long time before he turned back to the window.

The velvet lullaby of night faded into the cold, prosaic morning. Frances awoke to a crow's harsh caw that came from opaque gray mist outside the window. Landry came to sit beside her, cross-legged like a schoolboy, and pared an apple for her with a penknife he had found abandoned in a corner. A night's lost sleep showed little on him. There was a faint trace of blond beard at the line of his jaw, however, and his clothes, like hers, had not come through the previous day unscathed. She was not accustomed to seeing him otherwise than impeccably groomed, and the intimacy of their shared dishevelment increased her awareness of what had passed between them the night before.

He made a number of suggestions to her. They should find an inn, try to return to London. It was unusual for her that she agreed to everything without comment. He accepted her embarrassment with the same amused tolerance with which he had met her quaint independence, her parson's-daughter manners. In the yard by the stables there was, underneath a ruined awning, a crumbling well. Landry drew water in a leaking wooden bucket for Frances to drink and splash on her face, and, the sheep tagging after them like children on a

181

picnic, they began their walking journey down the stony road. He smiled and shrugged as she pointed ruefully to a patch of blue silk flapping in a tree.

Years of disuse had whittled the country lane down to a stony footpath flanked by running ditches that were full of water dark with clay from the newly plowed fields. The wind sighed through faraway belts of conifers, started a mill-sail into a slow spin, and set to waving the knee-high grass of the hedgerow, where budding dog daisies and yellow kingcups nodded. The air was scented with sweet violets and wet grass.

The nearest village was a four-mile tramp, and by the time the first thatched cottage came into distant view, Frances had long since abandoned her attempt to keep her hem hitched above the muddy lane. Only Landry, with a hidden grin of pity, and a fat black pig rutting in a roadside turnip patch watched her while she attempted to make herself respectable by stuffing her snarled curls under the bedraggled bonnet and brushed at her rain-spotted and wrinkled mantle. It was a fruitless effort, and as they approached the tiny plastered inn with its tulip-planted windowboxes, Landry said:

"Better let me do the talking." No sooner were the words out of his mouth when he realized they had been a grave mistake. Frances turned on her heels to face him.

"*You* do the talking?"

"Our story may sound a little off, so I'll make up some satisfying tale . . ."

"Do you mean to say—" Frances' gold-dusted hazel eyes flashed with indignation for the first time since he had been with her in the stable. "—that you will bespeak a lie, Lord Landry? I find lying abhorrent under all circumstances!"

"Under *all* circumstances?" he remarked unwisely. "Miss Brightcastle?"

She blushed painfully as she remembered the numerous occasions she had lied at the theater and at Chez la Princesse, and wondered aloud why it was that Lord Landry felt impelled to belabor every inconsistency of her character when there might be a deficiency or two in his own that needed attention, then marched into the inn, followed at a leisurely pace by Lord Landry.

Normally the inn's cozy public room would be empty at this early hour, but Mr. Odiham's prized Suffolk Punch had foaled a fine colt last night, and a group of his friends had joined to celebrate with him, taking ale before they went to the fields. The host, one Mr. Monson, whose sense of propriety was exceeded only by his ample girth, was irritated to be interrupted in the middle of a florid toast to the new colt when Frances stepped through the door. The omens for the interview were ill from the beginning. The sheep slipped through the door after her and gamboled exuberantly across the well-scrubbed wood floor with muddy hooves before they could be caught and thrust outside. When she introduced herself to the landlord as Miss Atherton, that worthy had replied scathingly that he begged her pardon, he had thought to be confronting Little Bo Peep. By the time Frances had described herself as the victim of a runaway balloon and admitted under cross-examination to having come from Wrenleigh, where she had spent the night among the ruins, it was obvious that she would receive no sympathy from her hostile, snickering audience.

Landry, in the meantime, had taken a relaxed posture against the doorframe, grinning sardonically. The host turned to him and demanded:

"Ho! And what has the lady's husband to say about this?"

Landry achieved a knowing leer, and replied, "I find lying abhorrent under all circumstances. I'm not the lady's husband."

They were put from the house in a trice.

The next inn was located at a crossroad three mucky miles further along the lane. Frances had been resolutely mute since leaving Mr. Monson's establishment and was forced to listen in frigid silence while Lord Landry introduced her to the innkeeper's wife as his bride, Mrs. Prudence Whiterose. Landry sketched the story of attacking highwaymen who had stolen their baggage, their money, and even (the cold-blooded knaves!) Madame's wedding ring! By the time Landry had done, he had woven the tale so skillfully that Frances almost believed it herself. She muttered:

"I don't wonder you can write *fiction*."

"Pardon me?" inquired the innkeeper's wife, looking in a kind way at the shy bride.

Landry glanced at Frances with exactly the right combination of simulated embarrassment and manly pride before bending to whisper a brief word in the ear of the innkeeper's wife.

Chapter Ten

Sunshine pierced the window of Miss Sophie Isles'
parlor like a solid gold beam on Tuesday afternoon
as that lady talked with her niece. Aunt Sophie was
respectably prepared to be among the audience on the
opening night of Lord Landry's new play *Marie*, predicted to be one of the season's great events. Her brown
hair was caught up in a poppy-colored turban, and she
wore an evening gown of matching color decorated at
the bodice with crystalized gauze dotted with glass
beads. An objective scan of her niece revealed the high
color in the poor girl's cheeks to almost match the
shade of Miss Isles' evening dress. It was an attractive,
if pitiful, effect, and left Miss Sophie wondering if
Frances would go through with her onstage appearance
this evening.

Frances was costumed for the farce in a stomacher-
front gown printed in coral chintz on white. As the
part required, Frances had, with Henrietta's help, arranged her hair in curls accented with a dainty branch
of silk cherry blossoms.

"Considering everything, I think you've survived in
good form," remarked Aunt Sophie, making delicate
adjustments to the elbows of her long net gloves. "What
did that innkeeper's wife give you to eat?"

"Ham with pork pies," said Frances with a shudder,

"and baked whiting, buttered spinach, eggs, and a Sutherland pudding. It was humiliating, Aunt Sophie! She watched every mouthful I took and said in a motherly way that I mustn't forget I was eating for two! Then she asked if she ought to send for the mid-wife to have me examined *just in case*. I wish now that I'd said yes! That would have exposed Lord Landry and his odious lies. And as for his introducing me as Mrs. Whiterose . . ." Frances struggled to find words that could express her degree of chagrin.

"Was for your own good that he *did* lie," said Aunt Sophie, in a fair-minded way. "If it ever gets about that you spent the night with Lord Landry, you'd have to move to America and change your name."

"I wish, dear Aunt Sophie," said Frances tersely, "that you would not keep referring to my ballooning accident as 'the night you spent with Lord Landry.' I've told you, we didn't *do* anything."

Her aunt looked sympathetic. "I wasn't born last Wednesday, niece. You can unlace your stays around me."

Frances sought again the handkerchief she had only recently abandoned and applied it briefly to her misty eyes. "Very well. The truth is that we didn't do *everything*. But I . . . we . . ." It was a moment before she was able to go on. Finally she said miserably, "If I am ruined, it's no more than I deserve."

"I can't agree. Landry's such a dazzler that if you held yourself off from him you ought to win a medal for chastity. Besides," Miss Isles added in a practical spirit, "the story of your adventure is in safe hands. I admit that when Richard Rivington came here Sunday night to bring back the parrot and tell me what happened, I did suffer a qualm or two. You must know, though, that Rivington and his father showed the nicest discretion in their handling of the matter! None of the teams were hitched, so they couldn't chase the balloon directly, but they were not such fools as to raise a general alarm. 'Never fear,' young Rivington told me, 'David will find some way to put that balloon down safely. But it could happen that we might not find them tonight, so it would be best not to let it become general knowledge.' "

Frances smiled through her tears. "Small good that would have done if we had landed in a town square."

"Nonsense," said Aunt Sophie, in a practical spirit. "A public descent would have been the best. Everyone knows, my dear, that even such great rakes as Landry *rarely* choose to consummate their affairs on town squares, whatever you may have heard about Lord Byron and that Millsmith tart in the Clarence Hotel foyer!" Since Frances' very shocked expression informed her aunt that she had *not* heard that particular piece of scandal broth, Miss Isles cleared her throat and said hastily, "Never mind that! How did you pay your shot at the inn and two tickets home on the mail coach? Rivington admitted that he didn't believe Landry had any money with him."

"The innkeeper's wife insisted that I lie down for the hour, and while I was resting, Lord Landry sold the sheep to a farmer. He *told* me later that he would send one of his footmen this week to buy them back for Captain Zephyr."

"There's a circumstance," chuckled Aunt Sophie. "The noble Lord Landry on a common mail coach!"

"He was perfectly at home, I assure you! We rode with a butcher and his family, and Lord Landry swept the husband into an animated converse about what effect the depressed price of pig iron will have on the Shropshire blast furnaces. Then he flirted abominably with the daughter, played 'How Many Coaches?' with the four-year-old son, and settled comfortably in the corner and dropped off to sleep, leaving me to the mercy of the butcher's inquisitive wife, who had the story of our supposed robbery from the innkeeper and interrogated me for every detail. I'm sure if she caught me in one lie, she caught me in a dozen. Never have I been so mortified! Crowning everything, I have missed the chance to penetrate Fowleby Place during the masked ball."

"The hand of Providence, my dear child. If only now you would stop behaving so mulishly and permit me to talk you out of appearing on the stage tonight."

"Aunt Sophie, you know I must, if I'm to keep up my imposture. I can't quit now!" A tap interrupted the ladies, directing their attention to the parlor door, where Henrietta was hovering with a folded sheet of stationery in her hand.

"Yes, Henrietta, what is it?" said Aunt Sophie. She received the note and read the envelope with a disappointed air. "It's from Priscilla Bolton. I hope this doesn't mean she intends to be late!" said Miss Isles as she broke the seal and opened the missive. "I don't want to miss the first minutes of the play. Drat the woman! She's turned her ankle. And she has the effrontery to beg me to come and sit the night with her."

"You must go to her, of course," said Frances, trying to hide her dismay.

"And leave you alone at the Lane tonight? I couldn't; it wouldn't do."

Frances smiled bravely. "Nonsense, Aunt Sophie. I have to be there so much earlier than you, we weren't even going to ride together. I'm incognito, so we can't acknowledge each other. It would be a comfort to

188

know you were there, but it will be quite as comforting if you come tomorrow night instead."

Miss Bolton was a gentle lady of fragile health; Miss Isles allowed herself to be persuaded. Since she had made an absolute secret of Frances' participation in the play, she could hardly use those grounds now to refuse Priscilla. Besides, Aunt Sophie thought with an inward smile, Frances would not be friendless at the Lane. Lord Landry was sure to be there.

Drury Lane Theatre was packed with spectators, as would be expected for the opening of one of Lord Landry's plays. The French Revolution was a popular theme, Landry was a popular playwright, and with Edward Kennan and Sheila Grant in the lead roles there was every anticipation of a handsome return on a three-shilling-and-sixpence ticket.

"Oranges, ginger beer, bills of play!" cried the orange-girls as they fanned out through the crowded pit, exchanging jibes with the audience, coquetting, and making change. Over two thousand playgoers were jostling for seats on the benches of the theater floor. The wait for the heavy green curtain to rise provided an opportunity for the expression of alarming exuberance. The fops strutted with chests inflated, the better to display the amethyst buttons of their snowy white shirts and the intricate arrangements of their cravats. With shirt collars so high that it was impossible for them to turn their heads, they moved with elegant stiffness as they hailed their comrades with the wave of an ivory-knobbed cane or a white evening glove. Artisans, young lawyers, tailors, shopkeepers, and street toughs mingled in a roaring melee, stomping, fighting, shaking rattles, blowing whistles, posthorns, and trumpets. One fellow wearing a false nose banged on a dustman's bell as he was paraded through the crowd on the shoulders of his comrades. Four university students had decided to race from the front of the pit to the rear, and many a fellow reveler suddenly found himself knocked flat by the rushing quartet.

The pit was surrounded by three gilded tiers of private boxes, exclusive territory available to those able to pay as much as twenty-five hundred pounds for a season's subscription. The Prince Regent sat in the Royal Box, the only one equipped with a fireplace, surrounded by a champagne-sipping crowd of celebrities clad in silks and precious hardware. The Prince was laughing uproariously over a bon mot offered by no less a personage than Lord Landry himself, who looked incomparably fine in a dark-blue coat and superbly cut breeches that accented the long line of his legs. Surrounding the Royal Box like planets circling the sun were the boxes of the Royal Dukes of Cumberland and Gloucester, the Duchess of Richmond, the Duchess of Argyll, Lady Jersey, and other celestial objects. It was a seat of fluttering fans and twinkling quizzing glasses, all trying to see and be seen at once, the ladies graciously ignoring and the gentlemen sneaking glances at the boxes containing the beautiful Fashionable Impures, shimmering with the jeweled favors of their wealthy admirers. There was much cross-traffic between the boxes as the patrons pursued the answers to the major questions of the evening: Who is sitting where and with whom? Who is being seen talking to whom?

The uppermost tier was called the gallery. Here a seat could be had for ten shillings, which was cheap enough unless one considered that an oversight in the theater's design had left an angle so extreme that all

190

that could be seen of the stage was the actors' feet. Gallery occupants were therefore apt to show their displeasure with the poor accommodations by throwing orange peels and glasses of water on the spectators in the pit, and by releasing pigeons to wheel near the ceiling, to the indignation of those below.

The audience's tumult penetrated backstage to the ladies' dressing room, where Frances Atherton sat on a cushioned bench, obediently holding her lips parted while a wardrobe maid applied a waxy coat of lip rouge. The room was crowded with hothouse lilies and roses sent to the actresses by friends and lovers, and the scent of the flowers mingled with perfume, sweat, and stage makeup. A score of women stretched long legs to roll on silk stockings and paced the room reciting lines. At a small dressing table next to the one at which Frances sat, Theresa Sea expertly powdered her nose with a hare's foot. Beyond her, Sheila Grant was reclining on a Grecian lounge calmly studying her lines and twirling a single yellow rose.

"The audience sounds as if they've come to a riot," remarked Frances apprehensively.

Theresa Sea gave her a condescending glance. "This is nothing—a little high spirits," she said sourly. "I only hope it doesn't get worse. Did you see the *Chronicle* this morning? There was a rumpus at the Covent Garden last night." Theresa reached in the cloth bag at her feet and pulled out the newspaper, spreading it on her dressing table. "Here it is: 'We attribute to the unhappy influence of gin the events last night at the Covent Garden Playhouse. Without the least plea or pretense whatever, the gentry in the upper gallery began midway into the second act to call for and demand a hornpipe, though nothing of the sort was expressed in the bills. They went so far as to throw a quart bottle and two pint bottles upon the stage, which happily did no mischief, but might have been productive of a great deal!" She flipped a page. "Let's see if Hazlitt has anything about it in his column." After reading for a moment, she looked curiously at Frances. "I see someone's been busy on your behalf. It says: '. . . where I had the privilege of meeting Miss Brightcastle in the green room at the Drury Lane. This dainty newcomer will move across the stage like a gay creature of the elements in her role in the farce presented after Lord Landry's new play, *Marie*. Her eyes like dark pools, her lips like two sweet summer strawberries . . .'"

Frances squeaked, "What!" and slid over to the bench beside Theresa Sea. "Who could have written that?" She wondered at the name heading the column. "I've never met Mr. Hazlitt."

The wardrobe girl who had been doing Frances' makeup said, "You don't have to *know* him, Miss Brightcastle. 'Tis puffery—the theater manager, John Rawson, slips him a couple of guineas and he says nice things about you in his column. Gives the audience the good prejudice in your favor. It's a fine thing to be bragged up in the paper."

Frances was about to protest indignantly, when Charles Scott entered the room without knocking and walked over to kiss Sheila Grant on the cheek. He seemed oblivious to the various stages of undress exhibited in the room, and neither did any of the actresses take undue notice of his presence.

"You look magnificent, darling," he said to Sheila. "How do you feel?"

Miss Grant gave him the cool, self-assured smile of a woman who had reigned as a beauty from her cradle. "Very well, naturally. I hope you've sent word to Mrs. Parkington to stay in her sickbed."

Scott offhandedly fastened the top two hooks and eyes of Theresa Sea's gown while he spoke. "I have, though she's on the mend from her flu. She said she'll be able to come in tomorrow night, and I'm glad. I don't like to have you working without an understudy."

"Charles, you're unjust," Sheila Grant remarked with teasing reproach, a smile curling one side of her mouth. "Miss Brightcastle has worked with me so much on my lines that she knows them as well as I." There was a delicate trace of hostility in her slanting eyes. "Would you be eager to see if you could step into my shoes, Miss Brightcastle?"

Scott gave Frances an apologetic shrug and sat by Miss Grant, assuring her of the irreplaceable nature of her contributions to the company.

They were soon interrupted by the call-boy's whistle and shout of, "If you please, Miss Grant, one minute 'til curtain!" The flurry of activity ceased as Sheila Grant composed herself; and when she turned from the mirror, all present were awed into a respectful silence when they realized that she had dropped her everyday mask to reveal the regal features of Marie Antoinette; it was a reincarnation that explained much concerning Miss Grant's position as the theater's primary actress. With royal condescension, she accepted Scott's escort from the room, followed by the cast members who were to appear in the first act.

Frances heard the crowd's uproar turn musical as they sang the National Anthem. The rising curtain caused a storm of applause that threatened to bring down the house. Then voices came dimly from the

193

stage. Two actresses left in the dressing room with Frances began some desultory gossip about a rumor that Lord Byron would turn his hand to a stage play.

Frances, feeling a surfeit of nervous energy, turned to mending handkerchief hems from the basket she had brought from Aunt Sophie's. This proved an unsatisfactory diversion, as it served to occupy her hands but not her mind. If only she had able to get evidence against Kennan earlier—she might not be facing the prospect of an appearance on stage for which she felt wholly unsuited!

There was another thunder of applause as Kennan made his entrance, and a moment later Frances heard his strong dramatic voice as he worked his magic on the crowd. Her feelings of agitation increased, and she cast about for a distraction: she noticed the newspaper Theresa Sea had left open on the dressing table and began scanning it as she sewed.

An item of particular interest caused her to lay her basket aside and read the newspaper with intense concentration. It concerned the Duke of Fowleby's masked ball. The Duke, mentioned in the headline, was the focus of her attention. There was a column and more of a guest list studded with "the Lady L. and the Duke of R." and carrying a description of the colored fairy lights used to decorate the gardens, and the cost of the fireworks display. At the close of the article, the author pointed out a tragic note to the festivities; in the midst of the ball, the quiet attack of some undiscovered bold thief had augured the loss of the Duke's Tintoretto canvas of Mary Magdalene; the priceless painting was slit from its frame and spirited away as though by some evil specter. Three previous thefts of paintings from the Duke had been carried out in the same manner, and it was thought, smuggled from the

194

country, since the paintings were too well known to be sold in England.

Smuggling. Evil specter. The thought snapped into her mind that Edward Kennan was more dangerous and diabolical than even she had thought! Motive had been there, and opportunity. Frances realized with horror that her father was only one of many wronged by Kennan. She guessed—no, she *knew*—that Edward Kennan was pillaging the treasured collection of his own benefactor! Frances suffered the overwhelming feeling that she must confide this terrible secret at once. Her first vision was of a handsome face with hair like a new-minted gold piece, and perceptive green eyes. How odd that her love for Landry should inhibit her from seeking him now, but her pride couldn't bear it.

But sensible advice she must have. If only Aunt Sophie were in the audience! What profit to think of that? She wasn't, and so . . . Richard Rivington! Last week he had assured Frances that he would take a place in the box of his aunt, Lady Bloxham. In Mr. Rivington Frances knew she could be assured a sympathetic auditor.

Frances waited impatiently for the finish of the second act. Finally there was a riotous burst of hurrahs from the audience, and the cast flooded back into the room. Each actress beamed with delight at the positive reception of the play; painted cheeks flushed with the heady glow of success. The hallway outside quickly filled with well-wishers wanting to offer felicitations and share in the cachet of what was obviously to be an astoundingly well received play. Frances threaded her way through the jostle to Charles Scott, who was standing with Kennan and Sheila Grant in a crush of congratulators.

A liveried lackey arrived with an invitation to Kennan and Miss Grant from the box of the Prince Regent. Sheila Grant was to appear in the beginning of the next act. She must respectfully decline the invitation of His Royal Highness until a later time. Edward Kennan would come. Wine was offered—Miss Grant refused hers, saying she would take some before her final scene, and Frances seized the opportunity to ask Charles Scott the number of Lady Bloxham's box. He gave it to her absently.

It was well into the next act before Frances attempted to find her way to Rivington; the corridors were crowded with people waiting at refreshment stations until the play started again, and she wished to avoid the stragglers.

Frances arrived at the box to find its entrance door firmly shut and a wolf on the ducal crest of Bloxham glaring at her with forbidding hauteur. When she knocked, the door was opened by a young man of about eighteen years that Frances was able to recognize as yet another of Rivington's cousins; he was attractive and slender, with that oddly attentive air that characterized members of the clan.

He was obviously surprised to face one of the young Drury Lane actresses, but not at all displeased. Frances became uncomfortably aware of her stage makeup and the low cut of her bodice, and quickly said:

"May I please—that is, is Mr. Rivington here?"

There was a rustle of fine silk from the interior of the box, and Frances saw a foursome of ladies in elegant pastels turn interestedly in her direction. The younger two snapped open their chicken-skin fans and raised them to shield their faces for a quick, giggling exchange of whispers. A haughty matron in a feathered headdress who was undoubtedly Lady Bloxham tapped her fan in the palm of her hand, and the two younger ladies promptly faced forward. As Rivington rose from his seat to look questioningly in Frances' direction, Lady Bloxham sent him a reproachful glance that conveyed subtle but massive disapproval. Rivington returned his aunt's gaze with a cool stare that abashed his aunt not at all. Frances reflected miserably that she was becoming only too familiar with the frequent mortification suffered by females with a questionable claim on respectability. As he closed the door behind them, Frances said:

"I'm dreadfully sorry—I can see that Lady Bloxham has put the worst possible construction on our acquaintance!"

"I'm sorry *you* should suffer that kind of an insult, Frances." Rivington drew her protectively behind the screen of a dark column. "I don't make my aunt the arbiter of my conduct, I promise you. And I'm very glad to see you! I've been wanting to hear from you directly the story of your adventure with Landry in the balloon—the last time I saw Frances Atherton, she was a small, receding speck in the sky!"

Frances examined the ruffled flounce on her hem. "Have you not spoken to Lord Landry, then?"

"No, I haven't—I had a note from him saying we could call off the search, that you'd landed safely at a ruined manor in Suffolk."

"He said nothing else?"

Rivington hesitated. "Only that he was grateful to me for putting you into the balloon, because the ride might have been dull without you." He looked at her searchingly. "I've had a fairly anxious afternoon trying to interpret the significance of that remark, if it has any. David's having a small gathering at his home after the play. He said he'd talk to me about it then."

Frances looked unhappy. "My aunt says that my reputation would be gone if it were to become known that I'd spent the night alone with Lord Landry in an abandoned manor."

His mouth gave an ironic twist. "Oh, are we worried about that when we're about to appear on the stage? It's not too late, Frances—please let me take you home."

His concern touched her, but she had to protest. "I can't, I can't—especially not now. I think I know who has been stealing the Duke of Fowleby's paintings. And the thief is here, in Drury Lane!"

Into the silence of Frances' dramatic pronouncement came the soft stroke of footsteps on carpet, and the murmur of voices. Frances looked behind herself distractedly and saw that she had been observed, perhaps overheard! She was confronted by Edward Kennan's merciless black stare. Kennan, on his return from the Prince Regent's box, had been walking a few paces ahead of Lord Landry and the banker-poet Samuel Rogers.

Frances stood still, her heart nearly ceasing to beat. Suddenly Kennan's gaze flicked from her and he turned to address Rogers. There was an avalanche of applause from the theater signaling the end of the act, and the little group was engulfed by playgoers as the doors of the boxes opened, disgorging their occupants once again into the corridor.

Frances felt Rivington touch her arm. He indicated that their chances of being overheard were good, and said, "Frances, if you won't let me take you home, then you had better go back now. It won't do you any good to be seen with me. I'll wait on you first thing in the morning and we'll talk then."

Aunt Ambarrow, wife of Frances' uncle, the Bishop,

had been waiting with well-bred patience for the act's end so she could make her way to a refreshment station to procure herself a jelly. As she stepped from her box, she paused to look in a three-quarter-length mirror hanging on the door, pleased with the aspect of her reflection. She recollected with satisfied complacency how correct she had been to have ignored the hints of her dressmaker that the soft pink of her gown and its molded fit were more appropriate for a girl in her first season than a lady on the leeward side of forty-five. Mrs. Ambarrow noted also, not with conceit, but in mere pardonable pride, that her ostrich-plumed headdress was taller and more elaborate than any other she had been able to discover in her survey of the other private boxes that evening. With these agreeable thoughts, she left her box and went into the corridor.

Suddenly, as during an absurd sequence in a dream, she saw her eldest niece, that paragon of maidenly integrity, berouged like a common prostitute and seemingly ringed by the delighted countenances of several of society's most devastatingly charming libertines.

"Fran-*ces Ath*-er-ton!"

Later the young lady so emphatically addressed decided that she ought to have had the presence of mind not to respond, but her poise was already so shaken by Kennan's appearance in the very midst of her denunciation of him, that her stock of ingenuity had run out. Frances turned and exclaimed in accents of horror:

"Aunt Ambarrow!"

Her aunt came bearing down upon her like a runaway bread wagon. "Frances, Frances, what in the name of creation are you doing here? Where is your mother? *What* are you doing here with your face—"

Aunt Ambarrow's eyes bulged nearly from their sockets. "—covered with paint? Where is your mama?" She looked up and down the hall as though she expected to find that lady slouched in a near coma against the corridor wall from the shock of seeing her daughter so disgracefully displayed. "You've guilt written all over your face! You're up to some trick, aren't you? You and that brother Joe of yours. I don't wonder—time and again I told your father that it betokens nothing but trouble to let a girl spend so much of her time with her brothers. It fills her head with *masculine* notions of independence, and now this! Are you so dead to propriety that you can have forgotten the duty you owe to your family in Beachy Hill? And your poor father, jailed like a common criminal. You will follow me immediately! I shall convey you to the presence of your uncle."

It was not a prospect that would have pleased Frances at the best of times. She had always been careful to show every respect to her Aunt and Uncle Ambarrow, but there was a tacit consent in her family that the Ambarrows were *not* the mentors of Atherton conduct. Aunt and Uncle Ambarrow were of the same guild: rigid standards and no imagination. Frances was sure they would have viewed the whole of her London experience as a distastefully sordid intrigue, ignored everything she had to say about Kennan, and confined her to a windowless room for a week of memorizing Bible passages on a diet of stale bread and mineral water. And her situation with Kennan was already approaching disaster. Frances forced her frozen mind to function. The first directive it gave her was to look at Kennan, to determine his reaction to her exposure. But there was little to be seen of him save his back as he strode away down the corridor through the clustering, milling knots of people.

Her second thought was a particularly irrelevant urge to glance up at Lord Landry. She thought to find him laughing, but she was amazed to find instead an expression of interested empathy. Unable to bear his pity, she looked quickly away. The door to Lady Bloxham's box opened and the young man who had admitted Frances originally, strolled over, smiled at Frances, and asked if Richard could introduce him to his pretty friend, with so pronounced a youthful licentiousness that Frances feared for her aunt's health, so purple did her coloring become.

Aunt Ambarrow swelled like a pigeon and rapped, in a tone that lent credit to the theatrical surroundings, "Frances, we will leave *this place* at once."

Frances' heart beat so high in her chest that she had to clear her throat to talk. "I beg your pardon, ma'am," she said, "you're mistaken. I am not Frances Atherton."

Her aunt gave Frances a look that would have exploded gunpowder at fifty paces. In the moment that it took Mrs. Ambarrow to find her voice, Frances saw with ill-concealed dismay that the scene had gained further witnesses as Lady Bloxham stepped into the hall with her three pretty daughters.

"Not my niece?" said Mrs. Ambarrow in a ringing tone. "Not my niece! You tell me I don't know my own niece when it was I that you spat your milk on upon the morning of your baptism."

"I am sorry, ma'am," said Frances, quaking inwardly at her own temerity, "I fear you've mistaken me for another."

"Mistaken!" said Aunt Ambarrow. "I'll show you

201

who's mistaken. I'll show the management of this theater who's mistaken when they find themselves brought to court for soliciting an underage girl to parade herself like a strumpet in their theater."

The air throbbed with tension, and then Landry took a single step toward Frances, passed a glance of haughty amusement at Mrs. Ambarrow, and said in a pleasant voice, "What nonsense about nothing."

Frances' aunt was no lightweight, but his expression was such that the color darkened in her cheeks.

"I'm sure you won't mind telling me your name, my good woman," he continued. Frances had no time to recover from the shock of hearing her self-important aunt addressed as "my good woman" before Mrs. Ambarrow rebutted with:

"That, sir, is no concern of yours."

"I won't deny it," drawled Landry, who, to Frances' amazement, had suddenly assumed the bored air of a lounging beau. "I can't imagine anything that would interest me less. But I wondered by what name I should introduce you when we go before the—I believe you said the theater management?"

"I've not the slightest need for *you* to introduce me, sirrah," snapped Ambarrow. "I'm more than capable of making myself known to the villains who have undertaken the corruption of my niece!"

Landry scrutinized her from under eyelids heavy with contempt, and said without hesitation, "*That's* clear. Shall we proceed then? Because I find that I'll have to accompany you to verify that this young lady here is not your niece."

"Then you, sir," said her aunt, the feathers on her headdress quivering dangerously, "are a liar."

As soon as she had spoken, Mrs. Ambarrow knew

she had made a mistake. The sympathy of at least some members of the crowd had been with her, but now she felt it veer sharply away. Frances was startled, though no more so than Lady Bloxham's attendant offspring and nephews when that lady stepped forward, and in a clear, carrying tone, said:

"My nephew Landry may be many things, but I shall not stand by to suffer him called a liar. Your relationship to this young woman is immaterial. What matters clearly is that she doesn't want to accompany you. That being the case, I think you ought to be off before my nephew is forced to lay aside the deference he owes to the female sex and act toward you with a rudeness that is, I assure you, repugnant to a gentleman of his good breeding." Lady Bloxham turned to her nephew Landry's admiring countenance and commanded, "David, you will escort this young person back from whence she came. Immediately, if you please."

The battle light was still militant in Mrs. Ambarrow's eyes, but for the moment there was nothing she could do short of following Lord Landry and Frances through the corridors demanding the return of a young girl who had shown herself intent on denying their connection.

Frances exhaled with relief as they turned the first corridor, and, looking at Landry, found he was anointing her with a conspirator's grin.

"Relax, if you like," he said, lifting his hand to acknowledge an acquaintance. "I don't *think* she's going to give chase. What a dragon!"

"Do you mean your aunt—or mine?"

"Both," he retorted. "Pluck to the backbone, your— what did you call her, Aunt Ambarrow? I'd give a monkey to see her matched against Jem Beamer. Is your family full of these formidable females? If so, I can see how you developed your style."

Frances stopped so suddenly that a young man behind her carefully juggling three cups of lemonade laid waste two of them and seriously depleted the third.

"I'm *nothing* like Aunt Ambarrow!" she exclaimed.

"Oh, no, not now," admitted Landry with a cheerfulness that made Frances long to do him violence. "But in another twenty years . . ."

Frances glared at him as she tried to conjure a suitably biting retort, but Landry's expression was so invincibly genial that she began instead to laugh.

"Not with you around always," she said, "to burst my bubble."

There was a moment of curious intimacy as hazel eyes gazed into green eyes; her smile faded as she realized that she'd committed the hideous faux pas of assuming he would *be* there in twenty years. Her embarrassment saw their silence as awkward, and to end it quickly, she said:

"I can't stand here, of course! They will be expecting me in the dressing rooms." Her hand fluttered self-consciously to her throat. "Don't accompany me, please. P-people gossip so over the merest nothing! Good-bye! And thank you for the help you've been with my aunt."

She turned and sped off through the crowd before he had time to reply. There was a common hall that strung the dressing rooms together like beads on a necklace, and as Frances entered, she saw at once that something was very wrong.

The faces of the players were stiff with distress, and Charles Scott rushed toward Frances, running his hands wildly through his disheveled hair.

"Where have you been, Brightcastle?" he shouted. "Come with me! Hurry! You'll have to go on in the next act."

"The next . . . but it's not time for the farce," said Frances.

Scott pulled her briskly after him, his hand on her elbow. "Who said anything about the farce?" he flung over his shoulder. "We're in the middle of one of those charming little situations known as a crisis. Sheila Grant has collapsed."

"She's what?" exclaimed Frances, nearly tripping on a discarded bill of play.

"When she had her exit five minutes ago, she took half a glass of wine and went into a swoon."

"Has a doctor seen her?" asked Frances.

"Of course," snapped Scott. "The pulse is strong, her lungs are steady; the best guess he could make is that she appears to have been drugged."

"Oh, no, it can't be—who would have done such a thing?" said Frances.

"God knows. A rival playhouse or a competing actress perhaps. We'll hire the runners to find out what we can tomorrow. Right now our biggest problem is filling her spot. It would take more than an hour for the understudy to arrive. By that time we're likely to have a riot in the pit, especially when they hear they're not going to get Sheila Grant. I'm going to have to let *you* take the final scene."

Chapter Eleven

It was a gift from the gods, a once-in-a-lifetime smile of favor from the muses. "Take ten years of my life," went the centuries-old prayer of the bit player, "but let me have the star's role for one night. One chance, one chance to shine before an audience so they can see the genius in me." Frances' near-tearful objections that she didn't want to go on were regarded at first as an understandable fit of nerves. When her protests persisted, Frances saw that they were regarded with such suspicion that she had no choice but to silence them.

In perfect truth, Frances knew that Scott's confidence in her ability was so slim that only the most dire necessity would have made him risk the play's success on her meager store of talent. The play was so new, the final speech so long and complex, that except for Sheila Grant, Frances, and her understudy, not one of the Lane's actresses knew it through.

The curtain rose. In front of it an audience angry at being deprived of the stunning Sheila Grant, their beloved favorite, shifted and stirred like a wakening beast. There was a cough from the gallery, and the snap of a snuffbox.

Frances stood alone on the stage, still and straight,

her pallor subtly enhanced by the costume of Marie Antoinette's imprisonment, a plain black silk dress with a muslin fichu over the neck, the long ends falling to the skirt front. Her unpowdered hair was tied with a black ribbon, and she wore no ornament other than a black bow and a band of velvet encircling her slender neck. Behind her loomed the twin beams of the guillotine, joined by the heavy blacksteel blade, lined dramatically on the bottom by the silvery cold gleam of the cutting edge. The tall, gaunt executioner stood to the side of his instrument, dressed in the raffish style of the sans-culottes, his features hidden by an ominous black hood.

It was fortunate that when Frances began to speak, her voice was so low that the audience was forced into silence, if only to hear her words. Hecklers who would have called out were quickly shushed by their fellows.

Her performance was not, to say the least, what the audience was expecting. Broad effects were the dramatic style of the day. Sheila Grant would have strode in magnificent melancholy from one end of the stage apron to the other, gesturing beseechingly toward the heavens. Frances was so stricken with stage fright that she could only stand in one spot, gently wringing her hands and forcing the words out through her dry throat.

As she spoke, the growing rumble of the audience peaked and began to die away, and after a few shouts of "down in front" and "quiet, please," it ceased entirely. This so unnerved her that she forgot where she was in the speech, and had to make a long pause until she remembered her place. She felt lost on the wide stage, frightened of the crowd that seemed waiting to devour her. She closed her eyes and thought—best to speak the lines and get it over with—her presence in this play was an accident of fate, something to which she must resign herself.

The audience grew so still that she imagined they had become disgusted and had quietly left the theater; she was afraid to open her eyes to the rows of empty seats.

Then she could remember no more of her lines, and stood waiting for the shower of catcalls, boos, and (she was sure) rotting vegetables to descend upon her. The seconds ticked by, until she recalled that, yes, the audience had left the theater; and keeping her eyes closed, she took one timid step to walk from the stage. There was a rustle from the pit. Perhaps there was a straggler, someone who had fallen asleep during the last paragraphs, and Frances opened her eyes to look. To her surprise, the theater was full. She cast about agitatedly for her next course of action, and remembered: the guillotine! That is what I am to do.

It was in front of her—the gleaming blade, and hooded executioner. Frances took timorous steps toward the terrible duo, and meekly inspected the guillotine. Then she looked at the executioner—was it a different man under the hood than she had seen previously? His physical shape was different, his height perhaps a few inches shorter, his forearms less muscular. She hadn't recalled a change in this role. She looked back to the guillotine, and at precisely the instant the executioner laid his hand on her arm to lead her to it, she noticed one horrifying circumstance: The two metal pipes that had been pushed as safety catches through the holes on either side and just above the neck rest were missing! What had formerly been a stage prop was now a true instrument of death!

She was galvanized into action by the shock and

began to struggle—the executioner's grip became more powerful; she kicked and bit and fought; the crowd began to roar and applaud, making a gargantuan ruckus. Someone must have realized that something was amiss, and the curtain came rolling down on the scene. The stage was flooded with hands running toward the struggling couple, and the mysterious executioner released Frances and ran off into the wings, swinging wildly at a pursuer.

"Bravo! Bravo! Huzzah!" The appreciation of the crowd was approaching torrential dimensions.

There was spinning confusion as the company massed on stage, examining the guillotine, expressing concern for Frances, and speculating excitedly about the identity of the false executioner. Charles Scott dispatched stagemen to search the backstage areas and ordered the company to fall into line for the curtain. He sent a callboy for Kennan, who someone said was taking his ease at a tavern across the alley.

Scott put up his hand, signaling for attention, and over the hubbub he shouted, "Ladies! Ladies and gentlemen! We have to bring up the curtain and take our bows—remember now, poise is the watchword. Theresa, straighten Miss Brightcastle's hair ribbon. We must stay calm—a scandal like this could damage the theater's reputation. Calm!"

A stagehand entered the near end of the stage, carrying the abandoned executioner's mask and cape, causing a new stir of interest. Simultaneously, Edward Kennan strolled onto the stage from the opposite end, looking about curiously.

"Where have you been, Edward? It's not like you to be late for the curtain," said Scott. "Especially under these circumstances."

Kennan's smile was smugly bland. "The boy told

me; much ado . . ." He gave Frances a snide look. "Someone's been playing a practical joke on you again, Miss Brightcastle. Have you angered one of your lovers?"

Frances longed to expose him so desperately that the words burned in her throat, and she was prevented from uttering them by the lifting curtain. An avalanche of applause descended on the stage. Bow, smile, acknowledge the private boxes, step forward, throw a kiss to the pit, raise hands to the gallery. The curtain came down and went up again, and still the applause thundered. The stage became littered with fair-smelling petals as the playgoers ripped the flowers from the hands of the flowergirls and tossed them at the company. As the curtain touched down again, Frances saw Charles Scott bearing toward her. With a hand on her forearm he whisked her offstage.

"Enough of that for now," he said. "Landry's arranged for a private coach to carry you home."

"*Landry*'s arranged! I shan't go. Someone's just tried to take my life and . . ."

Scott interrupted. "Which is exactly why you'd better be conveyed safely home until we've had time to investigate. Edgar Murphy, who plays the executioner, was found unconscious, bound, and gagged in the prop room, and no one's caught the imposter."

"Mr. Scott, there's no need to investigate. I know who's tried to kill me. Where's Richard Rivington? Have you seen him? I must talk to him at once."

Scott looked like a person taxed beyond endurance. "Rivington, is it now? Listen to me; if you want to play fast and loose with Landry, don't involve me or the theater in it. Good God, girl, Landry is the last person I want to alienate."

"Pleasing Lord Landry is not my object!"

"Well, it *is* an object of mine!" said Scott, looking harassed. "Keeping Landry happy is everyone's concern here, or he'll have his next play produced at Covent Garden. Are you miffed because he hasn't come to see you himself? He didn't want to endanger your reputation; this is the first time I've seen him show that much concern for anyone. He gave me strict instructions to personally see you into the coach and deliver you safely inside your own door, and you're coming with me if I have to drag you."

"I—but what of my role in the farce?" she said with some confusion. "Who's going to fill it?"

"Don't worry about your role in the farce," he snapped. "Any twit can fill it."

Chapter Twelve

It had been a highhanded maneuver, decided Frances, for Landry to have ordered her hustled home; that he should have the audacity to assign her a bodyguard was outrageous. When Frances arrived at the sumptuous town carriage she was handed inside by a short man with massive shoulders, undulating biceps, a broken nose, and a merry eye, who announced himself as Nick Vent, at your service, and that Lord Landry had said he was to accompany Miss Brightcastle and watch over her house for the night, begging the lady's pardon. The carriage door had been closed, the mysterious Mr. Vent had scrambled nimbly to the box beside the coachman, and the horses put forward before Frances' indignation had time to crystalize into a protest. However, by the time they reached Miss Isles' front door, she was more than ready to give Mr. Vent his good-bye. She was not sure why Lord Landry should take the responsibility of providing her with a guard, but it was an action taken entirely without her knowledge or consent; Mr. Vent should consider himself released from any task contracted by Lord Landry.

She swept into the house and up the stairs, but when, a quarter hour later the yap of a prowling dog caused her to glance out of the window, she observed that Mr. Vent, far from having respected her dictates, instead had taken a stalwart post by the entrance door. A sigh of exasperation escaped her as she went downstairs to try to make him go away again, receiving only a cheerful negative shake of the head in return. Mr. Vent, as it happened, was Lord Landry's groom. And, as it happened, the son of Lord Landry's *father's* groom; and before that, Mr. Vent's grandfather had been Lord Landry's grandfather's—Frances put up her hand to stop the onslaught of genealogy. Mr. Vent would have her to understand that he would do naught to distress a lady, but when His Lordship sent him to a task—well! Nick Vent had never come short in his duty. In the end, Frances was forced to resign herself to the presence of the immovable Mr. Vent. The dictates of conscience would not allow her to leave him to cool his heels on the frigid pavement all night. She asked him if he wished to step into her aunt's parlor and partake, if he would care for it, of a light supper. Mr. Vent was agreeable. His shoulders were so wide he had to turn partially sideways to get through her aunt's parlor door, and Frances began to fear for the knickknacks. The grace and care with which he made his way to the small tea table put her fears to rest. It was no small thing to sustain that substantial frame, and to Frances' awe and Henrietta's admiration, Mr. Vent put away a quantity of salmon, some cold tongue, a pyramid of strawberries, three biscuits, two Seville oranges, and a dish of boiled cucumbers. To wine he said no; coffee would be just the thing, if it were not too much trouble. That's what was needed to keep a man awake at night. Frances made note that it was not through any wish of hers that Mr. Vent would spend a slumberless night, adding that she was sorry to find Mr. Vent in the thrall of an employer who would expect such a thing.

Vent answered with a grin that while there was nothing in the green land of England that he respected more than a sweet lady's opinion, he had to say that there wasn't a man in the world better to work for than Lord Landry. Mr. Vent had tried to make his name in the boxing ring for a time, but it was no life for a peaceable man, so he'd returned to the service of a man who'd been his boyhood friend. To hear Nick Vent talk, one would think Lord Landry a paragon of paragons, in kindness second only to the archangels, in generosity equal to the patron saint of alms. Frances was assaulted with anecdote after anecdote extolling Landry's virtues, mercifully brought to a close by a sudden eerie whistle of wind in the chimney grate that recalled Mr. Vent's mind to his responsibilities.

"If you don't mind then, ma'am, I'll set up in a straight-backed chair before the front door." He nodded to Frances with a good deal of kindness. "You can rest yourself easy, ma'am, for there's nobody that'll get in here by me; so you have the word of Nick Vent. It's a right bad scare you've had this night, so His Lordship tells me!" He tsked his sympathy. "There's some that will have it that it's a full moon that drives men mad. *I* say watch out for an eve like this one, for the dark of the moon."

"Dark of the—" Her stare was blank, into space; then she flew to the window and gaped raptly at the heavens. "It is! It is!" She held up one finger, begging silence, and then paced a short circle on the flowered carpet, her hands pressed to her cheeks in a worried and thoughtful posture. She came to rest before Vent and looked at him with troubled hazel eyes. "The smuggler's moon, they call it? The weather is clear, so I know they'll make a run! And Kennan with them, no doubt!"

"Kennan, you say?"

Frances looked at him sharply. "You look as though

—has Lord Landry mentioned something about Kennan to you?"

"Naught, ma'am, only that," Vent hesitated, "that if that fellow tries to approach you, I'm to keep him off, and damn the consequences—begging your pardon, miss."

"I must speak to Richard Rivington immediately! He lives downstairs." She was walking toward the door as she spoke. "No! He won't be there! He was going to Lord Landry's house. I shall go there at once." Heart thudding with excitement, she rushed to her bedroom and pulled from her wardrobe a wine-colored three-quarter-length coat lined in pink satin. With hurried fingers, she pulled a reticule jingling with sixpence over her wrist. As she returned to the hallway, she found herself confronting Vent.

"Ma'am, you don't want to be going to Lord Landry's house," he said concernedly. "It's a bachelor establishment, y'see, and not the right place for a young lady. And less tonight than most nights, when it will be filled with his lordship's friends, bright young bucks every one of them. And spirits flowin' like the Thames at flood tide."

Frances would have walked barefoot across pin grass to catch Kennan. After the guillotine, a few drunken young bluebloods were a mere nothing. Vent shifted uneasily on his feet as he saw the determined look in her eye. He lodged every argument he could think of to dissuade her, until at last he saw she was adamant, and he'd better take her or she'd make her way there herself. What Landry would say about it later would be another thing entirely.

Some fifteen years earlier, Lord Landry's father, a brilliant nobleman noted for his iconoclastic tenden-

215

cies, had sold his ancestral pile on Saville Row to a wealthy paper manufacturer and employed one Mr. Basevi to build him a handsome Greco-Roman mansion on Belgrave Square. If, on completion, he found Mr. Basevi's attics a bit too ornate and the porch a trifle pompous for his taste, he felt himself more than compensated by the particularly handsome interior with the many modern conveniences upon which he had insisted. His French chef had gone into raptures over the built-in Bodley range, the maids adored the modern plumbing, and even the lofty butler, Quelbream, was forced to concede the cellars adequate to hold his master's store of fine wine. Of course, Quelbream had been a more tolerant man fifteen years previous to the arrival of Frances Atherton and Nick Vent on his doorstep this moonless night. He had never approved of Mr. Vent, and looked at the groom with magnificent impassivity, while ignoring Frances entirely.

"Lord Landry," pronounced Quelbream, "is not at home." The yellow-lit windows and the bright ring of laughter from within belied Quelbream's words. Lord Landry was at home, but not to unknown females.

"As it happens," said Frances, with more confidence than she felt, "I have no wish to see Lord Landry. Would you be so kind as to summon Mr. Richard Rivington?"

Quelbream's nose tilted until it was nearly at right angles to the floor; he was much too dignified to allow a gleam of triumph to show in his eye as he said, "Mr. Richard Rivington is not within."

This statement at least had the virtue of being true. Quelbream noted with dismal satisfaction that he had given the encroaching young woman pause; but Nick Vent, like the unabashed plebeian he was, began an immediate protest, saying that Quelbream was a dried-up snakebait and he'd better let the young lady in or lay no blame tomorrow on Nicholas Vent when Landry gently nailed his hide to the cellar door. Quelbream made only a barely audible sniff. He knew himself to be on solid footing. Landry maintained a bachelor suite several blocks to the east where he withdrew when the extended visits of his female relations rendered his mansion an excessively nice atmosphere. At this apartment, it was said, Quelbream was happy to have no personal knowledge of such irregular goings on; his lordship might, should the mood suit him, see fit to receive a member of his enormous flock of female admirers. However, they did *not* press their claims on him at his family home. Lord Landry might be renowned for the sweetness of his temper, but there was a streak of steel beneath that brooked no uninvited familiarities. Vent was much in his young master's confidence, but Quelbream was smugly certain this time that the young ape had overstepped his bounds.

Vent was struggling with the unacceptable choices of leaving Frances outside while he fetched Landry, or napping Quelbream on the honker, when he saw at the far end of the foyer His Lordship's cousin, Sir Giles, take a step from the Egyptian room. Sir Giles was one of the closest of what he affectionately referred to as "His Lordship's cronies," so he hailed him by name, adding, "Could you give us a hand, guv?"

Sir Giles, at least two sheets of the proverbial three sheets to the wind, spun about uncertainly and peered searchingly down the length of the foyer. "Nick?" he said questioningly, then, "Nick! Hello, little man. What's toward?"

An intimate knowledge of Landry's intelligent if rakish young cousin ensured that Vent would know the quickest way to attract that young gentleman's some-

217

what erratic attention. "I've got a young woman here I'm trying to bring to Landry, but Quelbream won't let me in."

"A woman? Hell you say!" said Giles, sufficiently interested to begin the journey down the foyer in their direction. "Is she pretty?"

"I venture to say, sir, a beauty."

"Is she, by God? Quelbream, you chicken-necked fossil, clear the way! Here's David made another smash at the theater, and you cut up stiff about Vent's damsel," said Sir Giles amiably. He stopped, dismay spreading across his features as he recognized Frances. "Good God—Miss Atherton!"

It was a prologue that under any other circumstances might have set Frances writhing with embarrassment, but urgency has a single mind. "Please, Sir Giles, would you tell Richard Rivington that I'd like to speak with him?"

"I've already informed this"— Quelbream paused, majestically searching for Frances' category—"this young individual that Mr. Rivington is not within."

Giles shook his head to clear the pleasant fog in which it was enveloped and then glanced at the butler with an impatient frown. "That'll do, Quelbream. You may go." He waited for Quelbream to complete his disapproving retreat before continuing. "Frances, for the love of God, what are you doing here? David said you were safely home with Nick. And Quelbream was right, Richard isn't here."

"I have to find him." There was an urgent pleading expression in her eyes.

Giles was a man of no little sangfroid, but in the past hour he had been as unstinting as the next man in toasting his cousin Landry's success. It had never occurred to Sir Giles that he would be called upon to

218

pursue any later activity more challenging than to lift his foot so his valet could remove his boots before putting him to bed. From what he'd seen of Miss Atherton, she could be a formidable armful, approached from a sober state of mind; and here she was, beautiful eyes shining with suppressed agitation. He took a step back, shoved his hands distractedly into his hair, and bluntly said:

"Well, you can't. Zephyr's had a bet riding with Sefton that David could turn out a major piece of drama before this year was out, and somewhere after he'd broached his third bottle, he took it in his head to collect. No one knows where Sefton is except there was mention of him intending to play cards tonight, so very likely Uncle Zeph will spend half the night trying to chase him to earth. Richard's gone along with him to make sure he doesn't do himself a mischief, considering what he's consumed. Now listen, I'm no one to be telling you what to do, but there's been some hard drinking going on, which makes this no place for you, and Nick—David's going to wring your neck in the morning for letting her leave the safety of her home."

"Let's see if you can do better with her," remonstrated Nick Vent.

They were interrupted by an opening door and the sound of voices at the end of the hall. Sir Giles cut Nick's protest short with a wave of his hand, saying, "Oh, Jesus, someone's coming. We've got to hide the girl."

Vent grabbed Frances by the right arm and began to drag her across the foyer. "We'll put her in the south drawing room."

"No! Alvanley and Claremont are there having a hand of piquet!" Sir Giles seized her by the other arm, and she was rent nearly in two as he hauled her in the opposing direction. "It'll have to be the library. Wait!" Giles fumbled inside his jacket and produced a gold coin, flipping it to Vent. "Go to the kitchen and give this to Quelbream, and tell him to hold his tongue with the other servants. I'll send for you later."

Frances was in perfect sympathy with any attempt geared toward the prevention of her presence being detected in this bachelor household, but she found her transition down an elegant landscape-lined hall, through a charming breakfast room highlighted with yellow glass, and into the library was accomplished with more breath-stealing haste than even she could have wished for. She saw that the effort had also taken its toll on Sir Giles, who released her arm, leaned against the wall, and winced as he massaged his temples. This action apparently bringing him some measure of relief, he stood erect and put his hand on the door to leave. Over his shoulder he said:

"Wait here, will you? I'm going to get David."

"No," cried Frances. "I—my business is with Mr. Rivington, and I don't care to see . . ."

Her speech was cut short by Giles, who was on her in a second, slipping his arm around her shoulders and clapping his hand over her mouth.

"Hush! Just hush now! Or I'll kiss you. Want me to kiss you?"

Frances shook her head so vigorously that he gave a crack of laughter. "Damme if I don't want to kiss you anyway. Though I won't, so stop kicking." He gave Frances a rogue's grin. "You're adorable, but what a knack you have for injecting yourself into perilous situations! If you were my woman, I'd flog you. But I don't doubt David's too kind. Stay here."

Frances' indignant protest that she was *not* Lord Landry's woman was addressed to the empty air. She was left to stare in angry bewilderment around the library.

It was a large room, the walls covered by glass-enclosed bookcases separated by classical statues. On the west wall was an enormous Renaissance canvas of Venus sprawled lasciviously in her bath, and on the east wall the exquisite marble fragment of a nude male torso, far more anatomically detailed than Frances deemed necessary in a statue. Life-size busts of Homer and Shakespeare examined her impassively from recesses near the window. Frances turned toward the neat bundle of coals glowing in the grate. As she watched, their sharp red iridescence began to remind her of the cruel, hungry orbs behind the slits in the executioner's mask. Fox eyes—Kennan's eyes.

She gave a start as the latch clicked behind her, and Landry, dressed still in his deep-blue evening coat, came into the library. He crossed the room with a graceful stride and enfolded her gently in an embrace. His questing fingers curled into her hair, caressing the back of her neck, and his lips nuzzled at her throat.

Frances felt a sweet burst of pleasure, quickly stifled. She might have tried to throw him off, but it occurred to her that the slightly heavy weight of his body against her was not only an amorous advance. He was leaning on her as much for support as in passion. After a moment, he said thickly:

"I wish you were naked."

Frances exclaimed, and as she shook herself out of his arms, he said, "Will you do that for me sometime, Frances? Come and stand naked in my library? That would be beyond anything."

"Certainly not!" said Frances severely, her cheeks tinted pink. "Sometimes, I think, you have the oddest notions!"

He laughed and pushed her unsteadily into a cane-work chair, propping himself with a dangerous bang against the glass door of a bookcase. "I'm drunk as a monk, sweeting; though I'm also devilish glad to see you. Giles tells me that Nick brought you, and you came looking for Richard. I'm bereft. Won't I do as well?"

Frances eyed him somewhat nervously. "You don't look to me as if you'd be good for much."

This seemed to amuse him, and he swung his hand down to lightly pinch her cheek. "God, wouldn't I love to show you how wrong you are. Why don't you take off your cloak?" He bent to plant a kiss on her lips. "And your gown, your chemise, your . . ."

She wriggled from his grasp and put the cane chair between them and glared at him across its narrow width. "Do you think it's possible, my lord," she said in tones of honeyed sarcasm, "that we might have a *rational* discourse?"

"Possible, but unlikely. If it's important to you, though, I'll try." He spread his arms wide in an expansive gesture and flung himself into the chair's open arms. "Will you rub my shoulders?"

Frances gave a long-suffering sigh, and said with exasperation, "Oh, very well. If you'll promise to listen."

"I shall," he said. "Mmmmm. Would you object if I remove my coat?"

"Yes, I would," she said crossly. "And I don't mind saying that I think you are the most callous, indifferent, odious . . ."

"Is this a new score, or are you referring to the general tune of our relationship?"

"You know very well what I'm talking about. My

222

head was almost struck off this evening, and you sit here in your stupid lavish mansion soaking up spirits like a sea sponge, as though it made no matter at all to you whether I lived or died."

He put one hand back to capture her wrist, and brought it around to caress with his lips. "Of course I care, love. That's why I sent Nick with you. I have the deepest confidence in his ability to protect you, and besides, I hired three runners to watch the outside of your house."

"Three— Without consulting me? How dare you?"

"That's exactly what Quelbream would like to know, though he managed to convey it to me with much more diplomacy. The three have followed you here and have been lurking outside in a sinister style that, I have been assured, is giving the housemaids the notion that they are about to be ravished in their beds."

"I would be surprised if they deem that any departure from the normal." She regained her hand and set it to massaging his shoulder.

He half turned toward her and gave her his delightful smile. "I'm wounded, Prudence! Do you think I'm the kind of slyboots who grabs kisses from the dairymaids on the backstairs?"

Frances received an inner vision of the utterly beautiful Sheila Grant. "Perhaps you don't now, but I'll bet you did as an adolescent."

"Never. I learned my father's views on abusing one's dependents when I was seven years old and Giles and I lit Quelbream's coat-tails on fire." He laid his head sideways on her arm. "My parents' real worry was the tendency among the junior housemaids to accost *me* on the backstairs."

"Which accounts for your being so conceited."

"Partly," he admitted with a lazy grin. "By the way, who was it, do you think, that tried to do you in this evening?"

"*By the way*," repeated Frances, incensed by his casual tone, "I *know* it was Edward Kennan. If only one of the stagemen had caught him! You can't imagine what it was like, being dragged toward the guillotine like an animal to slaughter. I had a dreadful fancy that 'twas the grinning jaws of some terrible underworld monster come to devour me. And all the audience, sitting behind so terribly silent, as though it were all a part of the play. The horror of that moment was —David, are you asleep?"

"No," he said, suspiciously groggy. "You were about to describe the horror of the moment."

"I was, but I can see it's not the least use, since your concern appears to be near none."

He rose from the chair, placed his palm flat on her chest, and backed her up against the glass bookcase. Then he took her chin in his other hand; an emerald fire glowed in his eyes. "I care, I care, I care! What in God's name must I do to prove to you that I care? You damn little cynic."

Frances gave a squeak of alarm. "Watch yourself— you almost put your hand through the glass. I'm sorry if I said anything to—" Her lips were stopped by a hard, probing kiss. When he drew away, he said huskily:

"That's better." He kissed the tip of her nose. "What did you do to poor Kennan to make him want to decapitate you?"

"*Poor* Kennan! He's a vicious, scheming blackguard!" she said indignantly, then stopped and looked up at him with doubtful surprise. "Does that mean you believe it was Kennan?"

"I saw his face in the corridor, when he turned and

walked away—he had murder on his mind. Besides, Alvanley and I half suspected for more than a month that Kennan has been stealing Fowleby's paintings."

"And you've done nothing?" she said challengingly.

"Without proof?" He shrugged. "Alvanley did try to talk to the Duke, but Fowleby almost had him bounced out on his ear. Am I to understand by your tone that you *are* doing something about it?"

"Yes! Because, you see . . . I can explain that later! What matters now is that we catch Kennan, stolen painting in hand. That's why I was looking for Mr. Rivington. I want him to take me to Beachy Hill."

He tucked his finger under a lock of her hair and wound it slowly into a shining ringlet. "Frances, you must remember I'm feeling dim. Beachy Hill?"

"It's the base of Kennan's smuggling activities. He'll be there tonight because it's the dark of the moon, don't you see?"

"I see it in plural, as I've seen everything else since the second bottle."

"The smugglers always land when the moon is dark, and Kennan has just stolen one of the Duke's paintings and would be most eager to be rid of it. Of course, he can't sell it in England because it would be too well known, so he'll send it off with the boat when they go to pick up a cargo of illegal rum," she said earnestly. Frances waited for a sign of interest and finally challenged him, "Well, what do you say?"

"Farewell painting."

"How can you be so flippant?" she demanded angrily, then realized it was a method hardly likely to put him into a responsive frame of mind. "Naturally, though, it's not your painting, so perhaps as a *favor* to me would you be willing, please, to go with me to Beachy Hill and bring Kennan to justice?"

He stared at her blankly, then started to laugh. But for the circumstances, Frances would have thought him a handsome sight as mirth brought tears to his eyes. Finally he was forced to stop for breath, and leaned back in the chair, banging up against the glass bookcase, which swayed and rattled again. He looked at her with humorous amazement as she watched sternly, hands on her hips.

"Frances," he managed, "you cannot—you really cannot seriously mean that we leave—right now?"

"What's wrong with right now?" she said in frowning hauteur.

"First, I have a houseful of guests. Second, I'm so drunk I can barely stand. And third—God, I don't think there has to be a three."

"It would be a terrible inconvenience to you, and I have no right to ask . . ."

"My poor girl," he said, the hard lines of his laughter softening into a smile, "I've always considered myself to be a reasonably selfish person, and what I've ever done to persuade you otherwise is more than I can imagine. Frances—Beachy Hill, boats going out, that means the coast, doesn't it? Where—Sussex? That must be over three hours, even making good time, which we couldn't in the dark. Rest assured I'll do whatever is needed to protect you from Kennan, but the last thing you need is to become further entangled in his affairs, and the last thing I need is a starlight odyssey into Sussex."

"You're saying no, then." She drew herself up with pride.

His eyes were gentle but he agreed. "I'm saying no."

"Well," she said with dignity, "then there's nothing more to be said."

"About Beachy Hill, no," he said, not without sympathy.

"If you won't go, you won't go."

"All too true," he said.

She began to walk reluctantly to the door. The empathy in his expression did not mislead her into thinking that his mind could be changed. What profit to argue with him further? And indeed, he was hardly to be blamed. Why should he do this for her? Whatever had she done for him? It was asking much, indeed, of one who was in some ways little more than a stranger. The Blue Specter would not end his haunting this night; and her father would rest more yet in prison. The thought brought an ache to her tender heart so great she could scarcely bear it. That he should be so meanly lodged for one day longer because of her failure was too fearful a consequence. Landry must be persuaded! Frances thought of explaining the whole of her father's situation to him. If Lord Landry wouldn't go to Beachy Hill for her, whom he knew, what would make him go for her father, whom he didn't know? Reasonably selfish, he had said. But how was she to translate the trip into his own self-interest? She turned to look directly into the affectionate mocking green eyes.

"I have to go, really I do. I don't know where to locate Richard Rivington, and even if I did, there's no guarantee he'd be any more willing than you are to take me. And in looking, I'd lose valuable time. You must take me, David. And if you do—I sh-shall make it worth your while."

Frances saw grimly that for once she had reached a thought before him. It was the last thing, clearly, that he had expected her to say. His eyebrows rose and he strolled toward her slowly, holding her gaze in a quizzical regard.

"What, precisely, are you offering?"

Her cheeks burned with shame; there was a lump in her throat; she looked at her toes. "I'll do whatever you want."

There was a silence before he said:

"Anything?"

"Anything."

He gave a low whistle. "You *are* full of surprises. You're not under any illusions that I would be chivalrous in my interpretation?"

"No," she said in a breathless voice. "I understand what I'm promising."

"What a strange girl you are," he said mildly, and put his hands on her waist and pulled her close. "Payment in advance."

She gently pushed him away and frowned at him. "Payment on delivery."

His laugh echoed softly through the library. "Done," he said.

Chapter Thirteen

Frances was no horsewoman. Her own family was too poor to own horses; where they went, they walked. The only wealthy family in their parish was the foundry-owning Lynchams. The daughters of the house were giddy misses with nothing in common with Frances save age, but the stern hand of polite usage had dictated that they include Frances in certain of their entertainments. Since these usually consisted of riding to scenic vistas with which Frances was well familiar, in the company of a set of young people whom she didn't like, only Frances' good manners prevented her from pleading a toothache on the mornings of these excursions. A parson's daughter, even one so respectably connected as Frances, ranked low in the social priorities. Frances was loaned the oldest, most cantankerous mare in the stable, with the apt pet name of "Bonebuster," and sat on a saddle, the ill-tanned leather of which had split in ten places before the Americans had taken arms against colonial rule.

It was not surprising, therefore, that Frances' past experience brought a look of trepidation to her pink-cheeked face when Landry suggested they ride to the coast. She wasn't dressed for riding! Landry informed her with typical male nonchalance that his mother had a habit upstairs that she had worn last season for riding in the park. Frances was too shy to mention a possible disparity in size; instead, she said she was afraid the habit might be done some damage.

Landry gave her an ironic grin. "Frances, if you knew my mother, you'd realize that she'd as soon wear the same riding habit to Hyde Park for two years in a row as mount her stallion backwards."

When Frances appeared one half hour later in an imperial red riding costume, accented *à la militaire* (of a cut so dashing that it spoke volumes for the sophistication of Landry's mother), she found the worst of her suspicions confirmed, for the snorting, dancing animal Nick Vent had brought to the mounting block for her could only be the aforementioned wild stallion. Landry had gotten to the small cobbled yard before her; the yellow lamp glinted off his golden hair as he sat easily on the back of a prancing Arabian. He laughed when he saw the doubtful look she directed toward her mount; Nick Vent said kindly that she was not to worry, Castor was the sweetest-going prad in his lordship's stable, not one of those pretty-bodied killers that Landry himself was so fond of riding.

"I'm sure he is," said Frances. "But it's a long ride, and perhaps I would be more comfortable," and *safer*, she added to herself, "on a gentle mare. I've never ridden on a stallion before . . ." If it were not for her fear of being alone with Landry in a coach, she would not have agreed to go on horseback.

Landry interrupted to say that Castor was not a stallion.

"I suppose you've named a mare Castor!" said Frances irritably, suspecting that she was being made fun of.

Frances realized her rejoinder had been a mistake when Landry gave a gleeful whoop and said, "Frances, can't you tell that horse is a gelding?" He began, with an odious grin, to delineate Castor's difference from a stallion, and Frances could only make him hush by diverting him with her incompetent attempts to climb into the saddle.

The early part of the ride was little occupied with conversation. Landry was too preoccupied with a dreamy contemplation of the starlit landscape, and Frances was too busy trying to keep from falling off the horse.

They took the best roads, pausing only at the toll-houses to ring awake the tollkeepers, who appeared in duffel coats pulled hastily over their nightshirts and rubbing the sleep from their eyes to collect the toll and raise the gate. Landry set a rapid pace, and for that she was grateful. Lush pasture, forest, and fields planted in oats fell back behind them. In the middle of a field under a sleeping birch tree was a mysterious lump with which the meager starlight played tricks; was it an old hay rick? Slumbering cattle? The rush of the wind, the motion of the horses, the hoofbeats, mingled with the smell of dirt and night dampness. Suddenly they came upon a herd of fallow deer grazing under the stars. A white doe bounded in front of them, causing Frances' gelding to startle and rear, and only Landry's quick reach at the bridle saved her from being thrown.

The incident unsettled Frances, for it reminded her that what lay ahead in the swallowing dark could be such an unknown quantity.

Landry brought her gelding back by his side and began to tease away her fears. Sobering from the fresh air, his lively mind began to form questions about her home county. He asked Frances if she'd been to the flint works mined in antiquity by Sussex men chipping at the stone with their antler picks; had she ever, when a child, hunted in the hills for arrowheads manufactured in medieval times? Question and answer turned into discourse, and the dark became warm and intimate. Frances began to forget her ill-considered promise, the ache in her lower back that had earlier seemed to be growing with the passing moments, and the raw places under the heavy skirt where the leather had begun to bite into her skin. They were still far inland when the first nip of sea salt in the air gave her a jolt of homesickness.

The roads, as they neared the coast, changed from passable to poor; adequate avenues changing into miserable ruts crowded by a press of vegetation. Landry's questions seemed to focus with the narrowing of the roads. He asked her about Beachy Hill; how many people? How near the sea? Did she remember any particular terrain details, and did she know the size of the port? It was far into the questioning when Frances realized that, while he wore the mantle of an interested tourist, he was gently plumbing her to clarify the logistics of the coming adventure.

The roaring of the surf was the called greeting of the Sussex coastline, welcoming Frances home. The song grew stronger as they climbed a long slope; reaching the top, they saw Beachy Hill growing up the seaward slant toward them. It wasn't much of a village. Regional guidebooks were likely to dismiss it with the phrase "Visitors will find little to interest them here." Local advocates could tell one, however, that Beachy Hill had been privileged to exist as far back as the Domesday Book, where it was listed as a "hythe," or landing place. If, since then, the small sheltered harbor had become choked with sand, the fishermen would tell you that they didn't care to have big navy ships stopping there anyway, and it was plenty deep for the shallow port's picturesque fleet of yawls. And whatever was said about the famous "Whitstable Natives" farther down the coast, Beachy Hill was secure in the superior quality of their own oysters.

Rushlights illuminated the steep dirt paths between the huddled slab-roofed houses. A warm smile decorated Frances' face as she looked lovingly at the old-fashioned rambling outline of the parsonage. She saw the tiny figure of cross old Claudius, the goat Joe had trained to pull the children in a red-painted cart. Claudius was tethered in the middle of a circle of close-cropped grass. On a lumpy plateau next to the parsonage stood St. Andrews, her father's church. The dark disguised all things, but Frances knew that the low bump bordering the church steps was the holy-water stoup, and to the back lay the desolate churchyard, with its share of old sea-salt encrusted iron crosses marking the graves of shepherds buried with tufts of wool in their hands to show at the Gates of Heaven as explanation for their lack of church attendance. There were no mysteries here for Frances. She knew that behind the blacksmith's shop lay a slope, where deep puddles would collect every time it rained; she knew the rocky crevices near the landing where the water pipits nested. She knew which piece of Roman tile built into the church wall was loose—generations of sweethearts had used it to hide love tokens. Yet in the spare and brooding starlight, shivering under the ocean's ceaseless roar, Beachy Hill looked as isolated and lawless as a pirate's den. The rushlight's glow seemed like the phosphorescent sheen of wolf's eyes on a forest fringe. It was an odd fancy, Frances thought, and unlike her. She knew it would end if she could

233

go into her home and experience the warmth and security she had always known there. But there was no time for that now. Delayed cognizance made her aware that Landry had made a remark, received no answer, and was patiently repeating his words.

"How old is the church?" he was saying.

"The foundation dates from 936 A.D., the year after the miracle."

"I don't think I'm familiar with the miracle of 935."

"It wasn't spectacular," Frances admitted with a smile. "One morning four white oxen appeared on the village green, and as people watched, they turned rump to rump, in the shape of a cross. The villagers were so awed that they fell to their knees and vowed to build a church on that very spot."

"Very proper!"

"I expect our ancestors had a rather different frame of mind, before the development of scientific inquiry," explained Frances, noting Landry's grin. "Of course, there *were* some who thought it was a take-in. Rumor has persisted to this day that 'twas a trick—that the local abbott hired trained oxen from a band of traveling mummers. He owned the local inn, and there was a feeling that he wished to increase pilgrimage to the area."

"The true believers won the day?"

"Yes, because later the same year there was a second miracle! The village was attacked by Danish pirates, and among their plunder was the treble bell from the old church tower. As they sailed away, the abbott came from behind the cider press, where he had been hiding, and rang the remaining bell to sound 'all clear' to the villagers, who had fled to the hills."

"A courageous group!" noted Landry.

"I suppose they do sound a craven lot, but every excuse must be made for them," she said fair-mindedly. "Whatever one may say about the Danes now, they were a very fierce group then. Though on *that* occasion, they came to a melancholy, if richly deserved, end. As the abbott's bell began to toll, the treble bell on the pirate's boat miraculously joined its fellow, rocking and swaying with such violence that it caused the boat to capsize. All aboard were lost."

"So," Landry pointed out with a critic's fine eye, "were Beachy Hill's stolen possessions."

"There's the rub," admitted Frances. "My brother Charles always said it was a very good lesson that nothing in life is perfect, not even miracles."

"And does the abbott's ghost still walk?"

"Yes, of course! Many have seen his cowled shade stalking dolefully along the beach, accompanied by the sound of the treble bell chiming from somewhere far away in the night air. It's taken to be the worst of bad omens." She felt an internal tremor as she spoke, which was odd, because the story had never bothered her before.

Massive and pale, the chalk cliff rose like a gloomy phantom above the horseshoe ribbon of beach. As smugglers' landings went, it was superior. Rocks enclosed the cove from the cliff base to the tiny bay's narrow entrance; and the high jut of the cliff head concealed activities at its foot just as the belly of a fat man makes it difficult for him to see his toes. Like every well-planned foxhole, it had two exits. One was a track big enough for a two-wheeled cart cut deep into the rock by someone long forgotten. The other was a rocky, tortuous trail that edged between poorly balanced boulders and the dangerously eroded facing. It was down this path that Frances came with Lord Landry. They dared not risk a lantern. She had hitched the long riding-skirt ankle-high the better to negotiate the steep, crumbling trail. The horses had been left above, tethered to a wind-burned oak. Frances slipped once, when her heel hit a slippery hillock of thyme. Landry caught her at the waist before she could fall, and pressed a kiss on her lips as the fresh scent of the broken herb wafted around them, suspended in the sheltered air. She moved awkwardly and was instantly released.

As they moved lower, the smell of fish and dried seaweed grew stronger, and the echo of the surf boomed against the cliffside. Dropwort grew, stinking and poisonous, on the final shelf of rock; it was as though they were descending into a vast pit. At last the ground leveled, and after a wade through a scratching strip of mallow, they stood upon the beach.

Landry wandered to the water's edge, scooped up a handful of stones from the lip of the sea, selected a plate-shaped one, and sent it skipping into the water. After it hit and became wet, Frances could see it reflecting starlight as the stone bounced four times before becoming lost.

"What now, my dear?" he said.

Annoyed by his day-excursion attitude, Frances said, "I'm not your 'dear'!"

"Dearer than you think," he said, and smiled. Then, taking pity on her confusion, he said, "Are we going to cover each other with sand and pop up like sea monsters when the smugglers come? The dramatic possibilities are certainly intriguing."

Frances replied in a tone even she recognized as uncharitable, "I might have known that your greatest concern would be the dramatic possibilities. Very likely we'd find the boats dragged on top of us; though I suppose it wouldn't matter, because we'd surely have smothered—" She stopped, responding to his motion for silence. Trying to block out the noise of the wind and the surf, she heard, after a moment, the rhythmic slap of oars cutting into water as the smugglers' craft stealthily crawled toward shore.

Landry caught her arm and pointed toward the cliff base. "The humped rock, Frances—will it do?"

Frances nodded, and then ran beside him toward the sheltering bulk. No sooner had they hidden when the bobbing glimmer of a lantern began to move slowly down the cliffside.

"The Blue Specter!" Frances breathed in a hushed whisper. "The flame is covered with a blue globe."

"And when they arrive, you wish me to subdue them with fisticuffs?" whispered Lord Landry.

Frances frowned, managing to look austere and adorably doubtful at the same time. "We shall contrive something."

"Another Beachy Hill miracle?" he whispered. "We catch Kennan, *but* he shoots us?"

Frances was too ashamed to admit that she hadn't considered that Kennan might be armed. She stalled by saying, "Have you an idea?"

"Send for Jem Beamer."

"There isn't time," she said sweetly.

He clicked his tongue with mock regret. "If you're going to raise quibbling objections like that, it's going to be very hard to agree on a course of action."

"You," said Frances with resignation, "are incorrigible." She had reason enough to be afraid; rather, to her surprise, she felt a vivid and far from unpleasant exhilaration course through her. In the strangest of circumstances, Landry's presence could do that to her, in spite of his flippancy and all the things she knew he was that ought not to please a parson's daughter, and in spite of that dreadful promise that she could only pray he had been too drunk to remember.

Far out on the water, the oars ceased their creaking, and a beam of light shot out and was quenched as a bull's-eye lantern was flashed. Kennan answered by covering his own lantern with a cloth, then letting the cloth fall away. The oars began creaking again, and before too long the boat was close in, a long, low shape in the water. There were three men in it. Frances and Lord Landry could smell strong tobacco and hear the wooden scrape of sand on the bottom as one of the sailors stepped into the water and guided the craft to shore. There was some splashing and hollow knocking and a muttered oath, then the three men grouped by their beached rowboat. Their emphatic, serious words carried over the sand, and Frances recognized the gruff voice of the village blacksmith, Henry Johnson.

"I ain't sayin' I'm scared—I ain't sayin' that at all. But I don't know. I jest don't know," said Henry.

"Tell us again, then. What was it exactly was said?" Frances carefully peeked over the hump of the rock long enough to recognize the skinny, high-strung figure of Jonathan Green, a local ne'er-do-well tenant farmer. Landry's hand pulled her down with some force.

"Ain't nothing to add—nothing. Like I told you, when Miss Pam, the parson's gel, came by my missus this morning to get her eggs, she said right out that she'd seen it walk last night." Johnson's voice, which had begun the sentence with its usual harsh bravado, had developed a distinct tremor at the end.

"It?" said the third man, Peter Willis, who gardened for the Squire. "The monk?"

"Aye," said Johnson, his voice lowering two octaves, nearly dropping from the bass clef. "The undead. The old abbott! Miss Pam saw it on her way home from the Squire's. Peered out of the shadows, it did, and beckoned to her. Then it turned round and with one bony finger pointed straight at my cottage!" The night seemed to turn blacker, and the waves more alive. Frances shivered in their hideaway and drew closer to Landry. "She thought it was a trick by one of the lads, did little Miss Pam, so she run right up to it. Crazed with courage, every one of that Atherton brood —she put her hand on the cowl and yanks it back!" His two companions exclaimed at the foolhardiness of Miss Pam. "But there weren't no head there! Weren't nothing but a wisp of green vapor! Well, she turned and ran fast as you please back to the parsonage, and didn't come out 'til this morning's light."

A blue glow spread over the top of the rock over Frances' head as the Blue Specter joined the three.

"What's going on? Where's the rest of you?" Frances' apprenticeship in the theater had sharpened her ears. She recognized Kennan's voice even through his uncannily skilled attempt to disguise it, speaking in crisper than his normal tones. At his sharply spoken question, the Sussex men united in a wall of resistance.

"Wouldn't come," said Johnson.

"Why not?" Kennan's voice purred menace through the muffling shield of his mask. The men of Sussex were silent. "Well?" he demanded threateningly. The men shifted their feet uncomfortably on the gritty pebbles.

"The monk was walkin'. Ain't nobody comes out when the monk's walkin'," said Green.

"There's some," intoned Johnson in a hoarse whisper, "that say it's a judgment on us—that the abbott's spirit has come to curse the men of Beachy Hill for keeping their tongues quiet when the Blue Specter brought in thugs from Eastbourne to hide contraband in the church."

"Shut your mouth, you fool," hissed Kennan furiously. "By God, you lot are alike the world over. Peasants and ghost stories! Whenever was there the one without the other? Have you no more brains among you than a baboon? Some lying jackanapes sees a shadow and you scurry underneath your beds."

Pete Willis' distant shy devotion to Frances' pretty sister Pam predated his first pair of short pants, so Frances was not surprised when he cried, "Weren't no jackanapes, either, what saw it! 'Twas . . ." His sentence was cut by a fist striking flesh, and there was a soft thud as Willis hit the ground. Frances peered over the rock to see Willis, sitting dazed on the sand, Johnson bending over him. Jonathan Green stared at the Blue Specter with hate in his eyes.

"The fist is the only lesson you miserable wretches can understand! If you've come alone, you'll have to make the trip to Calais alone." Kennan knew well how to instill horror in his audience. His words carried the binding, horrific ring of a satanic pact. "On your return, tell the others to be back here next month or it will be the worse for them—and their families."

"Three men ain't enough to unload brandy quick as we might need," whined Green.

"Forget the brandy," Kennan ordered. "There's only one thing I want you to take." There was a sound of cloth drawing across cloth. "Do as you did the times before—you'll be met at dockside in Calais by the man calling himself Jean-Luc. Give him the parcel, and he will give you the envelope with the money. It's been arranged, and you'll be paid your usual sum . . . what the devil?"

His words died in a warm breeze that came across the waters from the open sea, a breeze that brought with it the high and bitter cry of metal striking metal, the peal of an ancient treble bell. Frances clutched at the rock for support as the world of nightmares, tales, and reality began to merge.

"Do you hear, too?" She turned to Landry. "Can you hear it?"

"Yes," he returned in a low voice. "And I wonder . . ."

There was a shrill, bone-chilling scream from Jonathan Green. Frances, who could not stand the suspense, looked over the rock to see Green pointing with a shaking arm at the top of the ridge, while his three companions stood transfixed. She followed his indication to see, on the edge of the cliff above them, a giant black-cowled figure stretching its robed arms wide in the wind, silhouetted eerily by an unearthly green light!

"The old abbott!" said Johnson hoarsely.

"The monk!" breathed Willis.

"It's Doomsday!" shrieked Green. "We're all lost!"

Landry, always an enemy of melodrama, pulled Frances down again, muttering something about a jack-in-the-box as the three men from Beachy Hill took to their heels and began to race screaming toward the boat. In spite of Kennan's vile curses, the yawl's bottom was slapped onto the water, and fear pulled the oars so hard that it was on its way in a matter of less than a minute.

Frighteningly profane in defeat, his cape swirling about his legs, Kennan stood at the water's edge, curs-

241

ing his legmen for superstitious yokels as they rowed out of sight. As they disappeared, he tore off his mask and cast it into the waves with violent disgust before he turned, dimmed his lantern, and began to make his way toward the trail with hurried strides.

"David, he's getting away!" said Frances, pleadingly urgent.

"It's all right, Frances, it's obvious that someone has . . ." It was too late; Frances had already left the shelter of the rock to make a headlong rush after Kennan. She caught up with Kennan just as he reached the foot of the trail. He turned to face her, lifting his lantern to see her face.

"It's you!" he hissed, and without another word pulled a pistol from his cape and lowered it straight for her heart.

She froze and then felt Landry's warmth as he came out of the darkness behind her, encircling her in his arms, pulling her to him. He gave Kennan a vaguely sardonic smile and said:

"And me."

Horror and rage transformed Kennan's face into taut, weasellike lines. When he spoke, his words whistled though his trembling jaw like steam spewing from an overheating pan. "So, *you're* with her, are you, boy genius? What are you doing here?"

"Not," said Landry, "sea bathing."

Kennan's teeth were bared by his tightly drawn skin. Even in the sparse light his complexion was ashen. "I hope what she's given you will be worth dying for."

"It's been the salvation of your career that you haven't had to write your own lines," replied Landry in an even tone. "Are you planning, by any chance, to leave the country? After you've shot me, you may find you have become . . . deathly unpopular with

242

certain of my kinsmen. I *had* mentioned Frances' suspicions to them before we left for Sussex."

"Damn you!" cried Kennan, his eyes glittering crazily in the blue lantern light. "I knew as soon as I saw you that you've come to ruin me! For that damn parson's brat whom you'll forget in a week!" The cove echoed with Kennan's coarse, desperate laughter. "By God, if I had a shilling for every wench you'd cast eyes over, I'd be as rich as you without ever a day's work."

Frances felt the frantic tattoo of her heartbeat as she stood in icy paralysis, gripped within the steady curve of Landry's arm. She watched helplessly as Kennan snapped the pistol's hammer with his thumb and pointed the cocked weapon at Lord Landry's head.

Kennan's voice was harsh as he growled, "By the time they find your decomposing body among the rushes, my fine lord, I shall be far quit of England, so I won't be around to hear the piteous gnashings of your distraught family. Farewell, monk-maker!"

"Monk-maker?" Landry repeated. "*I* didn't manufacture that apparition on the hill. I . . . my God, Kennan, look!"

The sudden urgency in Landry's tone caused Kennan to wheel without thought, gazing frantically toward the cliff top as Landry indicated. Frances had turned as well, and had barely time to realize that the monk had vanished when Landry's boot nipped her behind the ankles and set her flying to the sand with rough efficiency. Almost before she had hit the ground, Landry made a swift, clean lunge for Kennan and brought the heel of his hand up to deliver a powerful blow to the base of Kennan's chin. Bathed in flickering blue shadows, Kennan staggered into the writhing folds of his cape and began to topple. The pistol slipped from his hand and discharged harmlessly into the sea foam as Kennan fell backwards. His head made a brutal collision with a rock jutting from the sand and he was knocked quickly and completely into unconsciousness.

"That's what you get," observed Landry tersely, bringing his hands to rest on his flat hips as he stood over the fallen actor, "when you threaten the unoffending citizenry with firearms." He turned to look at Frances. "Well, here he is, my dear, in all his fatuous glory. What would you have me do with him?"

It was too soon for her to talk of it in a light way. Frances found her feet and, in a moment, the sanctuary of Landry's arms. He had just begun to involve her in one of his blissfully satisfying kisses when from the foot of the path came the rattle of dislodged pebbles and the sound of running feet. Two men came racing forward, their lanterns flooding the beach with yellow light.

The older was of medium height, with soft light hair and direct hazel eyes. He bent briefly to inspect Kennan and, turning his face toward Landry, said, "I don't know your name, sir, but you have my gratitude, and . . . Good God—Frances!"

Frances stared at the speaker through tear-clouded eyes.

"Charles! And Joe!" With sisterly joy, she abandoned Landry to embrace her oldest brother. He seemed leaner and harder than she remembered, and his face was tinted with a Mediterranean tan. Joe was, as ever, slim and graceful, but it seemed a million years since she had seen him. When she hugged him, he said:

"Oh, aye; have done, darlin'. I'm very glad to see you, but you know how I hate syrup."

"Horrid boy," she said, pushing him away, laughing through her tears. "And I'm more than very glad to see you—I'm in transports! And Charles—you're back in England! But what are you about *here*?"

"Catching Kennan, or so we thought. It seems this gentleman"—he smiled at Landry—"has beaten us to the punch." Charles laid his hands affectionately on his sister's shoulders. "Look at you! Two years and you've turned into a beauty."

"Told you she had," injected Joe complacently.

"He's told me other things, too," Charles went on, "about what you tried to do in London. Little lionheart! I got home yesterday morning and there wasn't time to travel into London and bring you home. Thank God we have you here, and safe! Whatever imbroglio you've left in the capital, I'm going to help you with the consequences! I want to hear everything—we'll have a long talk about it later. *Now*, you better introduce us to your friend or he'll think we're a family of gapeseeds."

Frances' association with Landry had been flamboyant by any standards and, compared with her stable family life, as fire to water. The humble ordinariness of Beachy Hill threw Landry's spectacular looks and exotic nature into high relief. Frances was glad she had mentioned little about Lord Landry in her letters to Joe, beyond that she had met him at the Drury Lane; she felt awkward enough making the introduction as it was. Her discomfort was covered by the excitement Joe, and even the usually poised Charles, expressed at meeting the nation's most lauded playwright. Joe had to say at once that Landry's play *The Conqueror* was the most rousing piece ever penned, and as Charles shook Landry's hand, Frances' older brother declared that since Sheridan had retired his

245

quill, Landry was the only major writer left in the British theater.

"Did you come with Frances after Kennan?" asked Joe. "What a kick-up! What did you think of *our* little drama, eh? Did you like the monk?"

"Very effective," said Landry. "Was it cloth over a straw body? How did you throw so much light on it?"

Charles had dropped a coiled rope from his shoulder and, with some effort, rolled the inert Kennan over and began to tie his wrists together. "Joe had a half-dozen lamps rigged to a pull-chain so he could open them with one yank." Glancing at Frances, he said, "The Bishop's here. He's sitting at the cottage right now with Mother. He is most disapproving of these left-handed Atherton goings-on. We forgive him all of it, though. He brought home Father from prison last evening."

Frances was transformed with joy. "Father's home— Oh, Charles, oh, Joseph . . ." Impulsively she turned to Lord Landry. "Did you hear that? My father's home!"

"I'm glad to hear it," said Landry amiably, "although I can't recall ever knowing that he was away."

"You mean to say she dragged you to Sussex without an explanation of how Kennan framed our father?" interrupted Joe, aghast. "If that isn't rich! Why on earth did you come?"

Innocently, Joe had steered the conversation onto treacherous conversational waters. Before Landry had a chance to open his mouth, Frances altered the subject with chattering inefficiency. "So—so the monk was a trick, to frighten the village men out of smuggling. Pam was in on it, too, wasn't she? We eavesdropped on Jonathan Green describing her sighting of the monk last night. How clever of her to have made up the story! But I heard the treble bell!"

Charles tugged tight the last knot on Kennan's bindings. "That was Dr. Sutter and the Squire passing by in a skiff banging on an old iron pot with a brass ladle."

"What a marvelous conspiracy!" exclaimed Frances, her cheeks glowing. She turned to Landry. "And you had it figured out—that's why you called me back when I was running after Kennan, because you knew they would be waiting to catch him at the top."

"It was either that," said Landry apologetically, "or believe it was really a strolling deceased monk."

"Indeed!" Frances raised her hands in a happy gesture. Then, in the golden lamplight, the three men saw the rich color drain from her face. "B-but Chez la Princesse, Drury Lane, the guillotine, and the . . . the promise—I did it all for nothing," she whispered, and fainted like a dead weight into Landry's arms.

Frances felt warmth, and softness. As she raised her head, she saw it had become light, a golden light. She was lying next to Landry. He seemed a creation of the light: golden hair, golden skin. Their bodies had formed a hollow in the sand, a safe haven. She looked out toward the sea, and had to shade her eyes from the slanting rays of the newly rising sun, which bounced from the glistening ripples before causing long shadows on the shore. It was a beautiful sight—it seemed as though the sun were bleeding and melting into the sea, which brought its light and warmth to their feet on the tireless wash of the waves.

Memory returned to her, and happiness that her share of the awesome burden of winning freedom for her father was finished. He was free, thank God, and soon she could see him, and her mother, and all the little ones at home. But her well-being was short-lived, disappointingly replaced by a curious sense of impending tragedy that had been her companion since the first moment she had fallen in love with Landry. The certain knowledge of the separation from him that she knew must come had shadowed her with the tenacity of a starved predator. Anxiety suddenly caused her to sit up and look behind her for the comfortingly familiar figures of her brothers. But they were not there!

"Where has Charlie gone? And Joe?" demanded Frances.

Landry opened his eyes and gave her the heavy-lidded look of one who has arrived at the coast with no better purpose than to sun himself on the beach. "After they assured themselves that you were all right, it was decided that they ought to begin dragging Kennan back to Beachy Hill. I told them we'd follow as soon as you were ready to walk again—oh, and you'll be glad to know that we found Fowleby's painting in an oilcloth wrapping in an inner pocket of Kennan's greatcoat."

Frances' interest in the painting was momentarily at a minimum. In disbelief she said, "My brothers left me alone with you?"

A smile came to the green eyes. "I'm afraid I was guilty of a small deception. I told them we were betrothed."

"I would say that was rather more than a small deception," said Frances. "Especially"—her shoulders slumped—"since they'll find out soon enough that it isn't true."

He stretched out a hand and gently stroked her hair. "And consider how reprehensible it will seem when the content of your promise to me becomes generally known."

"You didn't tell them, did you?" said Frances with lively alarm.

"Your brother Charles is no fool. And the dramatic way you blurted it out would have intrigued a corpse. However, I found the liberal width of your brother's biceps a definite inspiration and muddled through with a plausible explanation. One can't always depend on having a rock behind everyone one knocks down."

"I was hoping," she ventured in an experimental spirit, "that you would let the matter drop."

He took her shoulders in his hands and pulled her close to his chest. "The oceans may dry up, and the deserts grow trees, but rest assured, my sweet life, that is one notion I shall never let drop. It's no use, Frances. The only way to avoid spending your life enduring my constant unlawful importunities would be to marry me."

"M-marry?"

"I know in some ways you would be getting a very poor bargain. I'm incurably frivolous, probably; occasionally, I drink to excess; and my family has a notion of togetherness that would put an ant colony to shame. They're likely to encroach terribly. Giles and Richard have had the run of my house since infancy, and I doubt we will find it easy to break them of the habit. There are others, too, that you haven't met—dozens of them: aunts, uncles, grandmas, grandpas, infants."

Frances could hardly hear his words over the thunder of her accelerating heart. "Wh-what of my family, pray? My father will insist on conducting the ceremony himself at our village church. And afterward, they will visit us constantly! There'll be jammy fingerprints on the globe in your library, and river minnows in your crystal wineglasses. They'll bring the puppy, of course, and inevitably it will chew up the carpet fringe. Grandma Atherton will examine every door and window in your house for drafts. Privacy for us will be impossible."

"We'll be forced to improvise. Do you know, Frances, that ever since we were together in the balloon, I've been longing to . . ." and he whispered the rest of the sentence into her ear.

She blushed rosily. "If I'd known that, I wouldn't have felt safe with you for a minute. Not that I have anyway."

"My sweet, darling girl, there have been so many times when . . . Frances! Good Lord, are you crying?"

Her tears were beginning to dampen his shirtfront. "I c-can't help it. I'm just so—so amazed. I never thought you'd want to marry *me*. You told me yourself you didn't want—that commitment with a woman."

He stopped her words with a gentle kiss and smiled tenderly into her tear-brimmed eyes. "That was before I fell in love."

"But I can't understand how you could be in love with me, when you could be with women who are rich, and beautiful, and wellborn. David, you could marry so many people."

"No, I couldn't, they'll only let me have one." He produced a handkerchief for her from an inner pocket, and she accepted it, complaining with a broken sniff that he joked about everything. He pulled her closer, settling her comfortably against his chest, and leaned back into the sand. A gull cried overhead, its snowy whiteness transformed into a fiery orange by the sunrise. "Except," he agreed, "when I tell you that I love you very much—a sentiment which I have yet to hear requited." He lifted her shyly turned chin with one finger. "Do you love me too, sweetheart?"

The courageous Frances Atherton could only manage one small, affirmative syllable under her breath.

"Then say it," he whispered.

"I—don't feel so bold."

"I'm going to teach you much bolder things than that," he said. Her eyes were still downcast; he bent his head to kiss the bridge of her nose. "Say it, my love."

She looked up at him, her expression an arousing mixture of the earnest, vulnerable, and brave; and in a low, sweet voice, she said, "I do love you, David. And I have for a time, even though at first I didn't realize it."

He traced a finger across her brow, brushing a strand of hair away from her face. "Neither did I. You know, when I saw you at Chez la Princesse being handled by that damn St. Pips, I was so angry that I wanted to call him out. You'd think I would have been able to recognize it as decent, old-fashioned jealousy."

"So you went back and beat him at cards later that night? So he couldn't stay in London to recognize me?"

"Did Richard tell you that? What a rattlepate the boy's become. He's half in love with you himself— did you know that?"

"No, I didn't. But he's been very kind." She nestled her face against him. "Aunt Sophie will be so surprised."

He removed the small, elegant hat from her head and began to remove the pins with which she had hastily dressed her hair before leaving on the ride to Sussex. Then with a wry smile he said, "*Not* as surprised as you think. She came to my house yesterday and told me it was not her way to interfere, but did I or did I not intend to have her niece in lawful wedlock? And I said I did."

Frances giggled at the thought of her Aunt Sophie confronting Lord Landry, then suddenly pulled away

251

from him and knelt in the sand, the red dress spreading about her in the crimson sunrise. "Do you mean last night in the library you were intending to marry me? And you let me make that wretchedly horrendous promise to you anyway?"

He stood and scooped her up with him. "The temptation was irresistible," he admitted. His lips caressed her cheek. "Frances, after we're married, will you let me call you Fanny?"

"Certainly not!" she said, angry still, "and I shall have to wonder always whether or not you're marrying me because you couldn't have me otherwise."

He laughed and took her head in his hands. "We had better make love at once; when we marry in spite of it, your doubts will be laid to rest!" His lips found hers in a kiss thorough and penetrating as the sky's rich saturation of sun-soaked flame. It was a very long time before he was able to let her go, and then only so he could find her cheeks, her eyelids, the softness of her neck. As his lips wandered, she said in an unconsciously husky whisper:

"This won't do, David, it won't."

"My love, my innocent love." His voice was thick and love-filled. "It's already doing."

"Well, it mustn't!" Her voice was a poor thread of itself, but stoking, as always, for independence. "Because I intend to marry a virgin."

Were ever a pair of green eyes merrier than his? "Then I had better confess at once that I am not a virgin."

With dignity she corrected, "I meant, *as* a virgin."

"Oh, *as* a virgin." He let her go for long enough to reestablish her at his side and, with one arm tucked around her waist, began to stroll with her toward the steep trail that led up the cliffside.

"In that case," he said, "we had better stay away from secluded coves at dawn."

She let her head rest against his arm. "And ascending balloons . . ."

"And stables with haystacks . . ."

"And the interior of hackney carriages . . ."

So they walked on, together in the new sunlight, their voices and their laughter in mingling harmony with the ocean's eternal song.

Love—the way you want it!

Candlelight Romances

INTRODUCING...

The Romance Magazine For The 1980's

Each exciting issue contains a full-length romance novel — the kind of first-love story we all dream about...

PLUS

other wonderful features such as a travelogue to the world's most romantic spots, advice about your romantic problems, a quiz to find the ideal mate for you and much, much more.

ROMANTIQUE: A complete novel of romance, plus a whole world of romantic features.

ROMANTIQUE: Wherever magazines are sold. Or write Romantique Magazine, Dept. C-1, 41 East 42nd Street, New York, N.Y. 10017

INTERNATIONALLY DISTRIBUTED BY DELL DISTRIBUTING, INC.

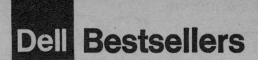

Dell Bestsellers

- [ ] TO LOVE AGAIN by Danielle Steel $2.50 (18631-5)
- [ ] SECOND GENERATION by Howard Fast $2.75 (17892-4)
- [ ] EVERGREEN by Belva Plain $2.75 (13294-0)
- [ ] AMERICAN CAESAR by William Manchester ... $3.50 (10413-0)
- [ ] THERE SHOULD HAVE BEEN CASTLES
      by Herman Raucher $2.75 (18500-9)
- [ ] THE FAR ARENA by Richard Ben Sapir $2.75 (12671-1)
- [ ] THE SAVIOR by Marvin Werlin and Mark Werlin . $2.75 (17748-0)
- [ ] SUMMER'S END by Danielle Steel $2.50 (18418-5)
- [ ] SHARKY'S MACHINE by William Diehl $2.50 (18292-1)
- [ ] DOWNRIVER by Peter Collier $2.75 (11830-1)
- [ ] CRY FOR THE STRANGERS by John Saul $2.50 (11869-7)
- [ ] BITTER EDEN by Sharon Salvato $2.75 (10771-7)
- [ ] WILD TIMES by Brian Garfield $2.50 (19457-1)
- [ ] 1407 BROADWAY by Joel Gross $2.50 (12819-6)
- [ ] A SPARROW FALLS by Wilbur Smith $2.75 (17707-3)
- [ ] FOR LOVE AND HONOR by Antonia Van-Loon .. $2.50 (12574-X)
- [ ] COLD IS THE SEA by Edward L. Beach $2.50 (11045-9)
- [ ] TROCADERO by Leslie Waller $2.50 (18613-7)
- [ ] THE BURNING LAND by Emma Drummond $2.50 (10274-X)
- [ ] HOUSE OF GOD by Samuel Shem, M.D. $2.50 (13371-8)
- [ ] SMALL TOWN by Sloan Wilson $2.50 (17474-0)

At your local bookstore or use this handy coupon for ordering:

DELL BOOKS
P.O. BOX 1000, PINEBROOK, N.J. 07058

Please send me the books I have checked above. I am enclosing $_____
(please add 75¢ per copy to cover postage and handling). Send check or money
order—no cash or C.O.D.'s. Please allow up to 8 weeks for shipment.

Mr/Mrs/Miss _____

Address _____

City _____ State/Zip _____